THEN SHE
WAS GONE

THEN SHE WAS GONE

A Novel

LISA JEWELL

ATRIA BOOKS

New York London Toronto Sydney New Delhi

ATRIA
BOOKS

An Imprint of Simon & Schuster, Inc.
1230 Avenue of the Americas
New York, NY 10020

ATRIA BOOKS and colophon are trademarks of Simon & Schuster, Inc.

Manufactured in the United States of America

ISBN 978-1-5011-5464-5

For Lor

THEN SHE
WAS GONE

PROLOGUE

Those months, the months before she disappeared, were the best months. Really. Just the best. Every moment presented itself to her like a gift and said, *Here I am, another perfect moment, just look at me, can you believe how lovely I am?* Every morning was a flurry of mascara and butterflies, quickening pulse as she neared the school gates, blooming joy as her eyes found him. School was no longer a cage; it was the bustling, spotlit film set for her love story.

Ellie Mack could not believe that Theo Goodman had wanted to go out with her. Theo Goodman was the best-looking boy in year eleven, bar none. He'd also been the best-looking boy in year ten, year nine, and year eight. Not year seven though. None of the boys in year seven were good-looking. They were all tiny, bug-eyed babies in huge shoes and oversized blazers.

Theo Goodman had never had a girlfriend and everyone thought maybe he was gay. He was kind of pretty, for a boy, and very thin. And just, basically, really, really nice. Ellie had dreamed about being with him for years, whether he was gay or not. She would have been happy just to have been his friend. His young, pretty mum walked to school with him every day. She wore gym gear and had her hair in a ponytail and usually had a small white dog with her that Theo would pick up and kiss on the cheek before placing it gently back down on the pavement; then he would kiss his mum and saunter through the gates. He didn't care who saw. He wasn't embarrassed by the powder-puff dog or his mum. He was *self-assured*.

Then one day last year, just after the summer holiday, he had struck up a conversation with her. Just like that. During lunch, something to do with some homework assignment or other, and Ellie, who really knew nothing much about anything, knew immediately that he wasn't gay and that he was talking to her because he liked her. It was totally obvious. And then, just like that, they were boyfriend and girlfriend. She'd thought it would be more complicated.

But one wrong move, one tiny kink in the time line, it was all over. Not just their love story, but all of it. Youth. Life. Ellie Mack. All gone. All gone forever. If she could rewind the time-line, untwist it and roll it back the other way like a ball of wool, she'd see the knots in the yarn, the warning signs. Looking at it backward it was obvious all along. But back then, when she knew nothing about anything, she had not seen it coming. She had walked straight into it with her eyes open.

PART ONE

1

Laurel let herself into her daughter's flat. It was, even on this relatively bright day, dark and gloomy. The window at the front was overwhelmed by a terrible tangle of wisteria while the other side of the flat was completely overshadowed by the small woodland it backed onto.

An impulse buy, that's what it had been. Hanna had just got her first bonus and wanted to throw it at something solid before it evaporated. The people she'd bought the flat from had filled it with beautiful things but Hanna never had the time to shop for furnishings and the flat now looked like a sad postdivorce downsizer. The fact that she didn't mind her mum coming in when she was out and cleaning it was proof that the flat was no more than a glorified hotel room to her.

Laurel swept, by force of habit, down Hanna's dingy hallway and straight to the kitchen, where she took the cleaning kit from under the sink. It looked as though Hanna hadn't been home the night before. There was no cereal bowl in the sink, no milk splashes on the work surface, no tube of mascara left half-open by the magnifying makeup mirror on the windowsill. A plume of ice went down Laurel's spine. Hanna always came home. Hanna had nowhere else to go. She went to her handbag and pulled out her phone, dialed Hanna's number with shaking fingers, and fumbled when the call went through to voicemail as it always did when Hanna was at work. The phone fell from her hands and toward the floor where it caught the side of her shoe and didn't break.

"Shit," she hissed to herself, picking up the phone and staring at it blindly. "Shit."

She had no one to call, no one to ask: *Have you seen Hanna? Do you know where she is?* Her life simply didn't work like that. There were no connections anywhere. Just little islands of life dotted here and there.

It was possible, she thought, that Hanna had met a man, but unlikely. Hanna hadn't had a boyfriend, not one, ever. Someone had once mooted the theory that Hanna felt too guilty to have a boyfriend because her little sister would never have one. The same theory could also be applied to her miserable flat and nonexistent social life.

Laurel knew simultaneously that she was overreacting and also that she was not overreacting. When you are the parent of a child who walked out of the house one morning with a rucksack full of books to study at a library a fifteen-minute walk away and then never came home again, then there is no such thing as overreacting. The fact that she was standing in her adult daughter's kitchen picturing her dead in a ditch because she hadn't left a cereal bowl in the sink was perfectly sane and reasonable in the context of her own experience.

She typed the name of Hanna's company into a search engine and pressed the link to the phone number. The switchboard put her through to Hanna's extension and Laurel held her breath.

"Hanna Mack speaking."

There it was, her daughter's voice, brusque and characterless.

Laurel didn't say anything, just touched the off button on her screen and put her phone back into her bag. She opened Hanna's dishwasher and began unstacking it.

2

What had Laurel's life been like, ten years ago, when she'd had three children and not two? Had she woken up every morning suffused with existential joy? No, she had not. Laurel had always been a glass-half-empty type of person. She could find much to complain about in even the most pleasant of scenarios and could condense the joy of good news into a short-lived moment, quickly curtailed by some new bothersome concern. So she had woken up every morning convinced that she had slept badly, even when she hadn't, worrying that her stomach was too fat, that her hair was either too long or too short, that her house was too big, too small, that her bank account was too empty, her husband too lazy, her children too loud or too quiet, that they would leave home, that they would never leave home. She'd wake up noticing the pale cat fur smeared across the black skirt she'd left hanging on the back of her bedroom chair, the missing slipper, the bags under Hanna's eyes, the pile of dry cleaning that she'd been meaning to take up the road for almost a month, the rip in the wallpaper in the hallway, the terrible pubescent boil on Jake's chin, the smell of cat food left out too long, and the bin that everyone seemed intent on not emptying, contents pressed down into its bowels by the lazy, flat-palmed hands of her family.

That was how she'd once viewed her perfect life: as a series of bad smells and unfulfilled duties, petty worries and late bills.

And then one morning, her girl, her golden girl, her last-born, her baby, her soul mate, her pride and her joy, had left the house and not come back.

And how had she felt during those first few excruciatingly unfolding hours? What had filled her brain, her heart, to re-place all those petty concerns? Terror. Despair. Grief. Horror. Agony. Turmoil. Heartbreak. Fear. All those words, all so melo-dramatic, yet all so insufficient.

"She'll be at Theo's," Paul had said. "Why don't you give his mum a ring?"

She'd known already that she wouldn't be at Theo's. Her daughter's last words to her had been: "I'll be back in time for lunch. Is there any of that lasagna left?"

"Enough for one."

"Don't let Hanna have it! Or Jake! Promise!"

"I promise."

And then there'd been the click of the front door, the sud-den dip in volume with one person less in the house, a dish-washer to load, a phone call to make, a Lemsip to take upstairs to Paul, who had a cold that had previously seemed like the most irksome thing in her life.

"Paul's got a cold."

How many people had she said that to in the preceding day or so? A weary sigh, a roll of the eyes. "Paul's got a cold." *My burden. My life. Pity me.*

But she'd called Theo's mum anyway.

"No," said Becky Goodman, "no, I'm really sorry. Theo's been here all day and we haven't heard anything from Ellie at all. Let me know if there's anything I can do . . . ?"

As the afternoon had turned to early evening, after she'd phoned each of Ellie's friends in turn, after she'd visited the library, who'd let her see their CCTV footage—Ellie had definitely not been to the library that day—after the sun had begun to set and the house plunged into a cool darkness punctuated every few moments by blasts of white light as a silent electrical storm played out overhead, she'd finally given in to the nagging dread that had been growing inside her all day and she'd called the police.

That was the first time she'd hated Paul, that evening, in his dressing gown, barefoot, smelling of bedsheets and snot, sniffing, sniffing, sniffing, then blowing his nose, the terrible gurgle of it in his nostrils, the thickness of his mouth-breathing that sounded like the death throes of a monster to her hypersensitive ears.

"Get dressed," she snapped. "Please."

He'd acquiesced, like a browbeaten child, and come downstairs a few minutes later wearing a summer holiday outfit of combat shorts and a bright T-shirt. All wrong. Wrong wrong wrong.

"And blow your nose," she'd said. "Properly. So there's nothing left."

Again, he'd followed her instruction. She'd watched him with disdain, watched him fold the tissue into a ball and stalk pitifully across the kitchen to dispose of it in the bin.

And then the police had arrived.

And then the thing began.

The thing that had never ended.

She occasionally wondered whether if Paul hadn't had a cold that day, if he'd rushed back from work at her first call, rumpled in smart clothes, full of vim and urgency, if he'd sat upright by her side, his hand clasped around hers, if he hadn't been mouth-breathing and sniffing and looking a fright, would everything have been different? Would they have made it through? Or would it have been something else that made her hate him?

The police had left at eight thirty. Hanna had appeared at the kitchen door shortly afterward.

"Mum," she'd said in an apologetic voice, "I'm hungry."

"Sorry," said Laurel, glancing across the kitchen at the clock. "Christ, yes, you must be starving." She pulled herself heavily to her feet, blindly examined the contents of the fridge with her daughter.

"This?" said Hanna, pulling out the Tupperware box with the last portion of lasagna in it.

"No." She'd snatched it back, too hard. Hanna had blinked at her.

"Why not?"

"Just, no," she said, softer this time.

She'd made her beans on toast, sat and watched her eat it. Hanna. Her middle child. The difficult one. The tiring one. The one she wouldn't want to be stranded on a desert island with. And a terrible thought shot through her, so fast she barely registered it.

It should be you missing and Ellie eating beans on toast.

She touched Hanna's cheek, gently, with the palm of her hand and then left the room.

3

The first thing that Ellie shouldn't have done was get a bad grade in maths. If she'd worked harder, been cleverer, if she hadn't been so tired the day of the test, hadn't felt so unfocused, hadn't spent more time yawning than concentrating, if she'd got an A instead of a B+, then none of it would have happened. But going further back, before the bad maths test, if she hadn't fallen in love with Theo, if instead she'd fallen in love with a boy who was rubbish at maths, a boy who didn't care about maths or test results, a boy with no ambitions, or better still no boy at all, then she wouldn't have felt that she needed to be as good as him or better, she'd have been happy with a B+ and she wouldn't have gone home that evening and begged her mum for a maths tutor.

So, that's where it was. The first kink in the time line. Right there, at four thirty or thereabouts on a Wednesday afternoon in January.

She'd come home in a temper. She often came home in a temper. She never expected to do it. It just happened. The minute she saw her mum or heard her mum's voice, she'd just feel irrationally annoyed and then all the stuff she hadn't been able to say or do all day at school—because at school she was known as a Nice Person and once you had a reputation for being nice you couldn't mess with it—came spitting out of her.

"My maths teacher is shit," she said, dropping her bag on

the settle in the hallway. "Just so shit. I hate him." She did not hate him. She hated herself for failing. But she couldn't say that.

Her mum replied from the kitchen sink, "What's happened, love?"

"I just told you!" She hadn't, but that didn't matter. "My maths teacher is so bad. I'm going to fail my GCSE. I need a tutor. Like, really, really need a tutor."

She flounced into the kitchen and flopped dramatically into a chair.

"We can't afford a tutor," her mum said. "Why don't you just join the after-school maths club?"

There was the next kink. If she hadn't been such a spoiled brat, if she hadn't been expecting her mum to wave a magic wand and solve all her problems for her, if she'd had even the vaguest idea about the reality of her parents' finances, if she'd cared at all about anything other than herself, the conversation would have ended there. She would have said, *OK. I understand. That's what I'll do.*

But she had not done that. She had pushed and pushed and pushed. She'd offered to pay for it out of her own money. She'd brought up examples of people in her class who were *way* poorer than them who had private tuition.

"What about asking someone at school?" her mum suggested. "Someone in the sixth form? Someone who'll do it for a few quid and a slice of cake?"

"What! No way! Oh God, that would be so embarrassing!"

And there it went, slipping away like a slippery thing, another chance to save herself. Gone. And she didn't even know it.

4

Between the day in May 2005 that Ellie had failed to come home and exactly two minutes ago there had been not one substantial lead regarding her disappearance. Not one.

The last sighting of Ellie had been caught on CCTV on Stroud Green Road at ten forty-three, showing her stopping briefly to check her reflection in a car window (for a while there'd been a theory that she had stopped to look at someone in the car, or to say something to the driver, but they'd traced the car's owner and proved that he'd been on holiday at the time of Ellie's disappearance and that his car had been parked there for the duration). And that was that. Her recorded journey had ended there.

They'd done a house-to-house search of the immediate vicinity, brought in known pedophiles for questioning, taken CCTV footage from each and every shopkeeper on Stroud Green Road, wheeled out Laurel and Paul to be filmed for a television appeal that had been seen by roughly eight million people, but nothing had ever taken them further than that last sighting of Ellie looking at her reflection at ten forty-three.

The fact that Ellie had been wearing a black T-shirt and jeans had been a problem for the police. The fact that her lovely gold-streaked hair had been pulled back into a scruffy ponytail. The fact that her rucksack was navy blue. That her trainers were bog-standard supermarket trainers in white. It was almost as though she'd deliberately made herself invisible.

Ellie's bedroom had been expertly rifled through for four hours by two DIs with their shirtsleeves rolled up. Ellie, it seemed, had taken nothing out of the ordinary. It was possible she might have taken underwear but there was no way for Laurel to know if there was anything missing from her drawers. It was possible she might have taken a change of clothing, but Ellie, like most fifteen-year-old girls, had way too many clothes, far too many for Lauren to keep an inventory. But her piggy bank still contained the few tightly folded ten-pound notes she forced into it after every birthday. Her toothbrush was still in the bathroom, her deodorant, too. Ellie had never been on a sleepover without her toothbrush and deodorant.

After two years, they'd downgraded the search. Laurel knew what they thought; they thought Ellie was a runaway.

How could they have thought that Ellie was a runaway when there was no CCTV footage of her at any train station, at any bus stop, walking down any road anywhere apart from the one from which she'd disappeared? The downgrade of the search was devastating.

Even more devastating was Paul's response to this pronouncement.

"It's a sort of closure, I guess."

There, right there—the final nail in the dry box of bones of their marriage.

The children meanwhile were shuffling along, like trains on a track, keeping to schedule. Hanna took her A levels. Jake graduated from university in the West Country where he'd been studying to be a chartered surveyor. And Paul was busy asking for promotions at work, buying himself new suits, talking about upgrading the car, showing her hotels and resorts on the Internet that had special deals that summer. Paul was not a bad man. Paul was a good man. She had married a good man, just as she'd always planned to do. But the way he'd dealt with the violent hole ripped into their lives by Ellie's disappearance had shown her that he wasn't big enough, he wasn't strong enough—he wasn't *insane* enough.

The disappointment she felt in him was such a tiny part of everything else she'd been feeling that she barely registered it. When he moved out a year later it was nothing, a small blip in her existence. Looking back on it now, she could remember very little about it. All she could remember from that time was the raw need to keep the search going.

"Can we not just do one more house-to-house?" she'd pleaded with the police. "It's been a year since we did one. That's long enough, surely, to turn up something we didn't find before?"

The detective had smiled. "We have talked about it," she said. "We decided that it was not a good use of resources. Not at this time. Maybe in a year or so. Maybe."

But then suddenly this January, out of the blue, the police had called and said that *Crimewatch* wanted to do a ten-year anniversary appeal. Another reconstruction. It was broadcast on 26 May. It brought no fresh evidence. No new sightings.

It changed nothing.

Until now.

 ᐠᑐᐟ

The detective on the phone had sounded cautious. "It could be nothing. But we'd like you to come in anyway."

"What have you found?" Laurel said. "Is it a body? What is it?"

"Please just come in, Mrs. Mack."

Ten years of nothing. And now there was something.

She grabbed her handbag and left the house.

5

THEN

Someone from up the street had recommended her. Noelle Donnelly was her name. Ellie stood up at the chime of the doorbell and peered down the hallway as her mum opened the door. She was quite old, forty maybe, something like that, and she had an accent, Irish or Scottish.

"Ellie!" her mum called. "Ellie, come and meet Noelle."

She had pale red hair, twisted up at the back and clipped into place. She smiled down at Ellie and said, "Good afternoon, Ellie. I hope you've got your brain switched on?"

Ellie couldn't tell if she was being funny or not, so she didn't smile back, just nodded.

"Good," said Noelle.

They'd set up a corner of the dining room for Ellie's first lesson, brought an extra lamp down from her room, cleared the clutter, laid out two glasses, a water jug, and Ellie's pencil case with the black and red polka dots.

Laurel disappeared to the kitchen to make Noelle a cup of tea. Noelle stopped at the sight of the family cat, sitting on the piano stool.

"Well," she said, "he's a big lad. What's he called?"

"Teddy," she said. "Teddy *Bear*. But Teddy for short."

Her first words to Noelle. She would never forget.

"Well, I can see why you call him that. He does look like a big hairy bear!"

Had she liked her then? She couldn't remember. She just smiled at her, put her hand upon her cat, and squeezed his woolly fur inside her fist. She loved her cat and was glad that he was there, a buffer between her and this stranger.

Noelle Donnelly smelled of cooking oil and unwashed hair. She wore jeans and a bobbly camel-colored jumper, a Timex watch on a freckled wrist, scuffed brown boots and reading glasses on a green cord around her neck. Her shoulders were particularly wide and her neck slightly stooped with a kind of hump at the back and her legs were very long and thin. She looked as though she'd spent her life in a room with a very low ceiling.

"Well now," she said, putting on the reading glasses and feeling inside a brown-leather briefcase. "I've brought along some old GCSE papers. We'll start you on one of these in a moment, get to the bottom of your strengths and weaknesses. But first of all, maybe you could tell me, in your own words, what your concerns are. In particular."

Mum walked in then with a mug of tea and some chocolate chip cookies on a saucer that she slid onto the table silently and speedily. She was acting as though Ellie and Noelle Donnelly were on a date or having a top secret meeting. Ellie wanted to say, *Stay, Mum. Stay with me. I'm not ready to be alone with this stranger.*

She bored her eyes into the back of her mother's head as Laurel stealthily left the room, closing the door very quietly behind her: the soft, apologetic *click* of it.

Noelle Donnelly turned to Ellie and smiled. She had very small teeth. "Well, now," she said, sliding the glasses back up to her narrow-bridged nose, "where were we?"

6

The world looked loaded with portent as Laurel drove as close to the speed limit as she could manage toward the police station in Finsbury Park. People on the streets looked sinister and suggestive, as if each were on the verge of committing a dark crime. Awnings flapping in a brisk wind looked like the wings of birds of prey; billboards looked set to fall into the road and obliterate her.

Adrenaline blasted a path through her tiredness.

Laurel hadn't slept properly since 2005.

She'd lived alone for seven years—first in the family home and then in the flat she moved into three years ago when Paul put the final nail in any chance of a reconciliation by somehow managing to meet a woman. The woman had invited him to live with her and he'd accepted. She'd never worked out how he'd done it, how he'd found that healthy pink part of himself among the wreckage of everything else. But she didn't blame him. Not in the least. She wished she could do the same; she wished she could pack a couple of large suitcases and say good-bye to herself, wish herself a good life, thank herself for all the memories, look fondly upon herself for just one long, lingering moment and then shut the door quietly, chin up, morning sun playing hopefully on the crown of her head, a bright new future awaiting her. She would do it in a flash. She really would.

Jake and Hanna had moved away too, of course. Faster, she

suspected, and earlier than they would have if life hadn't come off its rails ten years ago. She had friends whose children were the same age as Jake and Hanna and who were still at home. Her friends moaned about it, about the empty orange-juice cartons in the fridge, the appalling sex noises and the noisy, drunken returns from nightclubs at four in the morning that set the dog off and disturbed their sleep. How she would love to hear one of her children stumbling about in the early hours of the morning. How she would love the trail of used crockery and the rumpled joggers, still embedded with underwear, left pooled all over the floor. But no, her two had not looked backward once they'd seen their escapes. Jake lived in Devon with a girl called Blue who didn't let him out of her sight and was already talking about babies only a year into their relationship, and Hanna lived a mile away from Laurel in her tiny, gloomy flat, working fourteen-hour days and weekends in the City for no apparent reason other than financial reward. Neither of them were setting the world alight but then whose children did? All those hopes and dreams and talk of ballerinas and pop stars, concert pianists and boundary-breaking scientists. They all ended up in an office. All of them.

Laurel lived in a new-build flat in Barnet, one bedroom for her, one for a visitor, a balcony big enough for some planters and a table and chairs, shiny red kitchen units, and a reserved parking space. It was not the sort of home she'd ever envisaged for herself, but it was easy and it was safe.

And how did she fill her days, now that her children were gone? Now that her husband was gone? Now that even the cat was gone, though he'd made a big effort to stay alive for her and lasted until he was almost twenty-one. Laurel filled three days a week with a job. She worked in the marketing department of the shopping center in High Barnet. Once a week she went to see her mother in an old people's home in Enfield. Once a week she cleaned Hanna's flat. The rest of the time she did things that she pretended were important to her, like buying plants from garden centers to decorate her balcony with, like visiting friends she no longer really cared about to drink coffee she didn't enjoy and talk about things she had no interest in. She went for a swim once a week. Not to keep fit but just because it was something she'd always done and she'd never found a good enough reason to stop doing it.

So it was strange after so many years to be leaving the house with a sense of urgency, a mission, something genuinely important to do.

She was about to be shown something. A piece of bone, maybe, a shred of bloodied fabric, a photo of a swollen corpse floating in dense hidden waters. She was about to *know* something after ten years of knowing nothing. She might be shown evidence that her daughter was alive. Or evidence that she was dead. The weight on her soul betrayed a belief that it would be the latter.

Her heart beat hard and heavy beneath her ribs as she drove toward Finsbury Park.

7

THEN

Noelle Donnelly began to grow on Ellie a little over those weekly winter visits. Not a lot. But a little. Mainly because she was a really good teacher and Ellie was now at the top of the top stream in her class with a predicted A/A* result. But in other ways, too: she often brought Ellie a little something—a packet of earrings from Claire's Accessories, a fruit-flavored lip balm, a really nice pen. "For my best student," she'd say. And if Ellie protested, she'd brush it away with a "Well, I was in Brent Cross, y'know. It's a little bit of nothing, really."

She'd always ask after Theo as well, whom she'd met briefly on her second or third session at the house. "And how's that handsome fella of yours?" she'd ask in a way that should have been mortifying but wasn't, mainly because of her lovely Irish accent, which made most things she said sound funnier and more interesting than they actually were.

"He's fine," Ellie would say, and Noelle would smile her slightly chilly smile and say, "Well, he's a keeper."

GCSEs were now looming large on the horizon. It was March and Ellie had started to count down to her exams in weeks rather than months. Her Tuesday-afternoon sessions with Noelle had been building in momentum as her brain stretched and tautened and absorbed facts and formulae more easily. There was a snappy pace to their lessons now, a high-octane rhythm. So Ellie noticed it immediately, the shift in Noelle's mood that first Tuesday in March.

"Good afternoon, young lady," she said, putting her bag onto the table and unzipping it. "How are you?"

"I'm fine."

"Well, that's good. I'm glad. And how did you get on with your homework?"

Ellie slid the completed work across the table toward Noelle. Normally Noelle would put on her reading glasses and start marking it immediately but today she just laid her fingertips on top of it and drummed them absentmindedly. "Good girl," she said. "You are such a good girl."

Ellie watched her questioningly from the corner of her eye, waiting for a signal that their lesson was about to begin. But none came. Instead Noelle stared blindly at the homework.

"Tell me, Ellie," she said eventually, turning her unblinking gaze to Ellie. "What's the worst thing that ever happened to you?"

Ellie shrugged.

"What?" Noelle continued. "Like a hamster dying, something like that?"

"I haven't had a hamster."

"Ha, well then, maybe that. Maybe *not* having a hamster is the worst thing that ever happened to you?"

Ellie shrugged again. "I never really wanted one."

"Well, then, what did you want? What did you really want that you weren't allowed to have?"

In the background, Ellie could hear the TV in the kitchen, the sound of her mother vacuuming overhead, her sister chatting to someone on the phone. Her family just getting on with their lives and not having to have weird conversations about hamsters with their maths tutor.

"Nothing, really. Just the usual things: money, clothes."

"You never wanted a dog?"

"Not really."

Noelle sighed and pulled Ellie's homework toward her. "Well, then, you are a very lucky girl indeed. You really are. And I hope you appreciate how lucky you are?"

Ellie nodded.

"Good. Because when you get to my age there'll be loads of things you want and you'll see everyone else getting them and you'll think, well, it must be my turn now. *Surely.* And then you'll watch it disappear into the sunset. And there'll be nothing you can do about it. Nothing whatsoever."

There was a moment of ponderous silence before finally, slowly, Noelle slid her glasses onto her nose, pulled back the first page of Ellie's homework, and said, "Right then, let's see how my best student got on this week."

"Tell me, Ellie, what are your hopes and dreams?"

Ellie groaned inwardly. Noelle Donnelly was in one of those moods again.

"Just to do really well in my GCSEs. And my A levels. And then go to a really good university."

Noelle tutted and rolled her eyes. "What is it with you young people and your *obsession* with university? Oh, the fanfare when I got into Trinity! Such a big deal! My mother couldn't stop telling the world. Her only girl! At Trinity! And look at me now. One of the poorest people I know."

Ellie smiled and wondered what to say.

"No, there's more to life than university, Miss Smarty Pants. There's more than just certificates and qualifications. I have them coming out of my ears. And look at me, sitting here with you in your lovely warm house, drinking your lovely Earl Grey tea, getting paid a pittance to fill your brain with my knowledge. Then going home to nothing." She turned sharply and fixed Ellie with a look. "To *nothing*. I swear." Then she sighed and smiled and the glasses came up her nose and her gaze left Ellie and the lesson commenced.

Afterward Ellie found her mother in the kitchen and said, "Mum. I want to stop my tutoring."

Her mum turned and looked at her questioningly. "Oh?" she said. "Why?"

Ellie thought about telling her the truth. She thought about saying, *She's freaking me out and saying really weird things and I really don't want to be alone with her for an hour every week anymore.* How she wished she had told her the truth. Maybe if she'd told her the truth, her mother might have been able to work it all out and then everything would have been different. But for some reason she didn't. Maybe she thought her mother would say that it was a silly reason to want to stop having the lessons so close to her exams. Or maybe she didn't want to get Noelle into trouble, didn't want a *situation* to develop. But for whatever misguided reason she said, "I just honestly think I've gone as far as I can go with Noelle. I've got all the practice papers she gave me. I can just keep doing those. And it will save you some money." She smiled, winningly, and waited for her mother's response.

"Well, it does seem a bit strange, so close to your exams."

"Exactly. I think there are other things I could be using the time for now. Geography, for example. I could really do with some extra study time for geography."

This was a 100-percent untruth. Ellie was totally on top of all her studies. The extra hour a week would make no difference to anything. But still she smiled that Mum-pleasing smile, left the request hanging in the air between them, waited.

"Well, darling, it's up to you, of course."

Ellie nodded encouragingly, the echo of Noelle's loaded words, the tired aroma of old cooking and unwashed hair, the mood swings and the tangential, slightly inappropriate questions pulsing through her consciousness.

"If you're sure? It would be nice not to have the extra expense," her mother said.

"Exactly." Relief flooded through her. "Exactly."

"OK," said her mother, pulling open the fridge door, taking out a tub of Bolognese sauce, closing it again. "I'll call her tomorrow. Let her know."

"Great," said Ellie lightly, feeling an odd, sordid weight lifting from her soul. "Thank you."

8

The suited policeman who greeted Laurel was young and washed out, clammy-handed and slightly nervous. He led her through to an interview room. "Thank you for coming," he said, as though there'd been an option not to come. *Sorry, I have a lot on today, maybe next week?*

Someone went to fetch her a cup of water, and then a moment later the door opened again and Paul walked in.

Paul, God, of course, Paul. She hadn't even thought of Paul. She'd reacted as though this was all down to her. But clearly someone at the station had thought of Paul. He blew into the room, all floppy silver hair, rumpled suit, the dry smell of the City embedded in his skin. His hand reached for Laurel's shoulder as he passed her but she couldn't bring herself to turn to acknowledge him, just forced a small smile for the benefit of people watching the exchange.

He took the seat next to her, his hand pressed down against his tie as he lowered himself into the chair. Someone fetched him tea from a machine. She felt cross about the tea. She felt cross about Paul.

"We've been investigating a site near Dover," said the detective called Dane. "A dog walker called us. His terrier dug up a bag."

A bag. Laurel nodded, furiously. A bag was not a body.

Dane pulled some 10- by 8-inch photos from a hard-backed

envelope. He slid them across the table toward Laurel and Paul. "Do you recognize any of these items?"

Laurel pulled the photos toward herself.

It was Ellie's bag. Her rucksack. The one she'd had slung over her shoulder when she left the house for the library all those years ago. There was the small red logo that had been such a vital part of the police appeal. It had been virtually the only distinguishing feature on Ellie's person that day.

The second photo was of a black T-shirt, a loose-fitting thing with a slash neck and cap sleeves. The label inside said "New Look." She'd worn it partly tucked into her jeans at the front.

The third was a bra: gray jersey with small black polka dots. The label inside said "Atmosphere."

The fourth was a pair of jeans. Pale denim. The label inside said "Top Shop."

The fifth was a pair of scruffy white trainers.

The sixth was a plain black hoodie with a white drawstring. The label inside said "Next."

The seventh was a set of house keys. The fob was a small plastic owl with eyes that lit up when you pressed a button on its stomach.

The eighth was a pile of exercise books and textbooks, green and rotten with damp.

The ninth was a pencil case: black and red polka dots, filled with pens and pencils.

The tenth was a packet of tampons, swollen and obscene.

The eleventh was a tiny leather purse, purple and red patchwork, with a zip that went around three sides and a red pompom on the zipper.

The twelfth was a small laptop, old-fashioned and slightly battered looking.

The last was a passport.

She pulled the photo closer; Paul leaned toward her and she pushed it so it lay between them.

A passport.

Ellie had not taken her passport. Laurel still had Ellie's passport. She took it from the box of Ellie's possessions from time to time and gazed at the ghostly face of her daughter, thought of the journeys she'd never take.

But as she stared at the passport she realized it was not Ellie's passport.

It was Hanna's.

"I don't get it," she said. "This is my elder daughter's passport. We thought she'd lost it. But . . ." She stared down at the photo again, her fingers touching the edges of it. ". . . it's here. In Ellie's bag. Where did you find this?"

"In dense woodlands," Dane replied. "Not too far from the ferry port. One theory we're looking at is that she may have been on her way to Europe. Given the passport."

Laurel felt a burst of anger, of wrongness. They were looking for evidence that backed up their long-held theory that she'd run away from home. "But her bag," she said. "With just the things she had when she left, when she was fifteen? And you're saying that she took the same things with her to leave the country? All those years later? That doesn't make any sense."

Dane looked at her almost fondly. "We've analyzed the clothing. There's evidence of intensive wear."

Laurel clutched her chest at the mental image of her perfect girl, always so impeccably clean, so fresh-smelling and fragrant, stumbling around in the same clothes for years on end. "So . . . where is she? Where's Ellie?"

"We're looking for her."

She could sense that Paul was staring at her, that he needed her to engage with him in order to process this jumble of information. But she could not face his gaze, could not give him any part of herself.

"You know," she said, "we were burgled a few years after Ellie went missing. I told the police at the time that I thought it was Ellie. The things that were taken, the lack of forced entry, the sense of . . ." She pulled herself back from talking about unsubstantiated feelings. "She must have taken Hanna's passport then. She must have . . ."

She trailed off. Was it possible that the police had been right all along? That she'd run away? That she'd been planning an escape?

But from where? To where? And why?

At that moment the door opened and another policeman walked into the room. He approached Dane and he whispered something in his ear. Both men looked toward Laurel and Paul. Then Dane sat straighter, adjusted his tie, and said, "They've found human remains."

Laurel's hand instinctively found Paul's.

She squeezed it so hard she felt his bones bend.

9

THEN

"What shall we do this summer?"

Theo, whose head was in Ellie's lap, turned his face up to her and smiled. "Nothing," he said. "Let's do completely nothing."

Ellie put down her paperback and rested her hand on Theo's cheek. "No way," she said. "I want to do *everything*. Everything that isn't revising and learning and studying. I want to go paragliding. Shall we do that? Shall we go paragliding?"

"So your plan for the summer is basically to *die*?" Theo laughed. "You are so weird."

She punched him gently against his cheek. "I am not weird. I am just ready to fly."

"Literally?"

"Yes, literally. Oh, and Mum says we can use Grammy's cottage for a few days if we want."

Theo beamed at her. "Seriously? Like, just us?"

"Or we can take some friends."

"Or maybe *just us*?" He nodded, eagerly, playfully, and Ellie laughed.

"Yeah, I guess."

It was Saturday afternoon, May, a week before GCSEs. They were in Ellie's bedroom, taking a break from revision. Outside the sun was shining. Teddy Bear the cat lay by their side and the air was full of pollen and hope. Ellie's mum always said that May was like the Friday night of summer: all the good times lying ahead of you, bright and shiny and waiting to be lived. Ellie could feel it all calling to her from the other side of the dark tunnel of exams; she could feel the warm nights and the long days, the lightness of having nothing to do and nowhere to be. She thought of all the things she could do once she'd finished this chapter of her life, all the books she could read and the picnics she could eat and the funfairs and shopping trips and holidays and parties. For a moment she felt breathless with it all; it overwhelmed her and made her stomach roll over and her heart dance.

"I cannot wait," she said. "I cannot wait for it all to be over."

10

THEN

The police investigation into the burglary at Laurel's house all those years ago had come to nothing. They'd found no finger-prints of any distinction anywhere on the property, checks of CCTV footage from the two hours that Laurel had been out of the house showed no sign of anyone meeting the description of Ellie, or of any teenage girl for that matter. The "thief" had taken an ancient laptop, an old phone of Paul's, some cash that had been tucked into Laurel's underwear drawer, a pair of art deco silver candlesticks that had been a wedding present from some very rich people who they weren't friends with anymore, and a cake that Hanna had baked the day before that had been sitting on the kitchen counter waiting to be iced.

They hadn't taken any of Laurel's jewelry—including her wedding and engagement rings, which she'd stopped wearing a few months before and which had been sitting in plain sight on a chest of drawers in her bedroom. They hadn't taken the Mac, which was newer and more valuable than the laptop they had stolen—and they hadn't taken her credit cards, which she kept in a drawer in the kitchen so that if she was mugged on the street, they wouldn't get stolen.

"It's possible they ran out of time," said one of the police officers who arrived at her front door ten minutes after she'd called them. "Or they were stealing to order and knew what they could sell and to who."

"It feels strange," Laurel had said, her arms folded tight around her middle. "It feels—I don't know. My daughter disappeared four years ago." She looked up at them, eyed them both directly and uncompromisingly. "Ellie Mack? Remember?"

They exchanged a glance and then looked back at her.

"I could sense her," she said, sounding mad and not caring. "When I walked into the house I could sense my daughter."

They exchanged another glance. "Are any of her things missing?"

She shook her head and then shrugged. "I don't think so. I've been in her room and it looks exactly as it was."

There was a beat of silence as the police officers moved awkwardly from foot to foot.

"We couldn't see any broken locks or windows. How did the burglar gain access?"

Laurel blinked slowly. "I don't know."

"Any windows left open?"

"No, I . . ." She hadn't even thought about it. "I don't think so."

"Do you leave a key out?"

"No. Never."

"Leave one with a neighbor? Or a friend?"

"No. No. The only people who have keys are us. Me, my husband, our children."

As the words left her mouth she felt her heart begin to race, the palms of her hands dampen. "Ellie," she said. "Ellie had a key. When she went missing. In her rucksack. What if . . . ?"

They stared at her expectantly.

"What if she came back? From wherever she's been? Maybe she was desperate? It would explain the fact that only things we don't care about have been taken. She knows I don't like those candlesticks. I was always saying I was going to take them on the *Antiques Roadshow* one day because they were probably worth a fortune. And the cake!"

"The cake?"

"Yes. There was a chocolate cake on the counter. My daughter made it. My other daughter. I mean, what sort of burglar takes a *cake*?"

"A hungry burglar?"

"No," said Laurel, her theory solidifying quickly into fact. "No. Ellie. Ellie would have taken it. She loved Hanna's cakes. They were her favorite thing, they were—" She stopped. She was going too fast and she was alienating the people who were here to help her.

No neighbors had seen anything out of the ordinary: most of them had not even been at home at the time of the burglary. Nothing stolen from the house had ever been recovered. And that was that. Another dead end reached. Another gaping hole in Laurel's life.

For years, though, she'd stayed close to home, in case Ellie came back again. For years she'd sniff the air every time she returned home from her brief sojourns beyond her front door, looking for the smell of her lost daughter. It was during those years that she finally lost touch with her remaining children. She had nothing left to give them and they grew tired of waiting.

Then three years ago Laurel had finally given up on Ellie coming home again. She'd accepted that it had been a simple burglary and that she needed to start again, in a new place. Three years ago she'd stepped backward out of her lost daughter's bedroom for the last time and closed the door behind her with a click so soft that it nearly killed her.

For three years she had put Ellie from her mind as much as she was able. She'd strapped herself into a new routine, tight and hard, like a straitjacket. For three years she'd internalized her madness, shared it with no one.

But now the madness was back.

∼

She climbed into her car near the police station and as she put the car into reverse she stopped for a moment, stopped to suck the madness back down, suck it as far inside as she could get it to go.

But then she thought of her daughter's bones being placed at this very moment into plastic bags by strangers in rubber gloves and it burst back up and emerged into the silence of her car as a dreadful roar, her fists pounding the steering wheel, over and over and over again.

She saw Paul then, across the road, walking toward his own car, the terrible hang of his face, the sag of his shoulders. She saw him stare at her, the shock in his eyes as he registered her fury. And then she saw him begin to walk toward her. She put the car into gear and drove away as fast as she could.

11

THEN

Ellie had not thought too much about Noelle Donnelly since their final lesson.

According to her mother she had been a "bit arsey" about it, said that had she known her time with Ellie would be cut short, she might not have taken the job and now she had a slot she could not fill, and it was not really the done thing blah blah blah. Her mother had brushed it off when Ellie had said she felt bad.

"It's fine," she said. "I think she's just the type to take umbrage. She'll be OK. And she'll definitely find someone to take that slot so close to the exams. Some last-minute panicking parent will snap her up."

Ellie had felt reassured by this and removed Noelle Donnelly from the bit of her brain that concerned itself with the here and now. The here and now was oversubscribed as it was.

In fact it had taken her a moment to place Noelle Donnelly at all when she saw her on the high street that Thursday morning during the May half-term. She was on her way to the library. Her sister had a friend over who had a *really* loud, *really* annoying laugh. She needed some peace and quiet. And also a book about the workhouses in the nineteenth century.

So, in retrospect, she could have blamed her sister's friend with the loud laugh for her being there at that precise moment, but she really didn't want to do that. The blame game could be exhausting sometimes. The blame game could make you lose your mind . . . all the infinitesimal outcomes, each path breaking up into a million other paths every time you heedlessly chose one, taking you on a journey that you'd never find your way back from.

Noelle's face formed a complicated smile when she saw Ellie. Ellie scrambled around in the back rooms of her brain for a nanosecond, retrieved what she needed, and then returned the smile.

"My best student!" Noelle said.

"Hi!"

"How's it going?"

"It's fine! It's great! The maths is going really well."

"Oh, well, that is grand." She was wearing a khaki-green waterproof coat in spite of a forecast for warm, dry weather. Her red hair was clipped back from her face with tortoiseshell clasps. She had on cheap black trainers and was clutching a cream canvas bag to her shoulder. "All ready for the big day?"

"Yes, totally," she overstated, not wanting to give Noelle an opportunity to chastise her for stopping her tutoring sessions.

"Tuesday, yes?"

"Yes. Ten a.m. Then the second paper the week after."

Noelle nodded, her eyes never leaving Ellie's. "You know," she said, "I've been using a practice paper with my other students. They all say it's been superhelpful. And from what I've heard *through the grapevine* it has a lot of crossover with this year's paper. If you like I could give you a copy?"

NO, Ellie screamed at herself from beyond the beyond. *NO. I DO NOT WANT YOUR PRACTICE PAPER.* But the here-and-now Ellie, the one who wanted to spend her summer paragliding and losing her virginity, the one who was having pizza tonight and seeing her boyfriend tomorrow morning, *that* Ellie said, "Oh, right. Yes. That could be good."

"Now let me see," said Noelle, touching her lips with her forefinger. "I could drop by this evening. I'll be close to you then."

"Great," said Ellie. "Yes, that would be great."

"Or . . . you know, maybe better still"—she looked at her watch and then briefly behind her—"I'm just here." She pointed at a side road. "Literally four houses down. Why don't you pop in now? It'll take ten seconds."

It was busy that Thursday morning. People passed on either side of them. Ellie thought of those people afterward, wondered if they'd noticed, wondered if somewhere in someone's head there lay an untouched memory of a girl with a rucksack, wearing a black T-shirt and jeans talking to a woman in a khaki waterproof with a Daunt Books shoulder bag. She imagined a *Crimewatch* reenactment of these moments. Who would they cast as her? Hanna, probably. They were almost the same height these days. And a red-haired female police officer togged up in an ugly green coat, pretending to be Noelle.

"Were you there," Nick Robinson would say afterward, eyes narrowed at the camera, "on the morning of Thursday the twenty-sixth of May? Did you see a middle-aged woman with red hair talking to Ellie Mack? They were outside the Red Cross charity shop on Stroud Green Road. It was about ten forty-five a.m. You might remember the weather that day; it was the day of an electrical storm over London. Did you see the woman in the green coat walking with Ellie Mack toward Harlow Road?" The screen would shift to some grainy CCTV footage of Ellie and Noelle walking together up Stroud Green Road—Ellie would look tiny and vulnerable, turning that last corner, heading toward her fate, like a prize idiot. "Please," Nick would say, "if you remember anything from that morning, if you saw Ellie Mack on Harlow Road, please get in touch. We're waiting for your call."

But nobody had seen Ellie that morning. No one had noticed her talking to a woman with red hair. No one had seen her walking with her toward Harlow Road. No one had seen Noelle Donnelly unlock the door of a small scruffy house with a flowering cherry tree outside and turn to Ellie and say, "Come on then, in you come." No one had seen Ellie walk through the door. No one had heard the door close behind her.

12

Paul and Laurel buried the partial remains of their daughter on a sunny afternoon at the tail end of an indolent Indian summer. They buried her femurs, her tibias, and most of her skull.

According to the forensics report, her daughter had been run over by a vehicle, her broken body then dragged some distance through the woodland, buried in a shallow grave, and left for animals to take her bones and scatter them through the woods. For days dogs had swarmed through the woods where she'd been found, looking for more pieces of their daughter, but they'd found nothing else.

The police trawled local garage records for cars that had been brought in with damage commensurate with hitting a body. They also leafleted the surrounding areas, asking if anyone remembered a female hitchhiker, a passenger on a bus, a young woman with a navy-blue rucksack; had she stayed in your hostel, your home; did you come upon her sleeping rough; do you recognize this face, this girl of fifteen years old, this computer-generated woman of twenty-five? Photos of Laurel's candlesticks were circulated. Had anyone sold them, seen them, bought them? But no one came forward. No one had seen anything. No one knew anything. After a twelve-week flurry of activity everything went still again.

And now Ellie was dead. The possibility was gone. Laurel was alone. Her family was broken. There was nothing. Literally nothing.

Until one day, a month after Ellie's funeral, Laurel met Floyd.

PART TWO

13

Laurel hands the young girl who washed her hair a two-pound coin. "Thank you, Dora," she says, smiling nicely.

Then she gives the hairstylist a five-pound note and says, "Thank you, Tania, it looks great, it really does. Thank you so much."

She eyes her reflection one more time in the wall-length mirror before leaving. Her hair is shoulder-length, blonde, shiny and swishy. Her hair is entirely unrepresentative of what lies beneath. If she could pay someone in Stroud Green eighty pounds to give her psyche a shiny, swishy blow-dry, she would. And she would give them more than a five-pound tip.

Outside it is a blowy autumn afternoon. Her hair feels light as silk as it is whipped around her head. It's late and she's hungry and decides that she can't wait to get home to eat so she pushes open the door to the café three doors down from her hairdresser's and orders herself a toasted cheese sandwich and a decaf cappuccino. She eats fast and the cheese pulls away from the bread in unruly strings that break and slap against her chin. She has a paper napkin to her chin to wipe away the grease when a man walks in.

He is of average height, average build, around fifty. His hair is cut short, gray at the temples, receding, and darker on the top. He's wearing good jeans with a nice shirt, lace-up shoes, tortoiseshell glasses: the sort of clothes that Paul would wear.

And whatever her feelings are now about Paul—and they are conflicted and horribly confusing—she has to concede that he always looks lovely.

She finds, to her surprise, that she is almost admiring the man in the doorway. There is something about him: a low-key swagger and a certain—dare she say it?—twinkle in his eye. She watches as he queues at the counter, takes in more detail: a flat but soft stomach, good hands, one ear that protrudes slightly farther than the other. He's not handsome in the traditional sense of the word but has the air of a man who has long ago accepted his physical limitations and shifted all the focus to his personality.

He orders a slice of carrot cake and a black coffee—his accent is hard to place, possibly American, or a foreigner who learned English from Americans—and then carries them to the table next to hers. Laurel's breath catches. He didn't appear to have noticed her staring at him yet he's chosen the table closest to hers in a café full of empty tables. She panics, feeling as though maybe she's subconsciously, inadvertently, invited his attentions. She doesn't want his attentions. She doesn't want any attention.

For a few moments they sit like that, side by side. He doesn't look at her, not once, but Laurel can feel some kind of intent radiating from him. The man plays with a smartphone. Laurel finishes her cheese sandwich in smaller, slower mouthfuls. After a while she begins to think maybe she was imagining it. She drinks her coffee and starts to leave.

Then: "You have beautiful hair."

She turns, shocked at his words, and says, "Oh."

"Really pretty."

"Thank you." Her hand has gone to her hair, unthinkingly. "I just had it done. It doesn't normally look this good."

He smiles. "You ever had this carrot cake before?"

She shakes her head.

"It's pretty amazing. Would you like to try some?"

She laughs nervously. "No, thank you, I . . ."

"Look, I have a clean spoon, right here." He pushes it across his table toward her. "Go on. I'm never going to eat all this."

A blade of light passes across the café at that moment, bright as torchlight. It touches the spoon and makes it glitter. The cake has the indents of his fork in it. The moment is curiously intimate and Laurel's gut reaction is to back away, to leave. But as she watches the sparkles on the silver spoon she feels something inside her begin to open up. Something like hope.

She picks up the spoon and she scoops a small chunk of cake from the end that he has not touched.

◦

His name is Floyd. Floyd Dunn. He offers her his hand and says, "Pleased to meet you, Laurel Mack." His grip is firm and warm.

"What's your accent?" she asks, pulling her chair closer to his table, feeling the blade of sunlight warming the back of her head.

"Ah," he says, dabbing his mouth with a paper napkin. "What isn't my accent would be a better question. I am the son of very ambitious Americans who chased jobs and money all around the world. Four years in the U.S. Two in Canada. Another four in the U.S. Four in Germany. A year in Singapore. Then three in the U.K. My parents went back to the States; I stayed here."

"So you've been here for a long time?"

"I've been here for"—he scrunches closed his eyes as he calculates—"thirty-seven years. I have a British passport. British children. A British ex-wife. I listen to *The Archers*. I'm fully assimilated."

He smiles and she laughs.

She catches herself for a moment. Sitting in a café in the middle of the afternoon, talking to a strange man, laughing at his jokes. How has this happened, this day? Of all the days, all the hundreds of dark days that have passed since Ellie went? Is this what closure does? Is this what happens when you finally bury your child?

"So, do you live around here?" he asks.

"No," she says. "No. I live in Barnet. But I used to live around here. Until a few years ago. Hence the hairdresser." She nods in the direction of the shop a few doors down. "Total phobia of letting anyone else touch my hair, so I trek down here every month."

"Well . . ." He eyes her hair. "It looks like it's worth it to me."

His tone is flirtatious and she has to ask herself if he's weird or not. Is he? Is there something odd about him, anything a bit off? Is she failing to read warning signs? Is he going to scam her, rape her, abduct her, stalk her? Is he mad? Is he bad?

She asks these silent internalized questions of everyone she meets. She was never a trusting person, even before her daughter vanished and then turned up dead ten years later. Paul always said he'd taken her on as a long-term project. She'd refused to marry him until Jake was a toddler, scared that he was just going through a phase and would stand her up at the register office. But she asks these questions even more these days. Because she knows that the worst-case scenario is not simply a terrible thing that isn't likely to happen.

But she's staring at this man, this man with gray eyes and gray hair and soft skin and nice shoes, and she cannot find one thing wrong with him. Apart from the fact that he is talking to her. "Thank you," she says in reply to his compliment. And then she moves her chair back, toward her table, wanting to leave, but also wanting him to ask her to stay.

"You have to go?" he says.

"Well, yes," she says, trying to think of something she needs to do. "I'm going to see my daughter."

She is not going to see her daughter. She never sees her daughter.

"Oh, you have a daughter?"

"Yes. And a son."

"One of each."

"Yes," she says, the pain of denying her gone daughter piercing her heart. "One of each."

"I have two girls."

She nods and hitches her bag on to her shoulder. "How old?"

"One of twenty-one. One of nine."

"Do they live with you?"

"The nine-year-old does. The twenty-one-year-old lives with her mum."

"Oh."

He smiles. "It's complicated."

"Isn't everything?" She smiles back.

And then he tears a corner off a newspaper left on the table next to his and finds a pen in his coat pocket and says, "Here. I've really enjoyed talking to you. But it hasn't been for long enough. I'd really like to take you out for dinner." He scribbles a number on the scrap of paper and passes it to her. "Call me."

Call me.

So assured, so simple, so forward. She cannot imagine how a human could be that way.

She takes the piece of paper and rubs it between her fingertips. "Yes," she says. Then: "Well, maybe."

He laughs. He has a lot of fillings. "'Maybe' will do for me. 'Maybe' will do."

She leaves the café quickly and without looking back.

꧂

That evening Laurel does something she's never done before. She drops into Hanna's unannounced. The expression on her older daughter's face when she sees her mother standing on the doorstep is 90 percent appalled and 10 percent concerned.

"Mum?"

"Hello, love."

Hanna looks behind her as though there might be a visible reason for her mother's presence somewhere in her vicinity.

"Are you OK?"

"Yes. I'm fine. I just . . . I was just passing by and felt I hadn't seen you in a while."

"I saw you on Sunday."

Hanna had popped by with an old laptop for her but hadn't crossed the threshold.

"Yes. I know. But that was just, well, it wasn't proper."

Hanna moves from one bare foot to the other. "Do you want to come in?"

"That would be nice, darling, thank you."

Hanna is in joggers and a tight white T-shirt with the word *Cheri* emblazoned across the front. Hanna has never been much of a style maven. She favors a black suit from Banana Republic for work and cheap leisurewear for home. Laurel doesn't know what she wears in the evenings since they never go anywhere together in the evenings.

"Do you want a cup of tea?"

"Bit late for tea for me."

Hanna rolls her eyes. She has little patience with Laurel's caffeine sensitivity, thinks she makes it all up to annoy her.

"Well, I'm going to have a coffee. What shall I get you?"

"Nothing, honestly. I'm fine."

She watches her daughter moving around her small kitchen, opening and closing cupboards, her body language so closed and muted, and she wonders if there was ever a time when she and Hanna were close.

"Where've you been then?" says Hanna.

"I'm sorry?"

"You said you were passing?"

"Oh, yes. Right. Hair appointment." She touches her hair again, feeling the white lie burning through her.

"It looks lovely."

"Thank you, darling."

The piece of newspaper with the scribbled number and the name "Floyd" on it is in her pocket and she touches it as she speaks. "A funny thing happened," she begins.

Hanna throws her a look of dread. It's the same look she throws her any time she starts a conversation about anything, as though she's terrified of being dragged into something she hasn't got the emotional capacity to deal with.

"A man gave me his phone number. Asked me out for dinner."

The look of dread turns to horror and Laurel feels she would do anything, pay anything, *give* anything to be having this conversation now with Ellie, not with Hanna. Ellie would whoop and beam, throw herself at Laurel and squeeze her hard, tell her it was *amazing* and *incredible* and *awesome*. And Ellie would have made it all those things.

"Of course I'm not going to call him. Of course I'm not. But it got me thinking. About us. About all of us. How we're all floating about like separate islands."

"Well, *yes.*" There's a note of accusation in Hanna's voice.

"It's been so long now. And yet we still haven't found a way to be a family again. It's like we're all stuck. Stuck inside that day. I mean, look at you." She knows the moment the words leave her mouth that they are completely the wrong ones.

"What?" Hanna sits up, unknits her fingertips. "What about me?"

"Well, you're amazing, obviously you're amazing, and I am so proud of you and how hard you work and everything you've achieved. But don't you ever feel . . . ? Don't you ever think it's all a bit one-dimensional? I mean, you don't even have a cat."

"What! A *cat*? Are you being serious? How the hell could I have a cat? I'm out all day and all night. I'd never see it, I'd . . ."

Laurel puts a hand out to her daughter. "Forget about the cat," she says. "I was just using it as an example. I mean, all these hours you work, isn't there anything? Some other dimension? A friend? A man?"

Her daughter blinks slowly at her. "Why are you asking me about men? You know I don't have time for men. I don't have time for anything. I don't even have time for this conversation."

Laurel sighs and touches the back of her neck. "I just noticed," she says, "a few times recently, when I've been in to clean, you haven't been home the night before."

Hanna flushes and then grimaces. "Ah," she says, "you thought I had a boyfriend?"

"Well, yes. I did wonder."

Hanna smiles, patronizingly. "No, Mother," she says, "sadly not. No boyfriend. Just, you know, parties, drinks, that kind of thing. I stay at friends' places." She shrugs and picks again at the dry skin around her nails.

Laurel narrows her eyes. Parties? Hanna? Hanna's body language is all skew-whiff and Laurel doesn't believe her. But she doesn't push it. She forces a smile and says, "Ah. I see."

Hanna softens then and leans toward her. "I'm still young, Mum. There'll be time for men. And cats. Just not now."

But what about us, Laurel wants to ask, *when will this stop being our life? When will there be time for us to be a family again? When will any of us ever truly laugh or truly smile without feeling guilty?*

But she doesn't ask it. Instead she takes Hanna's hand across the table and says, "I know, darling. I do know. I just so want you to be happy. I want us all to be happy. I want . . ."

"You want Ellie back."

She looks up at Hanna in surprise. "Yes," she says. "Yes, I want Ellie back."

"So do I," says Hanna. "But now we know. We know she's not coming back and we're just going to have to get on with it."

"Yes," says Laurel, "yes. You're absolutely right."

Her fingers find the piece of paper in her pocket again; they rub against it and a shiver goes down her spine.

14

"Hi. Floyd. It's Laurel. Laurel Mack."

"Mrs. Mack."

That soft transatlantic drawl, so lazy and dry.

"Or are you a *ms.*?"

"I'm a *ms.*," she replies.

"Ms. Mack, then. How good to hear from you. I could not be more delighted."

Laurel smiles. "Good."

"Are we making a dinner plan?"

"Well, yes. I suppose. Unless . . ."

"'There's no *unless*. Unless you have a specific *unless* in mind?"

She laughs. "No, I have no *unless* in mind."

"Good then," he says. "How about Friday night?"

"Good," she says, knowing without checking that she will be free. "Lovely."

"Shall we go into town? See some bright lights? Or somewhere near me? Somewhere near you?"

"Bright lights sound good," she says, her voice emerging breathlessly, almost girlishly.

"I was hoping you'd say that. You like Thai?"

"I love Thai."

"Leave it with me then," he says. "I'll make us a booking somewhere. I'll text you later with the details."

"Wow, yes. You are . . ."

"Efficient?"

"Efficient. Yes. And . . ."

"Exciting?"

She laughs again. "That's not what I was going to say."

"No. But it's true. I am a thrilling guy. Nonstop fun and adventures. That's how I roll."

"You're funny."

"Thank you."

"I'll see you on Friday."

"You will," he says, "unless . . ."

◦⌒◦

Laurel has always taken care of her appearance. Even in the terrible early days of Ellie's disappearance she would shower, choose clothes carefully, blot out the shadows under her eyes with pricey concealers, comb her hair until it shone. She had never let herself go. Herself was all she had left in those days.

She's always made herself look nice but not worried about looking pretty for a long time. In fact, she stopped attempting to look pretty in approximately 1985 when she and Paul moved in together. So this, right now, her stupid face in the mirror, the open bags of cosmetics, the flow of nervous energy running through her that has her putting mascara on her eyelids instead of eyeliner, the terrible scrutiny and crossness at herself for allowing her face to get old, for not being pretty, for not being born with the genes of Christy Turlington, this is all new.

She grimaces and wipes the mascara away with a cleansing wipe. "Bollocks," she mutters under her breath. "Shit."

Behind her on her bed are the contents of her wardrobe. It's strange weather tonight. Muggy, for the time of year, but showers forecast, and a strong wind. And although her figure is fine—she's a standard size ten—all her going-out clothes are ones she's had since she was in her forties. Too high up the leg, too flowery, too much arm, too much chest. Nothing works, none of it. She surrenders, in the end, to a gray long-sleeve top and flared black trousers. Dull. But appropriate.

The time is seven oh five. She needs to leave the house in ten minutes to be on time for her date with Floyd. She quickly finishes her makeup. She has no idea if she's made herself look better or worse but she's run out of time to care.

At the front door of her apartment she stops for a moment. She keeps photos of her three children on a small console here. She likes the feeling of being greeted and bade farewell by them. She picks up the photo of Ellie. Fifteen years old, the October half-term before she went missing; they were in Wales; her face was flushed with sea air and ball games on the beach with her brother and sister. Her mouth was fully open; you could see virtually to the back of her throat. She wore a tan woolly hat with a giant pompom on the top. Her hands were buried inside the sleeves of an oversized hoodie.

"I'm going on a date, Ellie," she says to her girl. "With a nice man. He's called Floyd. I think you'd like him."

She passes her thumb over her girl's smiling face, over the giant pompom.

That's awesome, Mum, she hears her say, *I'm so happy for you. Have fun!*

"I'll try," she replies to the emptiness. "I'll try."

❧

The light is kind in the restaurant that Floyd's chosen for their date. The walls are lacquered black and gold, the furniture is dark, the lampshades are made of amethyst beads strung together over halogen bulbs. He's already there when she arrives, two minutes late. She thinks, He looks younger in this light, therefore I must look younger, too. This bolsters her as she approaches him and lets him stand and kiss her on both cheeks.

"You look very elegant," he says.

"Thank you," she says. "So do you."

He's wearing a black and gray houndstooth-checked shirt and a black corduroy jacket. His hair looks to have had a trim since their first meeting and he smells of cedar and lime.

"Do you like the restaurant?" he asks, faking uncertainty and fooling nobody.

"Of course I like the restaurant," she says. "It's gorgeous."

"Phew," he says and she smiles at him.

"Have you been here before?" she asks.

"I have. But only for lunch. I always wanted to come back in the evening when it was all gloomy and murky and full of louche people."

Laurel looks around her at the clientele, most of whom look like they just came straight from the office or are on dates. "Not so louche," she says.

"Yeah. I noticed. I am *very* disappointed."

She smiles and he passes her a menu.

"Are you hungry?"

"I'm ravenous," she says. And it's true. She's been too nervous to eat all day. And now that she's seen him and remembered why she agreed to share his cake with him, why she called him, why she arranged to meet him, her appetite has come back.

"You like spicy food?"

"I love spicy food."

He beams at her. "Thank God for that. I only really like people who like spicy food. That would have been a bad start."

It takes them a while even to look at the menu. Floyd is full of questions: Do you have a job? Brothers? Sisters? What sort of flat do you live in? Any hobbies? Any pets? And then, before their drinks have even arrived, "How old are your kids?"

"Oh." She bunches her napkin up on her lap. "They're twenty-seven and twenty-nine."

"Wow!" He looks at her askance. "You do not look old enough to have kids that age. I thought teens, at a push."

She knows this is utter nonsense; losing a child ages you faster than a life spent chain-smoking on a beach. "I'm nearly fifty-five," she says. "And I look it."

"Well, no you don't," he counters. "I had you at forty-something. You look great."

She shrugs off the compliment; it's just silly.

Floyd smiles, pulls a pair of reading glasses from the inside pocket of his nice jacket and slips them on. "Shall we get ordering?"

They overorder horribly. Dishes keep arriving, bigger than either of them had anticipated, and they spend large portions of the evening rearranging glasses and water bottles and mobile phones to free up space for them. "Is that it?" they ask each other every time a new dish is delivered. "Please say that that's it."

They drink beer at first and then move on to white wine.

Floyd tells Laurel about his divorce from the mother of his elder daughter. The girl is called Sara-Jade.

"I wanted to call her Sara-Jane, my ex wanted to call her Jade. It was a pretty simple compromise. I call her Sara. My ex calls her Jade. She calls herself SJ." He shrugs. "You can give your kids any name you like and they'll just go ahead and do their own thing with it ultimately."

"What's she like?"

"Sara? She's . . ." For the first time Laurel sees a light veil fall across Floyd's natural effervescence. "She's unusual. She's, er . . ." He appears to run out of words. "Well," he says eventually. "I guess you'd just have to meet her."

"How often do you see her?"

"Oh, quite a lot, quite a lot. She still lives at home, with my ex; they don't get on all that well so she uses me as an escape hatch. So, most weekends, in fact. Which is a mixed blessing." He smiles wryly.

"And your other daughter? What's her name?"

"Poppy." His face lights up at the mention of her.

"And what's she like? Is she very different to Sara-Jade?"

"Oh God yes." He nods slowly and theatrically. "Yes indeed. Poppy is amazing, you know, she's insanely brilliant at maths, has the driest, wickedest sense of humor, takes no shit from anyone. She really keeps me on my toes, reminds me that I am not the be-all and end-all. She wipes the floor with me, in all respects."

"Wow. She sounds great!" she says, thinking that he could have been describing her own lost girl.

"She is," he says. "I am blessed."

"So how come she lives with you?"

"Yes, well, that's the complicated part. Poppy and Sara-Jade do not have the same mother. Poppy's mum was . . . I don't know, a casual relationship that rather overran its limitations. If you see what I mean. Poppy wasn't planned. Far from it. And we did try for a while to be a normal couple, but we never quite managed to pull it off. And then, when Poppy was four years old, she vanished."

"Vanished?" Laurel's heart races at the word, a word so imbued with meaning to her.

"Yeah. Dumped Poppy on my doorstep. Cleared out her bank account. Abandoned her house, her job. Never to be seen again." He picks up his wineglass and takes a considered sip, as if waiting for Laurel to pick up the commentary.

She has her hand to her throat. She feels suddenly as though this was all fated, that her meeting with this strangely attractive man was not as random as she'd thought, that they'd somehow recognized the strange holes in each other, the places for special people who had been dramatically and mysteriously plucked from the ether.

"Wow," she says. "Poor Poppy."

Floyd turns his gaze to the tablecloth, rolls a grain of rice around under his fingertip. "Indeed," he says. "Indeed."

"What do you think happened to her?"

"To Poppy's mother?" he asks. "Christ, I have no idea. She was a strange woman. She could have ended up anywhere," he says. "Literally anywhere."

Laurel looks at him, judging the appropriateness of her next question. "Do you ever think maybe she's dead?"

He looks up at her darkly and she knows that she has gone too far. "Who knows?" he says. "Who knows." And then the smile reappears, the conversation moves along, an extra glass of wine each is ordered, the fun recommences, the date continues.

15

When she gets home, Laurel goes straight to her laptop, pulls on her reading glasses, and googles Floyd Dunn. They'd talked all night, until the restaurant had had to ask them very politely to leave. There'd been a gentle suggestion of going on somewhere else; Floyd Dunn was a member at a club somewhere ("Not one of those flashy ones," he'd said, "just a bar and some armchairs, a few old farts drinking brandy and growling"), but Laurel had not wanted to travel back to High Barnet after the tubes stopped running, so they'd said good-bye at Piccadilly Circus and Laurel had sat smiling dumbly, drunkenly at her reflection in the tube window all the way up the Northern line.

Now she is in pajamas with a toothbrush in her mouth. The clothes she'd left on her bed are in a pile on the armchair and her makeup is still scattered across her dressing table; she has no energy for practicalities; she just wants to keep herself tight inside the bubble that she and Floyd made together tonight, not let life crawl in through the gaps.

Within a few seconds Laurel discovers that Floyd Dunn is in fact the author of several well-reviewed books about number theory and mathematical physics.

She clicks on Google Images and stares at Floyd's face in varying stages of life and appearance; in some photos he is visibly younger: late thirties, long-haired, wearing a low-buttoned shirt. This is his author photo from his first few books and is slightly unsettling. She would not have shared a slice of cake with this man who resembles a lonely Open University lecturer from the early eighties. Later photos show him more or less as he is now, his hair slightly scruffier and darker, his clothing not quite so smart, but fundamentally the man she just had dinner with.

She wants to know more about him. She wants to envelop herself in him and his fascinating world. She wants to see him again. And again. And then she thinks of Paul, and his Bonny, the numb disbelief she'd felt when he'd come to her to inform her that he'd met a woman and that they were moving in together. She had been unable to comprehend how he had managed to get to such a place, a place of softness and butterflies in your stomach, of making plans and holding hands. And now it is happening to her and all of a sudden she aches to call him.

Paul, she imagines herself saying, *I've met a fabulous guy. He's clever and he's funny and he's hot and he's kind.*

And she realizes that it's the first time in years she's wanted to talk to Paul about anything other than Ellie.

                        ~

The next day is an agony of silence.

On Saturdays Laurel usually sees her friends Jackie and Bel. She's known them since they were all at school together in Portsmouth, where they were an inseparable gang of three. About thirty years ago, when they were all in their twenties and living in London, Laurel had met up with them in a bar in Soho and they'd told her that they had come out to each other and were now a couple. And then eleven years ago, in her early forties, Bel had given birth to twin boys. Just as Laurel was exiting the parenting zone, they'd walked straight into it, and in the years after Ellie disappeared, their home in Edmonton full of nappies and plastic and pink yogurt in squeezy tubes had been a refuge to her.

But they are away this weekend, taking the boys to a rugby tournament in Shropshire. And so the minutes pass exquisitely and the air in the flat hangs heavy around her. The sounds of her neighbors closing doors, calling to their children, starting their cars, walking their dogs, ratchets up the feeling of aloneness, and there is no call from Floyd, no text and she is too old, far too old for all this, and by Saturday night she has talked herself out of it. It was a mad idea. Nonsensical. She is a damaged woman with a ton of ugly baggage and Floyd was clearly just using his effortless charm to secure a night out with a woman, something he could probably manage every night of the week if he so chose. And he was probably sitting in a café somewhere right now, sharing a slice of carrot cake with someone else.

On Sunday Laurel decides to visit her mother. She usually visits her mother on a Thursday; having it as a weekly slot makes it less likely that she'll find an excuse not to go. But she cannot spend another day at home alone. She just can't.

Her mother's care home in Enfield, a twenty-minute drive away, is a new-build, redbrick thing with smoked-glass windows so that no one can peer in and see their own devastating futures. Ruby, her mum, has had three strokes, has limited vocabulary, is half-blind, and has very patchy recall. She is also very unhappy and can usually be counted upon to find the words to express her wish to die.

Her mother is in a chair when she arrives at half eleven. By her side is a plate of oaty-looking biscuits and a cup of milk as though she was four years old. Laurel takes her mother's hand and strokes the parchment skin. She looks into her dark eyes and tries, as she always does, to see the other person, the person who would pick her up by one arm and one leg and throw her in swimming pools when she was small, who chased her across beaches and plaited her hair and made her eggs over easy when she requested them after she'd seen them on an American TV show. Her mother's energy had been boundless, her curly black hair always coming loose from grips and bands, her heels always low so that she was free to run for buses and jump over walls and pursue muggers.

Her first stroke had hit her four months after Ellie's disappearance and she'd never been the same since.

"I went on a date last week," Laurel tells her mother. Her mother nods and pinches her mouth into a tight smile. She tries to say something but can't find the words.

"F-F-F-F . . . F-F-F . . ."

"Don't worry, Mum. I know you're pleased."

"Fan*tas*tic!" she suddenly manages.

"Yes," says Laurel, smiling broadly, "it is. Except now of course I'm really nervous, behaving like a teenager; I keep staring at my phone, willing him to call. It's pathetic . . ."

Her mum smiles again, or the facsimile of a smile that her damaged brain will allow. "N . . . Name?"

"His name is Floyd. Floyd Dunn. He's American. He's my age, ludicrously clever, nice-looking, funny. He's got two daughters; one of them lives with him, the other is grown up."

Her mother nods, still smiling. "You . . . you . . . you . . . you . . ."

Laurel runs her thumb across the top of her mother's hand and smiles encouragingly.

"You . . . you . . . you *call him!*"

Laurel laughs. "I can't!"

Her mum shakes her head crossly and tuts.

"No. Honestly. I called him the first time. I already made the first move. It's his turn now."

Her mum tuts again.

"I suppose," Laurel ponders, "I could maybe send him a text, just to say thank-you? Leave the ball in his court?"

Her mum nods and clasps Laurel's hand inside hers, squeezing it softly.

Her mother adored Paul. From day one she'd said, "Well done, my darling, you found a good man. Now please be kind to him. Please don't let him go." And Laurel had smiled wryly and said, "We'll see." Because Laurel had never believed in happy ever afters. And her mum had been sanguine about Paul and Laurel splitting up; she'd understood, because she was both a romantic and a realist. Which in many ways was the perfect combination.

Her mother puts out a hand to feel for Laurel's handbag She puts her hand into it and she pulls out Laurel's phone and hands it to her.

"What?" says Laurel. "Now?"

She nods.

Laurel sighs heavily and then types in the words.

"I will hold you fully responsible," she says, mock-sternly, "if this all blows up in my face."

Then she presses the send button and quickly shuts her phone down and stuffs it into her handbag, horrified by what she has just done. "Shit," she says, running her hands down her face. "You cow," she says to her mum. "I can't believe you made me do that!"

And her mother laughs, a strange, warped thing that comes from too high up her throat. But it's a laugh. And the first one Laurel can remember hearing from her mother in a very long time indeed.

Seconds later Laurel's phone rings. It's him.

16

Laurel and Floyd have their second date that Tuesday. This time they stay local, and go to an Eritrean restaurant near Floyd that Laurel had always wanted to try but Paul would never agree to because they had a three-star hygiene rating taped to their window.

Floyd is dressed down, in a bottle-green polo shirt under a black jumper, with jeans. Laurel is wearing a fitted linen pinafore over a white cotton blouse, her hair clipped back, black tights and black boots. She looks like a trendy nun. She had not realized, until she met Floyd, how stern, virtually *clerical* all her clothes were.

"You look amazing," he says, clearly missing all the signs of her sartorial struggle. "You are far too stylish for me. I feel like an absolute bum."

"You look lovely," she says, taking her seat, "you always look lovely."

She's amazed by how relaxed she feels. There are none of the nerves that plagued their first meeting last week. The restaurant is scruffy and brightly lit, but she feels unconcerned about her appearance, about whether or not she looks old.

She stares at his hands as they move and she wants to snatch them in midair, grab them, hold them to her face. She follows the movement of his head, gazes at the fan of smile lines around his eyes, glances from time to time at the just visible spray of chest hair emerging from the undone top button of his polo shirt. She wants, very badly, to have sex with him and this realization shocks her into a kind of flustered silence for a moment.

"Are you OK, Laurel?" he asks, sensing her awkwardness.

"Oh, God, yes. I'm fine," she replies, smiling, and he looks reassured by this and the conversation continues.

He talks warmly to the waitstaff, who seem to know him well and bring him bonus dishes and morsels of things to taste.

"You know," she says, tearing off a piece of flatbread and dipping it into a mutton stew, "my ex refused to bring me here because of the poor hygiene rating." She feels bad for a moment, belittling Paul, painting a one-note picture of him for a stranger when there is much more to know about him.

"Well, hygiene, schmygiene, I have never had a dodgy tummy after eating here and I've been coming for years. These people know what they're doing."

"So how long have you lived around here?"

"Oh, God, forever. Since my parents went back to the U.S. They gave me a piece of money, told me to put it down somewhere scruffy but central. I found this house; it was all split up into bedsits, just disgusting. Jesus, the way people live. Dead rats. Blocked toilets. Shit on the wall." He shudders. "But it was the best decision I ever made. You would not believe how much the place is worth now."

Laurel could believe it, having sold her own Stroud Green house only a few years earlier. "Do you think you'll ever go back to the States?"

He shakes his head. "No. Never. It was never home to me. Nowhere ever felt like home to me till I came here."

"And your parents? Are they still alive?"

"Yup. Very much so. They were young parents so they're

still pretty spry. What about you?" he asks. "Are your parents still with you?"

She shakes her head. "My dad died when I was twenty-six. My mum's in a home now. She's very frail. I doubt she'll be around this time next year." Then she smiles and says, "In fact, it was her who told me to call you. On Sunday. She can barely talk, it takes her an age to form a sentence; usually all she wants to talk about is dying. But she told me to call you. She said it was fantastic that I'd met you. She literally put my phone in my hand. It's the most"—she glances down at her lap—"the most maternal thing she's done in a decade. The most human thing she's done in months. It moved me."

And then Floyd reaches across the table and places his hands over hers, his nice gray eyes fixed on hers, and he says, "God bless your glorious mum."

She hooks her fingers over his and squeezes his hands gently. His touch feels both gentle and hard, sexual yet benign. His touch makes her feel everything she thought she'd never feel again, things she'd forgotten she'd ever felt in the first place. His thumbs move up her wrists and pass over her pulse points. His fingertips draw lines up and down the insides of her arms. She pulls at the soft hair on his forearms, and then pushes her hands deep inside the soft wool of his sleeves. She finds his elbows and his hands find hers and they grasp each other like that across the table for a long, intense moment, before slowly pulling apart and they ask for the bill.

❦

His house is exactly the same as her old house, just three roads down from where she used to live. It's a semidetached Victorian with Dutch gables and a small balcony over the front porch. It has a tiled path leading to a front door with stained-glass panels to each side and a stained-glass fanlight above. There is a small square of a front garden, neatly tended, and a pair of wheelie bins down the side return. Laurel knows what the house will look like on the inside before Floyd even has his key in the front door because it will look just like hers.

And yes, there it is, as she'd known it would be, the tiled hallway with a wide staircase ahead, the banister ending in a generous swirl, a single wooden step leading down to a large airy kitchen, and a door to the left through which she can make out a book-lined room, the flicker of a TV set, and a pair of bare feet crossed at the ankle. She watches the bare feet uncross and lower themselves to the stripped floorboards, then a face appears, a small, nervous face, a shock of white-blonde hair, a crescent of multiple earrings, a thick flick of blue liner. "Dad?"

The head retracts quickly at the sight of Laurel in the hallway.

"Hi, honey." Floyd turns and mouths *Sara* at Laurel before popping his head around the door. "How's your evening been?"

"OK." Sara-Jade's voice is soft and deep.

"How was Poppy?"

"She was OK."

"What time did she go to bed?"

"Oh, like half an hour ago. You're early."

Laurel sees the delicate head lean forward slightly, then snap back again.

"Sara"—Floyd turns to Laurel and gestures for her hand— "I've got someone to introduce you to." He pulls Laurel toward the door and propels her in front of him. "This is Laurel. Laurel, this is my elder daughter, Sara-Jade."

"SJ," says the tiny girl on the armchair, slowly pulling herself to her feet. She gives Laurel a tiny hand to shake and says,

"Nice to meet you." Then she falls back into the armchair and curls her tiny blue-veined feet beneath her.

She's wearing an oversized black T-shirt and black velvet leggings. Laurel takes in the thinness of her, wonders if it is an eating disorder or just the way she's built.

On the television is a reality TV show about people having blind dates in a brightly lit restaurant. On the floor by SJ's feet is an empty plate smeared with traces of tomato ketchup and an empty Diet Coke can. Crumpled on the arm of the chair is a wrapper from a Galaxy bar. Laurel assumes then that her build is all natural and immediately pictures her mother, some tremulous pixie woman with enormous eyes and size six jeans. She feels pathetically jealous for a moment.

"Well," says Floyd, "we'll be in the kitchen. Do you want a cup of tea?"

Sara-Jade shakes her head but doesn't say anything. Laurel follows Floyd into the kitchen. It's as she'd imagined: smart cream wooden units with oversized wooden knobs, a dark green range, an island surrounded by stools. Unlike her old kitchen it hasn't been extended into the return but just to the back where there is a pine table surrounded by pine chairs, piles of papers and magazines, two laptops, a pink fur coat slung over one chair, a suit jacket over the other.

She sits on a stool and watches him make her a mug of camomile tea, himself a coffee from a filter machine. "Your house is lovely," she says.

"Why thank you," he replies. "Although I feel you should know that that exact spot where you're sitting was where the guy who used to live in the back room kept his chamber pot. And I know that because he left it behind when he moved out. *Unemptied.*"

"Oh my God!" She laughs. "That's revolting."

"Tell me about it."

"You know, your house is the same as my old house. Exactly. I mean, not exactly, obviously, but the same layout, the same design."

"All these streets," he said, "all these houses, they were modern estates once upon a time, built at the same time to house the City workers." He passes her her tea and smiles. "Strange," he says, "to think that one day our ancestors might be charmed by a Barratt estate, desperately trying to preserve the period features. *Don't touch that plastic coving, it's priceless.*"

Laurel smiles. *"Can you believe, the people who lived here before took out the fitted wardrobes with mirrored sliding doors!"*

Floyd laughs and eyes her fondly. And then he stops laughing and stares at her intently. He says, "You know, I googled you. After our first date."

The smile freezes on Laurel's face.

"I know about Ellie."

Laurel grips her mug between her hands and swallows. "Oh."

"You knew I would, didn't you?"

She smiles sadly. "Oh, I don't know, I suppose it occurred to me. I would have said something. Soon. I was on the verge. It just didn't seem like first-date kind of fodder."

"No," he says softly. "I get that."

She turns the mug around and around, not sure where to head next with this development.

"I'm really sorry," he says. "I just . . ." He sighs heavily. "I wouldn't . . . I can't imagine. Well, I can imagine. I can imagine all too well, which makes it hard to bear. Not that me bearing it is of any relevance to anything. But the thought of . . . you . . . and your girl . . . it's just. *Christ.*" He sighs heavily. "And I wanted to say something all night, because it felt so dishonest to sit there making small talk with you when I had all this *knowledge* that you didn't know I had and . . ."

"I'm an idiot," she says. "I should have guessed."

"No," he says. "I'm an idiot. I should have waited for you to tell me, when you were ready."

And Laurel smiles and looks up at Floyd, into his misty eyes; then she looks down at his hands, the hands that just caressed her arms so seductively in the restaurant, and she looks around his warm, loved home and she says, "I'm ready now. I can talk about it now."

He reaches across the counter and places his hand upon her shoulder. She instinctively rubs her cheek against it. "Are you sure?"

"Yes," she says. "I'm sure."

∞

It is nearly 1 a.m. when Floyd finally leads Laurel up the stairs to his bedroom. Sara-Jade had taken a taxi home at midnight, saying good-bye to her father in hushed tones and without acknowledging Laurel.

Floyd's room is painted dark burgundy and hung with interesting abstract oil paintings he claims to have found in the basement of the house when he was renovating it. "They're kind of ugly, I guess. But I like them. I like that I liberated them from total obscurity, let them live and breathe."

"Where's Poppy's room?" she whispers.

He points above and behind. "She won't hear anything. And besides, she sleeps like the dead."

And then he is unzipping the back of her pinafore dress and she is tugging at the sleeves of his warm soft jumper and they are a tangle of limbs and clothes and tights and despite the fact that Laurel had decided a long time ago that she and sex were over, five minutes later it is happening; she is having sex and not only that but it is the best sex she has ever had in her life and within moments of doing it she wants to do it all over again.

They fall asleep as a dull brown dawn creeps through the gaps in his curtains, wrapped up in each other's arms.

17

"Morning! Are you Laurel?"

Laurel jumps slightly. It's ten o'clock and she'd assumed that Floyd's daughter would have been at school by now. "Yes," she says, flicking on a warm smile. "Yes. I'm Laurel. And you're Poppy, I assume?"

"Yes. I am Poppy." She beams at Laurel, revealing crooked teeth and a small dimple in her left cheek. And Laurel has to hold on to something then, the closest thing to her, the door frame. She grips it hard and for a moment she is rendered entirely mute.

"Wow," she says eventually. "Sorry. You look . . ." But she doesn't say it. She doesn't say, *You look just like my lost girl . . . the dimple, the broad forehead, the heavy-lidded eyes, the way you tip your head to one side like that when you're trying to work out what someone's thinking.* Instead she says, "You remind me of someone. Sorry!" and she laughs too loud.

Laurel used to see girls who looked like Ellie all the time, after she'd first gone. She'd never quite got to the point of chasing anyone down the street, calling out her daughter's name and grabbing them by the shoulder as people did in movies. But she'd had the butterflies, the quickening of her breath, the feeling that her world was about to blow apart with joy and relief. They were always so short-lived, those moments, and it hadn't happened for years now.

Poppy smiles and says, "Can I get you anything? A tea? A coffee?"

"Oh," says Laurel, not expecting such slick hostessing from a nine-year-old girl. "Yes. A coffee, please. If that's OK?" She looks behind her, to see if Floyd is coming. He'd told her he would be down in two minutes. He hadn't told her that his daughter would be here.

"Dad said you were really pretty," says Poppy with her back to her as she fills the filter machine from the tap. "And you are."

"Gosh," says Laurel. "Thank you. Though I must look a state." She runs her hand down her hair, smoothing out the tangles that this child's father put there last night with his hands. She's wearing Floyd's T-shirt and she reeks, she knows she does, of sex.

"Did you have a lovely evening?" Poppy asks, spooning ground coffee into the machine.

"Yes, thank you, we really did."

"Did you go to the Eritrean place?"

"Yes."

"That's my favorite restaurant," she says. "My dad's been taking me there since I was tiny."

"Oh," says Laurel. "What a sophisticated palate you must have."

"There's nothing I won't eat," she replies. "Apart from prunes, which are the devil's work."

Poppy is wearing a loose-fitting dress made of blue and white striped cotton, with navy woolen tights and a pair of navy leather pumps. Her brown hair is tied back and has two small red clips in it. It's a very formal outfit for a young girl, Laurel feels. The sort of thing she'd have had to bribe both her girls to wear when they were that age.

"No school today?" she inquires.

"No. No school any day. I don't go to school."

"Oh," says Laurel, "that's . . . I mean . . ."

"Dad teaches me."

"Has he always taught you?"

"Yes. Always. You know I could read chapter books when I was three. Simple algebra at four. There was no normal school that would have coped with me really." She laughs, a womanly tinkle, and she flicks the switch on the filter machine. "Can I interest you in some granola and yogurt? Maybe? Or a slice of toast?"

Laurel turns to look behind her again. There's still no sign of Floyd. "You know," she says, "I might just have a quick shower before I eat anything. I feel a bit . . ." She grimaces. "I won't be long."

"Absolutely," says Poppy. "You go and shower. I'll have your coffee waiting for you."

Laurel nods and smiles and starts to back out of the kitchen. She passes Floyd on the stairs. He's fresh and showered, his hair damp and combed back off his face, his skin uncooked-looking where he's shaved away yesterday's stubble. He encircles her waist with his arm and buries his face in her shoulder.

"I met Poppy," she says quietly. "You didn't tell me you home-schooled her."

"Didn't I?"

"No." She pulls away from another attempt at affection. "I'm going to have a shower," she says. "I can't sit chatting to your daughter smelling like an old slapper who's been up all night shagging her dad."

Floyd laughs. "You smell delicious," he says, and his hand goes between her legs and she's torn between pressing herself hard against it and slapping it away.

"Stop it," she says affectionately and he laughs.

"What did you think?" he says. "Of my Poppy?"

"She's charming," she says. "Totally delightful."

He glows at the words. "Isn't she just? Isn't she just magnificent?"

He leans down and he kisses her gently on the lips before descending the stairs and heading into the kitchen where Laurel hears him greeting his daughter with the words, "Good morning, my remarkable girl, and how are *you* today?"

She continues up the stairs and takes a long slow shower in her lover's en-suite bathroom, feeling a peculiarity and wrongness that she cannot quite locate the cause of.

～

Later that day Laurel goes to Hanna's flat to clean it. Other people might find the thirty pounds pinioned beneath a vase of flowers on the table slightly peculiar. Laurel is aware that being paid in cash to clean her daughter's flat is not entirely normal, but all families have their idiosyncrasies and this is just one of theirs. As it is, every week she puts the thirty pounds into a special bank account that she will one day use to spoil her as-yet-unborn grandchildren with treats and days out.

She folds up the notes and slots them into her purse. Then she does the detective sweep of Hanna's flat that she has begun to do since Hanna stopped sleeping here every night. She remains unconvinced by Hanna's explanation of late nights and sleepovers, this sudden rush of parties and good times. That is simply not the daughter she knows. Hanna has never liked having fun.

The flowers are of particular interest: not a hastily bought bunch of Sainsbury's tulips or Stargazer lilies, but a bouquet. Dusky roses, baby's breath, lilac hyacinths, and eucalyptus. The stems are still spiraled together in the middle where the twine would have tied them together.

In the kitchen she takes out the cleaning products and eyes the work surfaces, looking for clues. Hanna was not home the night before, as evidenced once again by the lack of cereal bowl and makeup detritus. The problem, Laurel can see, is that if there is a man, then Hanna is spending all her time at his house so there will be no evidence to find at her house. She sighs and leans down to the swing bin to pull out the half-full bag, which, as always, weighs nothing, as Hanna has no life. She scrunches it down to tie the top in a knot and notices the crackle of cellophane. Quickly she puts her hand into the bag and locates the flower packaging. She pulls it out and unfurls it, and there is a tiny card taped to it, a message scrawled on it in scruffy florist's handwriting:

Can't wait to see you tomorrow. Please don't be late!

> *I love you so much,*
> *T x*

Laurel holds the card between her thumb and forefinger and stares at it for a while. Then she shoves it back into the bin bag and ties a knot in it. There, she thinks, there it is. Hanna has moved on. Hanna has a man. But why, she wonders, is she not talking to me about it?

18

Laurel has not seen Paul since Ellie's funeral. There they had stood side by side; Paul had not brought Bonny and had not even asked if he could.

Yes, he is a good man.

A good man in every way.

He had held her up that day when she felt her legs weaken slightly beneath her at the sight of the box going through the curtains to the sound of "Somewhere Only We Know" by Keane. He'd passed her cups of tea at his mother's house afterward, and then found her in a corner of the garden and lured her back into the house with the promise of a large Baileys and ice, her all-time favorite treat. They'd sat together after everyone else had gone and rolled the ice around the insides of their glasses and made each other laugh, and Laurel's feelings had warped and contorted and turned into something both light and dark, golden and gray. He hadn't once checked his phone or worried about being late for Bonny and they'd left his mother's house together at ten o'clock, weaving slightly toward the minicabs that rumbled and growled on the street outside. She let him hold her deep inside his arms, her face pressed hard against his chest, the clean, familiar smell of him, the softness of his old Jermyn Street shirt, and she'd almost, almost turned her face toward him and kissed him.

She'd woken the following day feeling as though her world

had been upended and reordered in every conceivable way. And she hadn't spoken to him since.

But now she feels as though all that ambiguity has melted away. She is a clean slate and she can face him once more. So when she gets back from Hanna's flat, she calls him.

"Hello, Laurel," he says warmly. Because Paul says everything warmly. It's one of the many things that made her hate him during Ellie's missing years. The way he'd smile so genuinely at the police and the reporters and the journalists and the nosy neighbors, the way he'd reach out to people with both of his warm hands and hold theirs inside his, keeping eye contact, asking after their health, playing down their own nightmare, trying, constantly, to make everyone feel better about everything all the time. She, meanwhile, had pictured herself with her hands around his soft throat, squeezing and squeezing until he was dead.

But now his tone matches her own state of mind. Now she can appreciate him afresh. Lovely, lovely Paul Mack. Such a nice man.

"How are you?" he says.

"I'm fine, thank you," she says. "How are you?"

"Oh, you know."

She does know. "I wondered," she began, "it's mine and Hanna's birthday next week. I was thinking maybe we could do something. Together? Maybe?"

Hanna had arrived in the world at two minutes past midnight on Laurel's twenty-seventh birthday. It was family lore that she'd been born determined to steal everyone's limelight.

"You mean, all of us? You, me, the kids?"

"Yes. Kids. Partners, too. If you like."

"Wow. Yes!" He sounds like a small boy being offered a free bicycle. "I think that's a great idea. It's Wednesday, isn't it?"

"Yes. And I haven't asked her yet. It's possible she may be busy. But I just thought, after the year we've had, after, you know, finding Ellie, saying good-bye, we've been so fractured, for so long, maybe now it's time to—"

"To come back together," he cuts in. "It's a brilliant idea. I'd love to. I'll talk to Bonny."

"Well," she says, "wait till I've spoken to the kids. It's hard, you know, they're so busy. But fingers crossed . . ."

"Yes. Definitely. Thank you, Laurel."

"You're welcome."

"It's been a long journey, hasn't it?"

"Arduous."

"I've missed you so much."

"I've missed you, too. And Paul—"

He says, "Yes?"

She pauses for a moment, swallows hard, and then reaches down into herself to retrieve the word she never thought she'd say to Paul. "I'm sorry."

"What on earth for?"

"Oh, you know, Paul. You don't have to pretend. I was a bitch to you. You know I was."

"Laurel." He sighs. "You were never a bitch."

"No," she says, "I was worse than a bitch."

"You were never anything other than a mother, Laurel. That's all."

"Other mothers lose children without losing their husbands, too."

"You didn't lose me, Laurel. I'm still yours. I'll always be yours."

"Well, that's not strictly true, is it?"

He sighs again. "Where it counts," he says. "As the father of your children, as a friend, as someone who shared a journey with you and as someone who loves you and cares about you. I don't need to be married to you to be all those things. Those things are deeper than marriage. Those things are forever."

Now Laurel sighs, an awkward smile twisting the corners of her mouth. "Thank you, Paul. Thank you."

She hangs up a moment later and she holds her phone in her lap for a while, tenderly, staring straight ahead, feeling a sense of peace she never thought would be hers to feel again.

Hanna sounds annoyed even to be asked about it.

"What do you mean, *all of us*?" she asks.

"I mean, me, you, Dad, Jake, Bonny, Blue."

"Oh God," she groans.

Laurel stands firm. She'd known Hanna wouldn't leap head-first into the concept. "Like you said," she explains, "it's time for us all to move on. We're all healing now, and this is part of the process."

"Well, for you maybe. I mean, you've never even met Bonny. How awkward is that going to be?"

"It won't be awkward because me and your father won't let it be awkward." How long had it been since she'd used those words? *Me and your father.* "We're all grown-ups now, Hanna. No more excuses. You're almost twenty-eight. I'm virtually an OAP. We've buried Ellie. Your father has a partner. He loves her. I have to accept that and embrace her as part of this family. The same with Jake and Blue. And, of course, with you . . ."

"With me?"

"Yes. You. And whoever sent you those beautiful flowers."

There's a cool beat of silence. Then: "What flowers?"

"The bouquet on your kitchen table."

"There is no bouquet."

"Oh, well, then, the imaginary bouquet with the imaginary pink roses in it. *That one.*"

Hanna tuts. "That's not a bouquet. It's just a bunch. I bought them for myself."

Laurel sighs. "Oh," she says, breezily, disingenuously, "my mistake then. Sorry."

"Will you just stop trying to invent a boyfriend for me, Mum? There is no boyfriend, OK?"

"Fine. Yes. Sorry."

"And I really don't like the idea of this big family meal. It's too bizarre."

"Are you free?"

She pauses before she replies. "No."

"No?"

"Well, not on my actual birthday. On *our* birthday. No. But I could do another day next week."

"What are you doing on our actual birthday, then?"

"Oh, you know, just drinks after work. Nothing special."

Laurel blinks slowly. She knows her daughter is lying. That "T" is taking her out somewhere special. But she says nothing. "Well, then," she says measuredly, "how about the Friday?"

"Fine," says Hanna. "Fine. But if it's all a hideous disaster, I'll blame you for the rest of my life."

Laurel smiles.

As if that was anything new.

⸺

Laurel arranges to see Floyd again on Thursday night. She didn't need to fret and simmer this time. He'd texted her within half an hour of her leaving his house on Wednesday morning. *That was the best date I've ever been on. And Poppy loves you. Could I see you again? Please? Tomorrow?*

It had arrived on her phone as the tube burst out of the tunnel and into the daylight at East Finchley. She'd sucked her smile deep inside herself and texted back: *Maybe. Unless . . .*

She asked him if he'd like to come to her flat for dinner. He said that would be lovely, he'd ask SJ to sleep over at his.

And now she is shopping for that dinner, alarmed and exhilarated by the litany of choices she is having to make. For so long she has done everything by rote, out of necessity. She has eaten the same meals cooked from the same ingredients that she has picked up in the same aisles. All her meals are roughly calorie controlled. Three hundred for breakfast, four hundred for lunch and three hundred for dinner. Enough left over for a chocolate bar or some biscuits at work, two glasses of wine at the tail end of the day. That is how she views food: as calories.

She stopped cooking for Paul and the kids the day Ellie disappeared. Slowly they'd finished the contents of the fridge, and then the freezer, and then at some point Paul and Hanna had gone to Asda and filled a giant trolley to the brim with "staples"—pasta, canned fish, sausages, frozen meat—and Paul had, without any form of official handover or agreement, taken over the kitchen. And, God bless him, he was a terrible cook—no sense of taste, no idea about balanced meals—but the bland, well-intentioned food had appeared and the family had eaten and no one got rickets or died of malnutrition, and that was all that mattered, she supposed.

But now she has to cook a meal for a man. A man she's had sex with. A man she would be having sex with again. A man who took his daughter to an Eritrean restaurant when she was a toddler. And she feels completely out of her depth.

She's clutching a computer printout of a Jamie Oliver recipe for jambalaya.

Rice. How hard can it be?

She collects peppers, onions, chicken, chorizo. But it's the other elements that throw her. Nibbles. Aperitifs. Puddings. Wine. She has no idea. None. She piles her trolley with strange-sounding crisps made out of pita bread and lentils, then throws in some Walkers ready salted, just to be safe. Then tubs of taramasalata, hummus, tzatziki, all of which she throws back when she realizes that they didn't go with the main course. But what does go with jambalaya? What do they nibble on in Louisiana before dinner? She has no idea and picks up a Tex-Mex dip selection pack, which feels like something a student might buy for a house party.

She covers all her bases for pudding. He's American, so she chooses a New York–style cheesecake, but he's also an Anglophile, so she picks up a sticky toffee pudding, too. But what if he's too full for pudding? What if he doesn't *like* pudding? She buys a box of After Eight mints, imagining some kind of *well, you're not really English until you've eaten an After Eight mint* type of conversation and then finally she pays for everything and loads it all into the back of her car with a sigh of relief.

Her flat is another hurdle to cross. It's fine, essentially. She's neither messy nor tidy. Her flat is usually only a ten-minute run around with a vacuum and bin bag away from looking perfectly presentable. But it's the lack of personality that worries her. Her flat is smart but soulless. Shiny, new, low-ceilinged, small-windowed, featureless. She'd let the children take most of the things from the old house. She'd given a lot to charity, too. She'd brought the bare minimum with her. She regrets that now. It was as though she'd thought she'd be here for only a short time, as though she'd thought that she would just fade away here until there was nothing left of her.

She showers and shaves and buffs and plucks. She cooks in her pajamas to save her clothes and she finds the process of chopping and weighing and measuring and checking and tasting and stirring more enjoyable than she'd expected, and she remembers that she used to do this. She used to do this every day. Cook interesting, tasty, healthy meals. Every day. Sometimes twice a day. She'd cooked for her family, to show them that she loved them, to keep them healthy, to keep them safe. And then her daughter had disappeared and then reappeared as a small selection of bones, and the body that Laurel had spent almost sixteen years nurturing had been picked apart by wild animals and scattered across a damp forest floor and all of those things had happened in spite of all the lovely food Laurel had cooked for her.

So, really. What was the point?

But she is remembering now. Cooking doesn't just nurture the recipient; it nurtures the chef.

At seven o'clock she gets dressed: a black sleeveless shirt and a full red skirt and, as she's not leaving the house and won't have to walk in them, a pair of red stilettoes. At seven fifteen her phone pings.

Disaster. SJ blown us out. Can either come with Poppy or reschedule. Your call.

She breathes in deeply. Her initial reaction is annoyance. Intense annoyance. All the effort. All the hair removal. Not to mention the changing of her bedsheets.

But the feeling passes and she thinks, actually, why not? Why not spend an evening with Floyd and his daughter? Why not take the opportunity to get to know her a bit better? And besides, the bedsheets needed changing.

She smiles and texts back. *Please come with Poppy. It would be an absolute pleasure.*

Floyd replies immediately.

That's fantastic. Thank you. One small thing. She's obsessed with other people's photos. If you have any of Ellie, maybe best to put them away. I haven't told her about Ellie and think it's best she doesn't know. Hope that's OK. ☺

19

Poppy is wearing a knee-length black velvet dress with a red bolero jacket and red shoes with bows on them, and Laurel feels another jolt of unease about the way the girl is dressed. It screams of lack of peer influence and a mother's touch. But she puts the unease to one side and brings Floyd and Poppy into her living room where candles flicker and cast dancing shadows on the plain white walls, where bowls of crisps and Tex-Mex dips decanted into glass dishes sit on the coffee table, where soft background music blunts the hard edges of the small square room and where a bottle of Cava sits in a cooler and glasses sparkle in the candlelight.

"What a lovely flat," says Floyd, passing her a bottle of wine and prompting Poppy to pass her the bunch of lilies she'd been clutching when she arrived.

"It's OK," says Laurel. "It's functional."

Poppy looks around for a moment, taking in the family photos on the windowsills and the cabinets. "Is this your little girl?" she says, peering at a photo of Hanna when she was about six or seven.

"Yes," says Laurel. "That's Hanna. She's not a little girl anymore though. She's going to be twenty-eight next week."

"And is this your son?"

"Yes. That's Jake. My oldest one. He'll be thirty in January."

"He looks nice," she says. "Is he nice?"

Laurel puts the wine in the fridge and turns back to Poppy. "He's . . . well, yes. He's very nice. I don't really see much of him these days unfortunately. He lives in Devon."

"Has he got a girlfriend?"

"Yes. She's called Blue and they live together in a little gingerbread cottage with chickens in the garden. He's a surveyor. I'm not sure what she does. Something to do with knitting, I think."

"Do you like her? It sounds as if you don't like her."

Laurel and Floyd exchange another look. She's waiting for him to pull Poppy back a bit, rein her in. But he doesn't. He watches her in something approaching awe as though waiting to see just how far she will go.

"I barely know her," Laurel says, trying to soften her tone. "She seems perfectly OK. A bit, maybe, *controlling*." She shrugs. "Jake's a grown man, though; if he wants to be controlled by another human being, I guess that's his lookout."

She invites them to sit down and eat some crisps. Floyd does so, but Poppy is still stalking the room, investigating. "Have you got a picture of your husband?" she says.

"Ex-husband," Laurel corrects, "and no. Not on display. But somewhere, I'm sure."

"What's his name?"

"Paul."

Poppy nods. "What's he like?"

She smiles at Floyd, looking to be rescued, but he looks as keen to find out about Paul as his daughter. "Oh," she says. "Paul? He's lovely, actually. He's a really lovely man. Very gentle. Very kind. A bit daft."

"Then why did you split up?"

Ah. There it was. Silly her, not to have seen the conversational cul-de-sac she was walking straight into. And still Floyd does not come to her rescue, simply scoops some dip onto a pita chip and pops it into his mouth.

"We just . . . well, we changed. We wanted different things. The children grew up and left home and we realized we didn't want to spend the rest of our lives together."

"Did he marry someone else?"

"No. Not quite. But he has a girlfriend. They live together."

"Is she nice? Do you like her?"

"I've never met her. But my children have. They say she's very sweet."

Poppy finally seems sated and takes a seat next to her father, who grips her knee and gives it a quick hard squeeze as if to say *good job on grilling the lady*. Then he leans toward the coffee table and places a hand on the neck of the Cava and says, "Well, shall I?"

"Yes. Please. How did you get here? Are you driving?"

"No. We got the tube. Do you have an extra glass?"

She's confused for a moment and then realizes that he wants the extra glass for Poppy. "Oh," she says. "Sorry. I didn't think. It's the French way, isn't it?"

"What's the French way?" asks Poppy.

"Children drinking," she explains. "Not something that happens much in other countries."

"Only champagne," says Floyd. "Only a sip. And only on very special occasions."

Laurel pours the Cava and they make a toast to themselves and to her and to SJ for not showing up and meaning that Poppy gets to stay up late and wear her nice dress.

"That is a really lovely dress," Laurel says, sensing an opening. "Who takes you shopping for clothes?"

"Dad," she replies. "We shop online together mostly. But sometimes we go to Oxford Street."

"And what's your favorite clothes shop?"

"I haven't really got one. Marks & Spencer is really good, I suppose, and we always go into John Lewis."

"What about H&M? Gap?"

"I'm not really that kind of girl," she says. "Jeans and hoodies and stuff. I like to look . . . smart."

Floyd's hand goes to the knee again, gives it another encouraging *that's my girl* squeeze.

"So," says Laurel. "Tell me about the home-schooling? How does that work?"

"Just like real schooling," Poppy responds. "I sit and learn. And then when I've learned I relax."

"How many hours a day do you study?"

"Two or three," she says. "Well, two or three hours with Dad. Obviously he has to work. The rest of the time by myself."

"And you don't ever get lonely? Or wish you had kids your own age to hang out with?"

"Noooo," she says, shaking her head emphatically. "No, no, never."

"Poppy is basically forty years old," says Floyd admiringly. "You know, how you get to forty and you suddenly stop giving a shit about all the stupid things you worried about your whole life. Well, Poppy's already there."

"When I'm with kids my own age I tend to roll my eyes a lot and look at them like they're mad. Which doesn't really go down too well. They think I'm a bitch." Poppy shrugs and laughs and takes a mouthful of champagne.

Laurel simply nods. She can see how this self-possessed child might appear to other children. But she doesn't believe that it's the way it must be; she doesn't believe that Poppy couldn't learn to enjoy time with her peers, to stop rolling her eyes at them and alienating them. She doesn't know, thinks Laurel, she doesn't know that this isn't how you grow up. That wearing shiny shoes with bows on and rolling your eyes at other kids is not a sign of maturity, but a sign that you've missed a whole set of steps on the road to maturity.

This child, Laurel suddenly feels with the immediacy of a kick to the gut, needs a mother. And this mother, she acknowledges, needs a child. And Poppy, she is so like Ellie. The planes and lines of her pretty face, the shape of her hairline, of her skull, the way her ears attach to her head, the shapes her mouth makes when it moves, the precise angle of her cupid's bow, they're almost mathematically identical.

The differences are pronounced, too. Her eyebrows are thicker, her neck is longer, her hair parts differently and is a different shade of brown. And while Ellie's eyes were a hazel brown, Poppy's are chocolate. They are not identical. But there is something, something alarming and arresting, a likeness that she can't leave alone.

"Maybe you and I could go shopping together?" Laurel says brightly. "One day? Would you like that?"

Finally Poppy looks to her dad for his approval before turning back to Laurel and saying, "I would absolutely love that. Yes, please!"

∾

Laurel goes to work on Friday. She works Mondays, Tuesdays, and Fridays at the shopping center near her flat. Her job title is "marketing coordinator." It's a silly job, a mum job, a little local thing to fill some hours and make some money to pay for clothes and the like. She comes, she smiles, she makes the phone calls and writes the emails and sits in the meetings about the inconsequential things she's being paid to pretend she cares about and then she goes home and doesn't think of any of it again until the next time she walks through the door.

But she's glad to be there today. She's happy to be surrounded by familiar people who like her and know her, even if
it's only on a superficial level. The previous evening had been
strange and unsettling and she'd awoken thinking that maybe
she'd dreamed it. Her flat had felt odd in the wake of her dinner
guests, as though it didn't really belong to her. The cushions
on the sofa were in the wrong order, the result of Poppy's
attempt to tidy up after themselves, food was stacked in the
wrong parts of the fridge, and there was a pile of washing up
on the draining board that Poppy had insisted on doing in spite
of Laurel trying to persuade her that she needn't, that it would
all just go in the dishwasher. The lilies on the dining table gave
off a strange deathly perfume and Floyd had left his scarf in her
hallway, a soft gray thing with a Ted Baker label in it that hung
from a hook like a plume of dark smoke.

She'd been glad to leave the flat, to put some distance between last night and herself. But even as she switches on her
computer and stirs sweeteners into her coffee, as she listens
to the messages on her voicemail, it's there, like a dark echo.
Something not right. Something to do with Floyd and Poppy. She
can't pin it down. Poppy is clearly a strange child, who is both
charmingly naïve and unsettlingly self-possessed. She is cleverer
than she has any need to be, but also not as clever as she thinks.

And Floyd, who in the time that Laurel has spent alone with
him, is virtually perfect, warps into something altogether more
complicated when he's with his daughter. Laurel finally crystallizes
the issue while discussing her evening with her colleague, Helen.

"It was like," she says, "you know, like when you're supposed
to be having drinks with a friend and they bring their partner
along and suddenly you're at the pointy end of a triangle?"

The evening had essentially been the Floyd and Poppy Show
with Poppy as the star turn and Laurel as the slightly dumb-

founded audience of one. Floyd and Poppy shared the same sense of humor and lined up jokes for each other. And Floyd's eyes were always on his precocious child, sparkling with wonder and pride. There was not one conversation that had not involved Poppy and her opinions and there had not been one moment during which Laurel had felt more important, special, or interesting than her.

She'd closed the door on them at midnight feeling drained and somewhat dazed.

"Sounds like she's got the classic only-child syndrome," says Helen, neatly shrinking the issue down to a digestible bite-sized chunk of common sense. "Plus, you know, some fathers and daughters just have that sort of thing, don't they? Daddy's girls. They usually turn into the sort of women who can only be friends with men."

Laurel nods gratefully. Yes, that all makes perfect sense. She has seen that bond before between fathers and daughters. Not with her own daughters. Ellie was both a mummy's and a daddy's girl and Hanna is just a law unto herself. And maybe the surprise she is feeling is due to her own issues and nothing to do with Floyd and Poppy. Poppy is entertaining in a gauche kind of way and Floyd is clearly a wonderful, nurturing, and loving father.

By the time Laurel leaves the office at five thirty and gets into her car in the underground car park she is feeling clear-headed and right-footed.

She cannot wait to see Floyd again.

⟨◇⟩

Laurel and Floyd spend the whole of the following weekend together. It wasn't planned that way, but there never seemed to be a point at which leaving his house made any sense. They had dinner out on Friday night, a late breakfast on Saturday morning, a trip to the cinema with Poppy that afternoon followed by a detour to M&S for new underwear and a toothbrush, Chinese take-out on Saturday night, and then brunch in a café around the corner on Sunday before Laurel managed to tear herself away and back to her flat on Sunday evening, ready for work on Monday morning.

At the office Laurel feels as though she has shed a skin, that she is somehow reborn and that she needs to mark the transition in some landmark way.

She calls Hanna.

"How would you feel . . ." she starts tentatively, "if I invited my new boyfriend to our birthday dinner?"

The silence is black and heavy.

Laurel fills it. "Totally don't mind if you say no. Totally understand. I just thought, in the spirit of us all moving on? In the spirit of a brave new world?"

The silence continues, growing in depth and darkness.

"Boyfriend?" says Hanna eventually. "Since when did you have a boyfriend?"

"The guy," says Laurel, "the guy I told you about? Floyd."

"I know *the guy*," she replies. "I just wasn't aware that he'd made boyfriend status."

"Yes, well, if you ever answered your phone . . ."

Hanna sighs. Laurel sighs too, realizing she has just done the thing she always promised herself she would never do. When the children were small, Laurel's mother would occasionally make small, raw observations about gaps between phone calls and visits that would tear tiny, painful strips off Laurel's conscience. *I will never guilt trip my children when they are adults,* she'd vowed. *I will never expect more than they are able to give.*

"Sorry," she says. "I didn't mean to nag. It's just, yes, things are moving quite fast. I've met his kids. I've stayed at his. We talk all the time. We've just spent the whole weekend together. I just . . ." Ridiculous, she suddenly realizes. A ridiculous idea. "But forget I mentioned it. I mean, I haven't even asked Floyd yet if he'd like to come. He'd probably rather saw his legs off. Forget I said anything."

There's another silence. Softer this time. "Whatever," Hanna says. "Invite him. I don't mind. It's going to be so fucked up anyway, we may as well go the whole hog."

⌒

Floyd says yes. Of course Floyd says yes. Floyd has made it very clear from the moment she headed home after their second date that he is wholly committed to their romance and that he is not interested in playing games or hard to get.

"I would love that," he says. "As long as your family are OK with it?"

Paul had been OK about it. Hugely surprised, but OK. Jake had said it was fine. No one was jumping up and down about it but no one had said it was a mistake.

"And Poppy?" Laurel adds. "Would Poppy like to come too?" She half hopes he'll say no.

"She'll be thrilled," Floyd says. "She keeps saying how much she'd like to meet your children."

"And my ex-husband. And my ex-husband's girlfriend."

"The whole shebang."

The whole shebang. The whole hog.

She books a table for eight at a restaurant in Islington, a legendarily chichi place down a narrow cobbled alleyway off Upper Street.

She must be mad, she tells herself. She must be absolutely insane.

20

On her birthday, Laurel receives a large bouquet of purple hyacinths and laurel from Floyd. Paul always used to put laurel in her bouquets. But this doesn't take away from the pleasure of it, the startle of his thoughtfulness. And a comparison to her ex-husband is no bad thing, no bad thing at all.

Later on he takes her to a bar in Covent Garden called Champagne & Fromage, which delivers what its name promises. Throughout the evening Laurel keeps her eyes on her surroundings, hoping for a glimpse of Hanna, who said she was "going somewhere in town with mates" when Laurel had inquired about her birthday plans. But she doesn't see Hanna anywhere and so the mystery of the man called "T" stretches on.

"When's your birthday?" she asks Floyd, her knife breaking into a tartine.

"The thirty-first of July," he replies. "Roughly."

"Roughly?"

He shrugs and smiles. "Things were a bit chaotic when I was born."

"Really?"

"Yeah. It was a steep trajectory for my parents. From the gutter to the stars."

"And the gutter was . . . ?"

He narrows his eyes and she hears a small intake of breath. "My mum was fourteen when I was born. My dad was sixteen.

No one wanted to know. They were homeless for a time. I was born in a public toilet, I believe. In a park. They took me to a hospital . . . and left me there."

Laurel's breath catches.

"I was dressed in a blue suit and a fresh nappy, wrapped in a blanket. I had on a soft hat and mittens. I was in a box lined with a cushion. They'd written my name on a piece of paper. 'This is Floyd, please look after him.' My parents came back for me three days later. By that time I'd been taken into emergency foster care. There was no way they were giving an abandoned baby back to a pair of scrawny teens with no means of support. It took them nearly a year to get me back. I think it was the fight to do so that fueled my parents' ambition."

"And how did you find out about it? Did they tell you?"

"Yes, they told me. My God, they told me. All the time. Whenever I was misbehaving they'd march it out: 'We should have left you there in the hospital. We'll take you back there, shall we?'" A muscle twitches in Floyd's cheek.

"But do you remember anything about it?" she asks. "Anything about those days?"

"Nothing at all," he replies. "My very first memory is my dad bringing home a plastic car. It had a little ignition"—he mimes turning a key in a lock—"and it made a noise when you turned it, an engine starting. And I remember sitting in that car for an hour, maybe more, just turning that ignition, over and over. I was about four then and we were living in an apartment in Boston with a balcony, views across town, all the bright lights and the ocean. So, no, I don't remember the bad days. I don't remember them at all."

"You know," she says, "you're the first person I ever met in my whole life who didn't know their birthday."

He smiles. "Yup. Me, too."

Laurel glances about herself. For so long she has been the story: the woman whose daughter disappeared, the woman at the press conference, the woman in the papers, the woman who had to bury her daughter in tiny fragments. But now here is another human with a terrible story. What other stories surround her? she wonders. And how many stories has she missed all these years while she's been so wrapped up in her own?

"Your parents sound amazing," she says.

Floyd blinks and smiles sadly. "In many ways I suppose they are," he says. But there's a chip of ice in his delivery, something sad and dark that he can't tell her about. And that's fine. She'll leave it there. She understands that not everything is conversational fodder, not everything is for sharing.

<o>

They go back to Floyd's house after dinner. Sara-Jade is curled up in the big armchair again, a laptop resting on her thighs, headphones on. She jumps slightly as Laurel and Floyd walk into the room.

"Happy birthday," she says in her whispery voice. "Did you have fun?"

Laurel is taken aback by the unexpected overture.

"Yes," she says, "yes, thank you. We did."

Floyd squeezes Laurel's shoulder and says, "I'm just popping to the loo, be back in a minute," and Laurel knows his withdrawal is deliberate, that he's hoping she and SJ might finally have a chance to bond.

"I'm a bit tipsy," she says to SJ. "We went to a champagne and cheese place. Had more champagne than cheese."

SJ smiles uncertainly. "How old are you?" she says. "If you don't mind me asking?"

"No, of course I don't mind. I've never understood people

being ashamed of their age. As if it's a failure of some kind. I'm fifty-five," she says. "And a few hours."

SJ nods.

"Are you staying over?" Laurel asks.

"No," says SJ. "No. I think I'll go home and sleep in my own bed. I've got work tomorrow."

"Oh," says Laurel. "What sort of work do you do?"

"Bits and bobs. Babysitting. Dog walking." She lowers the lid of the laptop and uncurls her legs. "Modeling tomorrow. For a life-drawing class."

"Wow. Is that clothed, or . . . ?"

"Naked," SJ says. "Just as you say that there's no shame in getting older, I think there's no shame in being naked. And don't you think," she continues, "that if people say you shouldn't be allowed to ban burkinis on the beach then, really, the natural extrapolation of that is that full nudity shouldn't be banned either. Like, who decides which bit of a body should or shouldn't be seen in public? If you're saying that one woman legally has to cover her breasts and her minge, then how can you tell another woman that she's not allowed to cover her legs or her arms? I mean, how does that even make sense?"

Laurel nods and laughs. "Good point," she says. "I hadn't thought about it like that."

"No," she says. "No one thinks about anything properly these days. Everyone just believes what people on Twitter tell them to believe. It's all propaganda, however much it's dressed up as liberal right thinking. We're a nation of sheep."

Laurel feels suddenly very drunk and has to resist the temptation to say *baaaaa*. Instead she nods solemnly. She has barely absorbed another person's opinion for over a decade. She is no sheep.

"Your daughter was Ellie Mack," says SJ, as if reading the changing direction of Laurel's thoughts.

"Yes," Laurel replies, surprised. "Did your dad tell you?"

"No," she says. "I googled you. I've been reading everything on the Internet about it. It's really, really sad."

"Yes," Laurel agrees. "It's very sad."

"She was really pretty."

"Thank you. Yes, she was."

"She looked really like Poppy, don't you think?"

Laurel's head clears, suddenly and sharply, and she finds herself saying, almost defensively, "No, not really. I mean, maybe a little, around the mouth. But lots of people look like people, don't they?"

"Yes," SJ replies, "they do."

21

Laurel visits her mother the next day. She'd seemed a bit perkier during her visit last Thursday, interested in Laurel's romance, gripping Laurel's hand inside hers, her dark eyes sparkling. No talk of death. No empty gaze. Laurel hopes that she will find her in a similar mood today.

But the joy seems to have seeped out of her in the days between her visits and she looks gray again, and hollow. Her first words to Laurel are "I think there's not much time left for me now." The words are seamless, said without pause or hesitation.

Laurel sits down quickly beside her and says, "Oh, Mum, I thought you were feeling better?"

"Better," says her mum. And then she nods. "Better."

"So why the talk of dying again?"

"Because . . ."—she stabs at her collarbone with stiff fingers—". . . *old*."

Laurel smiles. "Yes," she says, "you are old. But there's more life left in you yet."

Her mother shakes her head. "No. No. No life. And y . . . y . . . you. Happy. *Now.*"

Laurel takes a sharp intake of breath. She feels the meaning of her mother's words. "Have you been staying here for me?" she asks, tears catching at the back of her throat.

"Yes. For y . . . y . . . you. Yes."

"And now I'm happy, you're ready to go?"

A huge smile crosses her mother's face and she squeezes Laurel's hand. "Yes. Yes."

A heavy tear rolls down Laurel's cheek. "Oh," she says. "Oh, Mum. I still need you."

"No," says her mum. "Not n . . . n . . . now. Ellie found. You happy. I . . ." She prods at her collarbone. "I go."

Laurel wipes away the tear with the back of her hand and forces a smile. "It's your life, Mum," she says. "I can't choose when to let you go."

"No," says her mum. "N . . . n . . . no one can."

⚬

That afternoon, Laurel takes Poppy shopping. It's raining, so she suggests Brent Cross as an alternative to Oxford Street.

Poppy greets her at her front door wearing smart trousers with a jade-green round-neck cardigan and a floral raincoat. Her hair is in two plaits, one on each shoulder. She loops her arm through Laurel's as they run through the rain to her car across the street. Then she rolls down her window and waves frantically at her father, who stands in the doorway in his socked feet waving back at her.

"How are you?" Laurel asks, turning to glance at Poppy as she pulls out of her road.

"I'm superexcited," she says.

"Good," Laurel replies.

"And how are you?"

"Oh, I'm OK, I guess. A little the worse for wear after last night."

"Too much champagne?"

Laurel smiles. "Yes. Too much champagne. Not enough sleep."

"Well," says Poppy, patting Laurel's hand, "it was your birthday after all."

"Yes. It was."

The rain is ferocious and Laurel switches on her headlights and pushes the wipers up to the top speed.

"What have you been up to this morning?" Poppy continues in the precocious way she has that Laurel is quickly becoming used to.

"Hm," she replies, "well, I've been to see my mum."

"You have a mum?"

"Yes, of course! Everyone has a mum!"

"I don't."

"Well, no, maybe not one you can see. But you have a mother. Somewhere."

"If you can't see something, it doesn't exist."

"That doesn't make any sense."

"It makes total sense."

Laurel frowns at her passenger. "So, what about New York? I can't see it. Neither can you. Does that mean it doesn't exist?"

"That doesn't count. We could see New York on a thousand webcams right now. We could call someone up in New York and say *please send me a photo of New York*. But with my mum, well, I can't see her on a webcam or in a photo, I can't call her up, I can't even go and look at her remains in a graveyard. So my mum does not exist."

Laurel feels thrown for a minute and breathes in sharply. "Would you like her to exist? Do you miss her?"

"No. I never even think about her."

"But she was your mum. You must think about her sometimes, surely?"

"Never. I hated her."

Laurel glances at Poppy quickly before returning her gaze to the road in front of her. "Why did you hate her?"

"Because she hated me. She was mean and ugly and neglectful."

"She can't have been that ugly, to have had a daughter as pretty as you."

"She didn't look anything like me. She was horrible. That's all I remember. Horrible and she smelled of chips."

"Chips?"

"Yes. Her hair . . ." She peers through the rain-splattered windscreen. "It was red. And it smelled of chips."

Laurel can't quite form a response. This awful woman with greasy hair sounds so far removed from anything she'd have imagined as a mother for this self-assured, groomed, and brightly shining girl. Not to mention as a romantic partner for Floyd. But then she remembers the photos she'd found online of Floyd when he was younger and rather more seedy-looking and she remembers that everyone blossoms at a different point in their life: clearly Floyd is blossoming right now and maybe his life was once much, much darker.

"Would you say that your father is happier now than he was then, Poppy?"

It's a leading question but she needs an answer. She's only known Floyd for a couple of weeks. He's without context, a man who walked into a cake shop and changed her life from the outside in. She'd love a little insight from someone who's been on the inside for a long time.

But what she gets is not what she expects. Instead of offering bland reassurances Poppy says, "What's happy got to do with anything? Look, we're here for absolutely no reason whatsoever. You do know that, don't you? People try and make out there's a greater purpose, a secret meaning, that it all *means something*. And it doesn't. We're a bunch of freaks. That's all there is to it. A big bunch of stupid, inconsequential freaks. We don't have to be happy. We don't have to be normal. We don't even have to be alive. Not if we don't want to. We can do whatever we want as long as we don't hurt anyone."

Laurel exhales audibly. "Wow," she says. "That's some philosophy you've got there."

"It's not a philosophy. It's life. Once you learn how to look at the world, once you stop trying to make sense of it all, it's blindingly obvious."

Laurel turns quickly to look at Poppy. "You're a very unusual girl, aren't you?"

"Yes," says Poppy firmly. "I am."

 ❧

In the shopping center they head straight to Nando's for something to eat. Laurel skipped lunch after seeing her mother and now she's starving.

"How do you get on with SJ's mum?" she asks as they sit and wait for the food to be delivered.

"Kate?"

"Is that her name?"

"Yes. Kate Virtue. She's nice. I like her. She's not very clever, but she's very sweet and kind."

"And SJ? Are you two close?"

"Ish. I mean, we're very different."

"In what sort of ways?" Laurel asks, thinking that they're both certainly rather strange.

"Well, she's an introvert, I'm an extrovert. She's good at art. I'm good at maths. She cares about everything. I care about nothing. She's humorless. I'm hilarious. She's not close to Dad. I'm superclose to Dad." She smiles.

"And why do you think that is?"

She shrugs. "I guess I'm just more like him. That's all."

They stop talking as their food is delivered. Laurel watches her for a moment, studies the intensity of her focus on a bottle of ketchup, the way her forehead bunches into lines, and suddenly she finds herself thrown headfirst out of her own continuum and into a moment from her past. She is here, in this very spot, with Ellie. She doesn't know where Jake and Hanna are in this isolated vignette; maybe it's an INSET day at Ellie's school? But she is sitting here and Ellie is sitting there and everything is exactly the same but completely different. Her head spins for a second and she grips the edge of the table and breathes deeply to center herself. She blinks and looks again at Poppy and now she is Poppy. Definitely Poppy. Not Ellie.

Poppy has not noticed Laurel's brief moment of extracorporeal time travel. She bangs the ketchup bottle to dislodge some sauce and then replaces the lid.

"I'm really looking forward to meeting your family tomorrow night," she says. "Do you think they'll like me?"

Laurel blinks slowly. "I'm surprised you care," she says drily.

"I don't care," Poppy replies. "I'm just interested in your opinion. Caring and being interested are two very different things."

"Yes," says Laurel, smiling. "Yes. They'll like you. You'll be a breath of fresh air."

"Good," says Poppy. "That's nice. I love being with other people's families. I sometimes wish . . ."

Laurel throws her a questioning look.

"Nothing," says Poppy. "Nothing."

Laurel takes Poppy into New Look. She takes her into Gap. She takes her into H&M and Zara and Top Shop and Miss Selfridge. But Poppy refuses to countenance anything fashionable. Eventually they find themselves in the John Lewis childrenswear department where Poppy heads steadfastly toward a rail of printed jersey dresses.

"These," she says. "I like these."

"But don't you already have a dress like this?" Laurel asks, thinking of something she'd seen her wearing that weekend.

"Yes," Poppy replies, pulling a dress sideways from the rail. "I've got this one. But they've got it in another print now. Look." She pulls another dress from the rail. "I don't have this one."

Laurel sighs and touches the fabric of the dress. "It's very pretty," she says, "but I thought we were going to, perhaps, break you out a bit, you know, of your usual style."

Now Poppy sighs. She looks mournfully at the dress and then up at Laurel. "We did say that, didn't we?"

Laurel nods.

"But all that other stuff. In the other shops. It's all so trashy. And scruffy."

"But you're young, and that is the *joy* of being young. You can wear anything and look amazing in it. Scruffy looks great when you're young. So does cheap. And trashy. You can save all the smart stuff for when you're my age. Come on," she urges. "One more whizz round H&M? For me?"

Poppy beams and nods. "Yes," she says. "Fine."

They pick out patterned leggings, a soft, slashed-neck sweatshirt, a brushed-flannel checked shirt, a fitted T-shirt with a mustache printed on it and a gray party dress with a chiffon skirt and jersey bodice.

Laurel stands outside the cubicle, as she has stood outside so many cubicles for so many years of her life and waits for the curtain to be drawn back. And there is Poppy, stern and uncertain in the leggings and T-shirt. "I look vile," she says.

"No," says Laurel, her hands going immediately to the waistband of the leggings to center them and make them sit properly. "Here." She pulls the flannel shirt from its hanger and helps Poppy thread her arms into the sleeves. "There," she says. "There." And then she removes the neat bands from the tips of Poppy's plaits, untangles them and fans the corrugated waves of her hair out over her shoulders.

"There," she says again. "You look incredible. You look . . ."

She has to turn then, turn and force half her fist into her mouth. She realizes what she has done. She has dressed this child up as her dead daughter. And the result is unnerving.

"You look lovely," she manages, her voice slightly tremulous. "But if you don't feel comfortable in it, that's fine. Let's go back to John Lewis. We'll get you that dress. Come on . . ."

But Poppy does not acknowledge Laurel's suggestion. She stands and stares at herself in the mirror. She turns slightly, from side to side. She runs her hands down the fabric of the leggings, plays with the sleeves of the shirt. She strikes a pose, and then another one. "Actually," she says. "I like this. Can I have it?"

Laurel blinks. "Yes. Of course you can. If you're sure?"

"I'm totally sure," she says. "I want to be different. It will be fun."

"Yes," says Laurel. "It will be."

"Maybe you could be different, too?"

"Different? In what way?"

"You always wear gray and black. All your clothes look like uniforms. Maybe we should find you something swishy."

"Swishy?"

"Yes. Or colorful. Something with lace and flowers. Something *pretty*."

Laurel smiles. "I was just thinking the same thing myself."

22

On Friday evening Laurel drives to Hanna's flat, from where they will get an Uber together to the restaurant in Islington.

"Wow," says Hanna upon opening her front door. "Mum, you look gorgeous."

Laurel swishes the skirt of her new dress. It's black with an Oriental print of birds and flowers. It has a halter neck, buttons down the front, and is made of silk. "Thank you!" she says. "Ellie helped me choose it."

An echoing silence spreads between them.

"Oh," says Laurel. "Did I just say Ellie?"

"Yes, you did."

"I meant Poppy. Obviously. Sorry. All this shopping with young girls must be messing with my time lines."

"Must be," said Hanna.

"And you look lovely, too," Laurel says, trying to leave her faux pas as far behind her as possible. "Have you had your hair done?"

"Yes, I had a cut and blow-dry on Wednesday."

For your big romantic night out with T, no doubt, Laurel thinks but does not say. "Very nice. I like it that length."

They sit in a companionable silence in the back of the mini-cab. It has always been thus with Hanna. She rarely feels the need to converse. It's taken Laurel a long time to lose her conviction that this is a symptom of her own failings as a mother.

Outside the restaurant Laurel breathes in hard. They're two minutes early and she has no idea of what lies inside, of who might be sitting at that table. It could be any number of awkward combinations of people, the most excruciating of which would be Paul, Bonny, Floyd, and Poppy. Her skin crawls at the very thought of it and she wishes she'd thought to meet Floyd elsewhere first.

But as they are led across the restaurant toward their table in a glass room at the back, she sees that only Floyd and Poppy are seated and she breathes a sigh of relief.

Floyd stands to greet them both. He looks incredibly attractive tonight. He is wearing a fitted ink-blue suit with a slim black tie and his salt and pepper hair is swept back off his forehead with some kind of product. And Poppy looks refreshingly normal in her new checked shirt worn over a fitted jersey dress with black leather lace-up boots. They look just right, thinks Laurel; they look like *us*.

"How incredibly good to meet you," says Floyd, his hand out to Hanna, his eyes bright with genuine pleasure.

Hanna gives him her hand. "You too," she says.

Then Poppy follows suit. "You're so pretty," she says. "I'm so happy to meet you."

Hanna flushes slightly at the bluntly delivered compliment and mumbles something under her breath that Laurel can't hear.

They take their seats and then all get to their feet again when Paul, Bonny, Jake, and Blue arrive. Laurel turns her hands into fists and plasters a facsimile of a smile onto her face. She's been told by both her children not to worry, that Bonny is a nice person, that she'll like her, that she's sweet, but still, it's a huge moment and magnified tenfold by the presence of her own boyfriend and the impending introductions that that will involve; for a brief moment Laurel feels as though she is going to turn liquid and pool to the floor.

But other people save her from herself. Bonny heads straight to Laurel, looks her directly in the eye, presses her hands against Laurel's forearms, then enfolds her inside her soft, welcoming body that smells of violets and talcum powder and says in the voice of a woman who has smoked and drunk and cried and sung, "At bloody last. At long bloody last."

Floyd meanwhile has made his way straight to Paul to shake his hand and tell him what an honor it is to meet him; there is a moment of gentle hilarity as they realize that they are dressed virtually identically and that they are in fact wearing exactly the same Paul Smith socks.

"Look," says Paul, pressing himself up against Floyd. "Twins!"

As onerous meetings between exes, new partners, old partners, and various children go, Laurel thinks, it really has been at the upper end of the scale.

She sits between Floyd and Bonny. Paul sits at Bonny's other side with Hanna at the head of the table, and Jake, Poppy, and Blue are opposite. Blue looks sour-faced and disgusted to be here and Laurel can only imagine the emotional wrangling that Jake must have undertaken to get her to agree to coming tonight. If Blue had her way, they would never leave their cottage.

But Blue is the only dark point in the proceedings. Laurel looks around the table and sees a best-case scenario. No one would ever guess, she thinks, no one would know how weird this is, how extraordinary. Even Hanna is smiling as she chats with her dad and opens his gift to her.

A waiter brings two bottles of preordered champagne and fills all their glasses. It feels as though someone should get to their feet to raise a toast to the birthday girls, but there is hesitation because, of course, who should it be? Without Floyd, Paul would be the obvious candidate: father to one, ex-husband to the other. But with Floyd it's not so clear-cut, and the hesitation builds and builds until suddenly, unexpectedly, Poppy gets to her feet.

She grips her half-glass of champagne between her hands and looks around the table from person to person, her focus not wavering. "I've only known Laurel for a couple of weeks," she begins, perfect diction, unerring poise. "But in that time I've got to know her well enough to consider her to be a true and beautiful friend. She's so kind and so generous, and my father and I are so lucky to have her in our life. And now I can see that she is not the only lovely person in her family. I know I've only just met you all, but I can feel how much you all love each other and I feel honored to be a part of all this. To Laurel"—she raises her glass—"and to Hanna. And to happy families!"

There's a brittle silence, just long enough to acknowledge the strangeness of Poppy's pitch-perfect speech, the irony of her comment about happy families, before everyone else raises their glasses and says, "To Hanna, to Laurel, happy birthday."

Paul catches Laurel's eye from the other end of the table and throws her a conspiratorial *whatthefuck* look. She smiles tightly at him. She wants to join in with his wry judging but she feels strangely loyal to Poppy. She's young. She has no mother. She doesn't go to school. She doesn't know.

Bonny turns to her as they all put down their glasses and says, "I hope you know I've been wanting this to happen for an awfully long time."

Bonny has an unruly face: a wide mouth that moves in all directions at once, a dip and a curve in her nose, one eyebrow sits higher than the other, and her chin has a scar running through it. But it all works together somehow and Laurel can see that she is beautiful.

"Yes," says Laurel. "I know. I'm sorry I wasn't ready before. It was never anything to do with you. I promise."

Bonny's hand covers hers. Her nails are short and painted red. "Of course I know that. And Paul has never spoken about you in any way that wasn't positive and generous. I've always understood. And I understand now, too. You're moving on, because you can. You couldn't before. There's a right time for everything. Don't you think?"

Laurel nods and smiles and thinks, Well, maybe not. Maybe, for example, there's not a right time to lose your child. But she doesn't say it because this nice woman is trying her hardest and this is an important conversation, one that will set the tone for a relationship that could last the rest of her life.

Paul reaches across and passes Laurel a wrapped gift. "Happy birthday," he says.

Laurel tuts. "Oh Paul," she says, "you didn't have to. That's just . . ."

"It's nothing, really."

"Shall I open it now?"

He shrugs. "Yes. Why not."

She unpeels the paper and uncovers a book. *The Goldfinch* by Donna Tartt.

"I hope you haven't read it?"

"No," she says, turning it over to read the back cover blurb. She hasn't read a book for ten years.

"Ooh, that book is *brilliant*," says Poppy.

"Oh," says Paul, "you've read it?"

"Yes," she replies. "I read two books a week. At least."

"Wow," says Paul. "And you enjoyed it?"

"Loved it." She picks the book up and holds it between her hands, caressing the sides of it lovingly. "It's about a boy who goes to a museum and his mum gets blown up by a bomb. He steals a small painting in the midst of the chaos and then spends the rest of his life trying to hide it from everyone. It's set in New York."

"Sounds brilliant," says Laurel.

Poppy nods. "It really, really is." Her face lights up as she talks.

"I must say," says Laurel, "that for a girl who thinks humanity is just a tedious mistake, you seem to have a lot of enthusiasm for novels. What is it about fiction that you enjoy?"

Poppy's hands fall onto the book. "Stories," she says, "are the only thing in this world that are real. Everything else is just a dream."

Laurel and Paul smile and nod. Then they turn to each other and exchange a look. Not a wry look this time, but one of disquiet.

Ellie used to read two books a week and when they teased her about always having her nose in a book, Ellie used to say, "When I read a book it feels like real life and when I put the book down it's like I go back into the dream."

Laurel picks up her champagne and raises it to Poppy. "Cheers to that, Poppy," she says, "cheers to that."

⌒

The evening is enjoyable. A success. Poppy does slightly attempt to hijack proceedings but as she is so obviously the youngest at the table and everyone is looking for some extra social glue to keep the whole precarious thing stuck together, she gets away with it.

"What a delightful girl," Paul whispers in her ear as they're filing out of the restaurant at eleven o'clock. "Doesn't she remind you in a funny way of . . ."

Laurel knows what he's going to say before the word is out

of his mouth. "Yes," she says. "Yes, in some ways. She really does."

"That thing about the book. The reality and the dreams." He shakes his head wonderingly.

"I know. I know. Weird."

"And looks like her, a bit, too?"

"A bit," she agrees. "Yes."

"Funny," he says, plucking his coat from a coat rack, "that you've found yourself in a lookalike family."

"A what?"

"Well, he looks a bit like me, too, doesn't he?"

His tone is light but Laurel blanches.

"Er, no," she says, "not really. Just the hair. And the clothes."

Paul looks at her fondly, realizing that he's crossed one of her many lines, the lines he knows so well. "Yes," he says. "That's true. I like him," he adds conciliatorily. "He seems like a good man."

"Well," she says, briskly, "it's early days yet. We'll see, won't we?"

"Yes." He smiles. "Of course, there's still plenty of time for him to prove himself to be an utter psychopath. Plenty of time."

She laughs. It's nice talking to someone who knows her better than anyone else in the world. It's nice talking to Paul.

"You know," he continues, "you know you deserve this, don't you? You know you're allowed it?"

She shrugs, feeling a rush of heat up the back of her sinuses. "Maybe," she manages quietly. "Maybe."

23

Laurel pulls herself from Floyd's bed at eight o'clock the following morning. He groans and turns to glance at his bedside alarm clock. "Come back," he growls, throwing an arm across the bed. "It's the weekend. It's too early!"

"I need to get home," she says, wrapping her hand around his where it lies on the wrinkled sheets.

"No you don't."

She laughs. "Yes I do! I told you, remember. I'm going for lunch at my friends' house."

He feigns defeat and throws himself back onto his pillow. "Use me for sex and then just abandon me," he says. "See if I care."

"I can come back later?" she says. "If you can find it in your heart to let me, after my betrayal."

He curls his pale naked body across the bed and he grasps Laurel's hands inside his, pulls them to his mouth and kisses each of her knuckles in turn. "I would really, really love it if you came back later. You know," he says, running her hands against the soft stubble on his cheeks, "I'm getting quite close to the can't-live-without-you zone. Really, really quite close. Is that pathetic?"

The pronouncement is both surprising and completely predictable. She can't process it fast enough and there is a small but prominent silence.

"Oh God," he says, "have I blown it? Have I broken a rule that someone somewhere wrote about dating that I don't know about?"

"No," Laurel says, bringing his hands to her mouth and kissing them very hard. "Just—I'm a bit of a cynic when it comes to matters of the heart. I can feel things, but never say them. And want things but then not want them. I'm . . ."

"A pain in the arse?"

"Yes." She smiles, relieved. "Yes. That's exactly what I am. But for what it's worth, you are absolutely allowed to not want to live without me. I don't have a problem with that at all."

"Well," he says, "I guess I'll just wait here patiently for your return and hope that by the time you get back you won't be able to live without me either."

She laughs and extricates her hands from his.

"See," he says, "you took your hands from mine. Is this how it is destined always to be for us? You take your hands from mine? You close the door without looking back? You put the phone down before I do? You leave first? You have the last word? I linger behind, in your wake?"

"Maybe," she says. "I'm pretty sure that's how I work."

"I'll take what I can get," he says, rolling back to his side of the bed and pulling the duvet over himself. "I'll take what I can get."

❧

Downstairs the house is quiet and filled with pools of morning sun. Laurel pokes her head around the kitchen door; Poppy is not in there. She walks in, the soles of last night's tights catching against splinters in the soft floorboards, and she switches on the kettle. Beyond the kitchen window a cat sits on the garden wall and observes her. There's a loaf of bread on the counter, a white bloomer, half-gone. She cuts a slice and searches the fridge for butter. Inside is evidence of the life that Floyd and Poppy live when she's not here: the remnants of half-eaten meals, the tin-foil containers of leftover takeaways, open packets of ham and cheese and pâté and pots of yogurt. She takes the butter and spreads the bread thickly. Then she makes herself a mug of tea and takes the bread and the tea to the table by the window. In solitude she thinks about Floyd's pronouncement. She'd been half expecting it. She'd wanted it. But now that she's got it, she's worrying at it, picking at it, overthinking it.

Why, she wonders, does he want me? What did he see when he walked into that café last month, what did he see that he liked so much? And why can't he live without me? What does it even mean anyway? When her children were small they'd sometimes say, "What would you do if I died?" And she would reply, "I would die too, because I could not live without you." And then her child had died and she had found that somehow, incredibly, she could live without her, that she had woken every morning for a hundred days, a thousand days, three thousand days and she had lived without her.

So maybe what Floyd meant was that he felt his life did not make as much sense without her and if that was what he meant, then maybe, yes, maybe she did feel that way, too. Paul had never made such proclamations. A simple "I love you" was how he'd announced the depth of his feelings. Still, she'd made him wait months before she'd reciprocated.

She wipes the crumbs from the plate into the bin, places her mug in the sink, and picks up her handbag and her coat. In the hallway she finds her shoes: last night's heels. She slips them on wishing she'd thought to bring a flat pair. She is about to leave when she remembers the bag of birthday gifts sitting in the kitchen: Paul's book, a necklace from Jake and Blue, a bottle of her favorite perfume from Hanna. When she comes back into the hallway she sees a figure beyond the front door, and then there is the clatter of metal as a bunch of letters is forced through the letterbox and lands on the doormat. She picks them up and places them on the console.

Her eye is caught, as she turns to leave, by the letter on the top. It looks formal, probably financial: a fat white A4 envelope.

Miss Noelle Donnelly

The name rings a bell.

She wonders for a moment why mail addressed to a complete stranger would be delivered here. But then she realizes. Of course. Noelle Donnelly must be Poppy's mum.

In the front garden she looks up and sees Floyd standing in his bedroom window, his mouth turned downward into a sad face, his hands pressed against the glass. She smiles and waves at him. He smiles and waves back, blows her a kiss, draws a heart in his breath on the windowpane.

Paul was right, she thinks; she is allowed this. She just needs to work out how to believe it.

❧

There are more gifts for Laurel at Jackie and Bel's house that day. The twins have made her a box of chocolate truffles, some more successfully truffle-shaped than others, and Jackie and Bel have bought her gift vouchers for a spa in Hadley Wood. They've made her a cake, too, the first cake of her birthday. It's a Victoria sponge, her favorite. She blows out the candles and smiles at the boys' singing of "Happy Birthday to You." She drinks a glass of champagne and she tells her friends all about the previous evening, the relating of which has them both agog. They tell her that she looks glowing, that her hair is shining, her eyes are sparkling, that she has never looked better. They say that they will invite them over for lunch next week, her and Floyd, and Poppy too maybe, that they cannot wait to meet this man who has brought light back into their friend's world.

And all the time Laurel is thinking that this feels like a normal Saturday at Jackie and Bel's, but also not like a normal Saturday at Jackie and Bel's. Because for the first time in years there's an energy somewhere outside her own body, an energy that belongs to her yet isn't of her. It calls her and it pulls her, and instead of lingering after tea and cake as she normally would, instead of trying to squeeze as much normality out of her time with her oldest friends as possible, she finds her hand on her handbag at five o'clock, words of thanks and farewell coming from her mouth. Her friends squeeze her hard in their hallway and there's a sense shared by all of them that things have changed, as they changed all those years ago when Jackie and Bel told her they were a couple, as they did when Ellie disappeared, as they did when the twins were born, and as they did when Paul left. The ebb and flow of need and priorities was moving things along again and Laurel knows that she will not need her Saturdays here as much as she once did.

She climbs into her car and she drives as fast as she can back to Floyd's house.

◦◦

The letter is still there, on the console when she walks in, but someone has crossed out the address and written "Return to Sender / Not known at this address" on it.

The name shouts out at her again.

Noelle Donnelly. Noelle Donnelly.

Why does she know that name?

"How was your lunch?" asks Floyd.

"Lovely," she says, "really lovely. Look"—she shows him the box of homemade truffles—"the boys made these for me. Isn't that sweet? And we're invited as a couple next weekend. If you want to go?"

"I'd love to," he says, hanging up her coat for her, and then her scarf.

Poppy rushes downstairs at the sound of Laurel's return and throws her arms around her.

"Oh!" says Laurel. "That's nice!"

"I missed you this morning," she says. "I thought I'd see you."

"Sorry," says Laurel. "I had to rush home to get ready for lunch."

Floyd has opened a bottle of wine in the kitchen and poured Laurel a large glass, which sits on the kitchen counter waiting for her.

"Funny," she says absentmindedly, swinging herself onto a stool. "I think maybe I might know someone who used to live in this house."

He puts the wine bottle back in the fridge and turns to her, an eyebrow raised. "Oh yes?"

"Yes. There's a letter on your console. For Noelle Donnelly. And I can't for the life of me remember how I know the name, but I do. I thought . . ." She treads carefully. "For a moment, I thought maybe it was Poppy's mum."

Floyd doesn't move. After a minute he turns toward the fridge and says, "Well, actually, it is."

Laurel blinks. She remembers Poppy's description of her mother's red hair, the smell of grease. "Was she Irish?" she asks.

"Yes. Noelle was Irish."

Laurel stares into her glass at the undulating reflections of halogen lights in the surface of the liquid. There's something wriggling beneath her consciousness. Something about the combination of the name and the hair color and an Irish accent—and she knows this woman. *She knows her.*

"Did she have any other children?" she asks. "Older children?" Maybe she was a mum at the school.

"No. Just Poppy."

"Did she work round here? Locally?"

"Well, kind of," says Floyd. "She was a tutor. Maths. I think she taught a lot of the local kids around here."

"Oh!" says Laurel. "Of course. That's it! She must have taught Ellie. Ellie did have a tutor for a while. A short while anyway. Just before . . ." Her words peter out.

"Well," says Floyd. "What a remarkable coincidence! That really is. To think that our paths came so close to crossing. Just one degree of separation."

"Yes," says Laurel, her hand tightening around the wineglass. "What a coincidence."

❦

She mentions it to Hanna when she phones her on Monday. "Remember," she says, "when Ellie had that tutor, the year she disappeared?"

"No," says Hanna.

"You must do. She was Irish—tall woman, red hair? She used to come on Tuesday afternoons?"

"Maybe."

Laurel can hear her typing as she talks. She swallows down a swell of irritation. "Well, weird thing," she continues, "but turns out that she was Poppy's mum."

"Who was?"

"The tutor! The maths tutor!"

There's a small silence and then Hanna says, "Oh *yeah*. Yeah. I remember her. Ellie hated her."

Laurel laughs nervously. "No," she says, "she didn't hate her. She thought she was wonderful. Her savior."

"Well," says Hanna, "that's not how I remember it. I remember her saying she was weird and creepy. That's why she stopped the lessons."

"But . . ." Laurel begins, pausing to try to order her memories. "She didn't say any of that to me. She said she needed more time to study other things. Or something like that."

"Well, she told *me* she didn't like her and that she was creepy." There's a note of triumph in Hanna's tone. She and Laurel had always vied for Ellie's attention.

"Anyway," says Laurel. "Isn't that strange? What a small world!"

She's talking in lazy clichés, using words that don't quite add up to the sum of her disquiet. In the hours since discovering that Noelle Donnelly was Poppy's mum, Laurel has remembered more and more about her: the slightly hunched back, the stale-smelling anorak and sensible rubber-soled shoes that squeaked against the tiled floor in the hallway, the nervous imperiousness, the pretty red hair left unbrushed and pushed back into clips and claws. She cannot reconcile that woman with Floyd, who may not be a classically handsome man but is groomed and stylish, fragrant and clean. How did they come together? How did they meet? How did they fit? And how, more than anything, did they make a baby together?

But she doesn't say any of this to Hanna. She sighs. She's been overthinking things as usual and now she's run out of steam. "How did you enjoy Friday night?" she asks. "It was fun, wasn't it?"

"Yeah. Yeah. It was good. It was nice, actually. Just to be together like that. Thank you."

"For what?"

"For organizing it. For suggesting it. For being the first person in this family to do something brave since Ellie went missing."

"Oh," says Laurel, taken aback. "Thank you. But I think you have Floyd to thank. He's the one who's given me courage. He's the one who's changed me."

"No," says Hanna. "You've changed you. You wouldn't be going out with him otherwise. I'm really pleased for you, Mum. Really pleased. You deserve it."

"Did you like him, Hans?"

"Floyd?"

"Yes."

"Yeah," says Hanna. "Yeah. He seems OK."

And that, coming from Hanna, is praise indeed.

24

Laurel doesn't see Floyd that evening. But he calls her at seven o'clock, just as he'd said he'd do, and Laurel is surprised to feel a little pulse of annoyance.

"I'll call you at seven," he'd said. And here he is, calling her at seven. She might have enjoyed a few moments' indulgent anticipation. For a minute she toys with the idea of not answering her phone, but then she checks herself. She's doing it again, keeping too much of herself back. And this was exactly why she and Paul had not survived the years of Ellie's disappearance, because of *her*, because she'd never allowed herself to be properly subsumed into her relationship with him, had disapproved of him for loving her so deeply and unquestioningly, felt gently suffocated by the lack of gaps in his feelings for her. At the first moment of mutual desperation, she'd escaped into the airlock inside herself that she'd deliberately kept empty all those years.

"Hi," she says brightly, "how are you?"

"I am very well indeed. Oh, apart from the gaping hole in my heart where you should be right now, of course."

"Stop it," she says teasingly, although she half means it.

"Do you not have a gaping hole in your heart, Laurel?"

"No," she says. "No. But I am missing you."

"I'll take that," says Floyd. "What are you up to?"

"Well, I have a glass of wine, naturally."

"Are you dressed?"

"Yes. I am fully dressed. I am even wearing slippers."

"Slippers, yes, carry on. What else?"

"A big cardigan."

"Ooh, yeah. A big cardigan. How big exactly is your cardigan?"

"It's huge. Gigantic. Really long sleeves that cover my hands. And a hole in the hem."

"Oh, tatty then? A tatty cardigan?"

"Very tatty. Horribly tatty." She laughs.

"No, no, don't stop!" he jokes. "Tell me more about your big tatty cardigan!"

She laughs again and looks down at her phone as she hears another call coming in. It's Jake's number and Jake only ever calls her on a Wednesday, and she feels an instant jolt of primal worry and says, "Floyd, I'm going to have to call you back. Jake's trying to get through to me."

"Quickly, quickly! What color is it? Tell me it's brown? Please."

"No," she says, "it's black! Now go! I'll call you back."

"Jake," she says, switching to his call.

"No," says a female voice. "It's not Jake. It's Blue."

"Oh," says Laurel. "Hi. Is everything all right? Is Jake OK?"

"Yes. Jake's fine. He's sitting right here."

Laurel's heart rate slows and she leans back into her sofa.

"What can I do for you, Blue?"

"Look," she says. "I've been wrestling with this all weekend. I haven't been able to think about anything else. Your boyfriend . . . ?"

Laurel's heart rate picks up again.

"I have a—a, like a sixth sense? And your boyfriend . . . his aura is all wrong? It's *dark*."

"I'm sorry?" Laurel shakes her head slightly, as if trying to dislodge something from her ear.

"I have this gift, I can see into people's psyches. Through the walls of their higher consciousness? Into their subconscious? And I'm really sorry, but the minute I sat down and saw him there, the minute he and I made eye contact, I knew."

"You knew what?"

"That he's hiding something. And I know you and I aren't close, Laurel, and I know that's mainly down to me because I'm so self-protective, but I do care about you, you're the mother of the man I love and I want you to be safe."

Laurel waits for a moment before forming her response, and then when it comes it's a slightly unkind, disparaging laugh. "Good grief," she says. "Can you put me on to Jake. Please."

"Jake thinks the same," says Blue. "It's all we've talked about all weekend. He totally agrees with me. He—"

"Just put him on to me please, Blue. Now."

She hears Blue tut and then her son's voice saying, "Hi, Mum."

"Jake," she says. "Seriously. Come on. What is this shit?"

"I don't know. It's just . . ."

"What, Jake? What is it?"

"I can't really explain it. It's what Blue said."

"Oh, come on, Jake. I know you better than that. You're not like her. That's not who you are. You don't have a . . . a *sixth sense*. You're the boy who never noticed when a girl liked you. The only member of the family who didn't notice when Granny Deirdre started losing her marbles. You've never been any good at reading people. So don't give me that. What the hell is going on?"

"Nothing, Mum. We just got a bad vibe off him. Floyd, or whatever he's called."

"No!" she snaps. "*Blue* got a bad vibe off him. You just got whatever vibe Blue told you to get because you're her little lapdog."

Jake falls silent and Laurel holds her breath. She has never, in all the time that Jake and Blue have been together, expressed any disapproval of their dysfunctional dynamic.

"Mum . . ." he starts. But he's whining and Laurel cannot possibly listen to her adult son whining, not now, not when everything is going so well, not when she's finally, finally happy.

"No, Jake. I'm sorry, I know she's your girlfriend and the center of your universe and I know you really, really love her. She's your rock; I get that. But I have been sad for so long and broken for so long and finally I have something good, something special, and I am *not* having you and your whacko girlfriend tell me that it's wrong. Dad liked him and Hanna liked him and that is more than enough for me."

"I'm sorry, Mum," says Jake.

But she can still hear the whine in his voice and she can't stand it and so she says, in a very quiet voice, "I'm going now, Jake. I'm going to hang up. Tell Blue that I know she means well but that I don't want to hear any more of her outlandish theories."

She's shaking when she hangs up and she feels nauseous. She grabs her wineglass and takes a huge gulp. She should phone Floyd back, but she can't. What would she say? *Oh, my son's partner just told me that she thinks you've got a dark aura and now I'm too upset to have jokey conversations about cardigans with you?*

So she sits instead and for an hour she slowly and deliberately works her way through her wine until her hands have stopped shaking enough to send Floyd a text: *Sorry about that. Jake had lots to say and now I'm tired and heading for bed. I will be wearing gray jersey pajamas. They're relatively old.* ☺

His reply arrives a few seconds later: *That will give me plenty of food for thought to get me through the night. Sleep tight my perfect girl. Speak tomorrow x.*

She turns off her phone, switches on the TV, finds something mindless to watch, and pours herself another glass of wine. For an hour at least she coasts through oblivion, feeling sweet numbness spread over her like a heavy cloak. Then when she feels nothing at all, she finally goes to bed.

⌘

"Oh," says Laurel, coming into the kitchen at Floyd's house the following evening. "Hi, SJ. I wasn't expecting to see you tonight."

SJ is standing at the sink, a pint glass of water in her hand. "I'm not supposed to be here," she says. "Me and Mum had a big fight last night." She shrugs, rests her left foot against her right foot and then the right against the left. She's wearing a black lace top with black joggers and scuffed silver tennis shoes. A constellation of hoops and drops glitters at her earlobes. She reminds Laurel of one of the fairies in a book she used to read to the children when they were small. The fairy was called Silvermist and had silver hair and silver lips and was always dressed in black. It was a sad fairy. Androgynous. It had secrets.

Floyd comes in after Laurel and sighs. "To be fair," he says, as though Laurel had said something, "it has been a very long time since Kate and SJ fell out."

"We haven't fallen out," SJ snaps.

"Well, had a fight, whatever."

"What did you fight about?" asks Laurel. "I mean you don't have to tell me, obviously . . ."

Sara-Jade casts her long-lashed gaze to the floor and says, "She doesn't like my new boyfriend."

Floyd makes a strange noise behind Laurel and she turns to give him a questioning look.

"He's forty-nine," SJ says.

Floyd makes another noise and looks pointedly from Sara-Jade to Laurel and back again.

"He's married," says Sara-Jade. "Well, sort of married. In a long-term relationship."

"Oh," says Laurel, wishing she hadn't asked.

"He has four children. The youngest is eight."

"Oh," says Laurel again.

"I've told her not to come here expecting validation or exemption from the usual rules of human decency."

"No," says Laurel. "No. I . . ." She tries and fails to find somewhere to bring her gaze to rest.

And then SJ starts crying and runs from the room, her thin arms bunched together in front of her chest.

Laurel looks from the door to Floyd and back again.

"You can go after her if you like," he says to her, slowly and calmly. "I've said all I've got to say on the subject."

Laurel looks away from Floyd and toward the hallway. SJ is brittle, like Hanna, but Hanna never cries. Sometimes Hanna looks like she might cry but her eyes stay dry and the opportunity to touch her, to hold her, to nurture her eludes Laurel. So it is some long untapped maternal longing that sends her out of the kitchen and into the hall where SJ is snatching her coat off the coatrack and sobbing uncontrollably.

"Sara," she starts. "SJ. Come into the living room with me. Come. We can talk."

"What is there to talk about?" she wails. "I'm a bitch. I'm *bad*. There's nothing else to say."

"Well, actually," says Laurel, "that's not true. I . . ." She inhales. "Come and sit with me. Please."

SJ rehangs her coat and follows Laurel. In the living room she curls herself into the armchair and looks at Laurel through wet eyelashes.

Laurel sits opposite her. "I had an affair with a married man once. When I was very young."

SJ blinks.

"To be fair, he didn't have any children. And he'd only been married for a year. We had an affair for two years. It was while I was at university."

"Was it a teacher?"

"No. Not a teacher. Just a friend."

"And then what happened? Did he leave her for you?"

Laurel smiles. "No. He didn't. I left university and moved to London and we thought we couldn't live without each other and that we were going to have all these wildly romantic rendezvous in country hotels. Of course, within six weeks it had totally fizzled out. Apparently he and his wife split up that same year. Too young to get married, basically. We were *all* too young. Did you know that the parts of the brain involved in decision-making aren't fully developed until you're twenty-five years old?"

SJ shrugs.

"Who is it?" Laurel asks.

"It's the course leader," SJ says, "at the art college where I model."

"How long has it been going on for?"

SJ drops her chin into her chest and mumbles, "A few months."

"And how often are you seeing him?"

"Most days," she says.

"Where?"

"At work. In his office." She shrugs. "Sometimes at his brother's place when he's out of town."

"Does he ever take you out anywhere? Drinks? Dinner?"

SJ shakes her head and plucks at the drawstring on her joggers.

"So it's just sex?"

SJ lifts her head quickly. "No!" she exclaims. "No! It's much more than that! We talk, all the time. And he draws me. I'm his . . ."

"Muse."

"Yes. I'm his muse."

Laurel sighs. Cliché after cliché after cliché.

"Sara-Jade," she starts carefully. "You are a very beautiful girl."

"Huh."

"You are very beautiful and very special. This man—what's his name?"

"Simon."

"Simon has very good taste. He can clearly see quality when it crosses his path. And I'm sure he's a wonderful man."

"He is," says SJ. "He really is."

"Of course. You wouldn't be with him if he wasn't. Has he said he'll leave his wife?"

"Partner."

"Partner, wife, it doesn't matter. They have children. They share a home. Has he said he'll leave her for you?"

She shakes her head.

"Do you want him to?"

She nods. And then shakes it again. "No. *Obviously.* I mean, you know, *his kids*, especially the little one. And I've been through it myself. So I know what it feels like."

"How old were you when your parents split up?"

"Six," she says. "Virtually the same age as Simon's son. So . . ."

"So you don't want him to leave her for you?"

"No. Only in an imaginary way, where no one gets hurt."

"But what if she finds out? His partner? What if she finds out? And then leaves him anyway?"

"She won't find out."

"How do you know?"

"Because we're discreet."

"SJ, this is the modern world. There is no privacy anymore. Everyone knows everything. All the time. I mean, look how quickly you googled me after we met. Found out about Ellie. Someone, somewhere will find out what's happening and they might just tell Simon's partner and then everything will be broken. Irreparably. And the only way you can avoid that happening is by walking away. Making it stop."

SJ sniffs and ties knots in her drawstring.

"Do you love him?"

"Yes."

"Do you love him enough to hurt a lot of people who don't deserve to be hurt?"

"How do you expect me to answer that?"

"It's a tough question, but you do need to answer it. Not now, but over the next hours and days. I'm not going to tell you that in ten years you'll look back and wonder what the hell you were thinking, because I remember being twenty-one and thinking that my personality was a solid thing, that *me* was set in stone, that I would always feel what I felt and believe what I believed. But now I know that *me* is fluid and shape-changing. So whatever you're feeling now, it's temporary. But what will happen to that family if they find out about their father's betrayal will have repercussions forever. The damage will never heal."

Fat tears coalesce in the rims of SJ's eyes and drop heavily onto her cheeks. Laurel thinks she sees her nod but she's not quite sure.

"Why did you and your husband split up?"

"Because of Ellie. Because I didn't think he was hurting enough. Because he tried to make me believe that things would be OK, and I didn't want things to be OK."

"Did it hurt your children when you split up? Do they hate you?"

The question takes Laurel by surprise. Not *did* they hate you, but *do* they hate you. She thinks of last night's awful phone call from Blue and Jake. She thinks of Hanna's refusal to engage with her on anything other than a very shallow level of human interaction, and the way both her children keep her at arm's length. She's always put it down to their responses to losing their sister when they were both at such a vulnerable age. She can't even remember how they reacted to Paul moving out. The separation was played out so slowly it was hard to pinpoint the moment it had actually ended. She doesn't remember tearful recrimination, she doesn't remember her children hurting, or at least hurting any more than they'd already been hurting.

"I don't know," she replies. "Maybe. But then we were already a broken family."

SJ nods; then she unfurls her limbs, sits forward in her chair, and engages Laurel on a different level entirely. "I've been reading lots of stuff about it. About Ellie. On the Internet."

"Have you?"

"Yes. I mean, I was only a kid in 2005 so I'd never heard of Ellie Mack before. And now, well, it's sort of weird that you're here, in my dad's house, and that this hideous terrible thing happened to you, a thing that just doesn't happen to people. And I keep thinking . . ." She pauses. "Do you believe that she ran away?"

Laurel feels herself almost physically pushed backward by the unexpectedness of the question.

"No," she says softly. "No I don't. But then I'm her mother. I knew her. I knew what she wanted and where she was heading and what made her happy. And I *know* she wasn't stressed about her GCSEs. So no, deep down I don't believe she ran away. But I have to because the evidence is all there."

"The burglary, you mean?"

"Yes, the burglary. Except I don't think of it as a burglary. She used her key. She just came home to collect some things. That's all."

"But . . . the bag. Don't you ever wonder about the bag?"

"The bag?"

"Yes. Ellie's rucksack. The one they found in the forest. Don't you think, I don't know, but surely after all those years on the run she'd have had some different things in it? Not just the things she had when she ran away from home?"

A chill runs through Laurel. She thinks of the hours she spent asking herself the same question at the time. Eventually she'd made peace with the theory that Ellie had deliberately kept a bag with her things from home in it as a kind of security blanket, in the same way that Laurel had kept Ellie's bedroom untouched for most of the years that she was missing.

"And you know," SJ continues, "there's another thing, something really strange, about Poppy's mum—" She stops talking and they both turn at the sound of the door opening. It's Floyd. He's holding two mugs of tea and he throws Laurel a grateful look.

"There you go," he says, putting the mugs down on the table and then sitting down next to Laurel. "Medicinal tea. For frayed nerves. Everything OK?"

Laurel touches Floyd's leg and says, "We've had a good chat."

"Yes," agrees Sara-Jade. "It's been a good chat. I'm going to think about things."

Laurel and Sara-Jade exchange a look. They have started a conversation that needs to be finished. But it will have to wait for another time.

25

The next morning Laurel awakes late and full of unsettling dreams. It takes her a moment to place her surroundings; they've conflated themselves with something she dreamed about. But a second later she remembers that she is in Floyd's bed, that it is Wednesday, that it is nearly nine, and that she really, really wants to go home.

She showers and dresses and finds Floyd and Poppy at the breakfast table, reading the papers together.

"Good morning," says Floyd. "I didn't wake you. You looked so peaceful."

"Thank you. I must have needed it. Morning, Poppy."

"Morning, Laurel!"

She's back in a classic Poppy outfit: pink cords and a black polo neck, hair clipped back at both sides.

"Let me get you some breakfast," says Floyd, rising to his feet.

"You know, actually, I'm going to head home, I think, and let you two get on with your day. I need to catch up with myself before I head over to Hanna's."

Floyd sees her off from his door with a long kiss and a plan for her to come back that evening. "I'll make you something delicious," he says. "Do you like veal?"

"I do like veal."

"Great," he says, "I'll see you later."

Laurel feels curiously relieved as she slides into her car and starts the engine. She'd thought that Floyd might try to guilt trip her into staying longer and was pleased when he didn't. Now she feels a sense of escape. The discovery that Poppy's mum used to teach Ellie maths, Hanna's comment about Ellie finding Noelle Donnelly creepy and weird, and her conversation last night with Sara-Jade have all left her feeling shaky and full of holes. She needs to get home and breathe in her own space. And she needs to do something else, something she hasn't done for a very, very long time.

$\backsim$

Laurel makes herself a mug of tea and takes it into the spare room. She sits on the edge of the bed and reaches down to pull a cardboard box toward her. Ellie's box. She remembers filling it in the old house. She'd been numb and drained and taken too long over it, a full day, touching and caressing, holding and smelling. She'd read Ellie's diaries. They were sporadic things that leaped about over the years, making it hard to work out what she was writing about half the time as she rarely dated the entries. Some of it Laurel had skipped over and she'd thrown one notebook bodily away from herself at a reference to giving Theo a hand-job.

There'd been nothing in those diaries then, nothing to indicate a secret life, a secret friend, unhappiness of any sort. She hadn't looked at them since.

But she pulls some out now, flipping through them to find the entries written in the months before she disappeared. They were messy records. Doodles and cartoons, homework and revision notes here and there, dates and numbers and lists of things to buy on a trip to Oxford Street:

Nice moisturiser
New trainers (not black or white)

Books: *Atonement, Lovely Bones*
Trainer socks
Birthday card for dad ☺

There were lipstick kisses and smudges of ink and glittery stickers. And, scattered in between, loose records of her days. And in those days and weeks before she ran away there were only two things going on in Ellie's world. Theo and revision. Theo and revision. Theo and revision.

Laurel peers closely at an entry from what seems to be January. Ellie is bemoaning her result in a maths test. A B+. She'd wanted an A. Theo had got an A. Laurel sighs. Ellie had constantly aligned herself with Theo, as though he was the only benchmark that mattered.

"Asked Mum for a tutor," she wrote. "Fingers crossed she says yes. I am *sooooo* shit at maths . . ."

And there, a few entries later: "Tutor came! She's a bit weird but a great teacher! A* here I come!"

Laurel turns the pages faster and faster. She's looking for something but she doesn't quite know what, something to tie all the loose fragments of her dreams together with the reality of the last few days' revelations.

Tutor today. I got 97% in the paper she set me. She gave me a set of lip balms. So sweet!

Tutor 5 p.m. She brought me a scented pen. She's so sweet!

Tutor 5 p.m. She said I'm the best student she's ever had! But of course!

Tutor 5 p.m. Bit weird today, asking me strange questions about what I want in life. Think she's having a midlife crisis!

Tutor 5 p.m. 100%!! I literally just got 100%!!! Tutor says I am a genius. She is 100% right!

Tutor 5 p.m. Think I'm over this now. She really freaks me out sometimes. She's so intense. And she smells. Am going to ask Mum to cancel her. I can do this by myself. Don't need bunny boilers in my life.

There's no more mention of the tutor after this entry.

Ellie simply slots back into her life. She sees Theo. She studies. She looks forward to the summer. Nothing more.

But Laurel's fingertip stays poised against the last entry, against the words "bunny boiler." What does that mean? Her understanding of the term is a woman who stalks and torments a man who has discarded her, unable to deal with the rejection. Clearly that is not the definition that Ellie was alluding to here. So if not that, then what? Had Noelle been overly fixated on Ellie? Obsessed with her, maybe? Maybe even physically attracted to her? Had she tried to touch Ellie inappropriately? Or maybe she was jealous of her, of her youth and beauty and unquestionable intelligence? Maybe she belittled her and made her feel bad? And if any of these scenarios was the case, what did this mean?

She squeezes her eyes tightly shut and her hands into fists. There's something in there, but she can't get to it. And what could it possibly be anyway?

The darkness lifts after a moment and life returns to its normal proportions. She slowly puts Ellie's books back into their box and slides it under the bed.

⌒

"Tell me more about Noelle," she says to Floyd that night over dinner.

She sees a muscle in his cheek twitch and there is a missed beat before he says, "Oh, God, must I?"

"Sorry. I know she's not your favorite person. But I'm curious." She rests her cutlery on her plate and picks up her wineglass. "I looked at Ellie's old diaries today. I wanted to see what she wrote about Noelle. And she called her . . . I hope you won't be offended, but she called her a 'bunny boiler.'"

"Ha, no. That about sums it up. She was a very needy woman. Very intense."

"How did you meet her?"

"Urgh." He swallows a mouthful of wine and puts down his glass. "Well, yeah. I don't come out of this too well. But she was a fan."

"A fan? You have fans?"

"Well, maybe it would be fairer to call them fervent readers. Maths groupies. That kind of thing."

"Well I never," says Laurel, sitting back in her chair and appraising Floyd teasingly. "I did not realize that I was facing such stiff competition."

"Oh, don't worry, those days are well and truly over. I had my moment in the sun with one book. My 'pay the bills book,' as I call it. Maths for dummies you could say, except we weren't that honest about it. I got to be a bit playful with that book and it got me a little fan club of slightly peculiar, maths-obsessed women. Wasn't my style at all. I soon went back to the big heavyweight tomes that no one with romantic yearnings would touch with a barge pole."

"So, Noelle, she was one of your groupies?"

"Yeah. I suppose so. And I'd just split up with Sara's mother and I was lonely and she was a bit crazy and a bit determined and I let her have her way with me and then spent the next few years repenting at leisure. She was like a leech. I couldn't get shot of her. And then she got pregnant."

"By you?"

He sighs and casts his gaze over her shoulder. He doesn't answer her question. "I didn't even really find her that attractive. I was just . . . I was just trying to be nice, I suppose."

Laurel laughs drily. She has never done anything "just to be nice" in her life. But she knows the type. Paul is the same, will go against all his basest instincts and feelings to make someone else feel good for five minutes.

"And then you were stuck with her?"

"Yeah. I was indeed." He runs his fingertips around the bowl of his wineglass and looks uncharacteristically pensive.

"Who ended it? Eventually?"

"That was me. And that was where the bunny-boiler bit came into it. She wasn't prepared to let me go without a fight. There were some bad nights. Really bad nights. And then one day she just said she'd had enough, dumped Poppy on my doorstep, and disappeared off the face of the earth." He shrugs. "Sad, really," he says. "Really sad. Sad woman. Sad story. You know."

The mood of the evening has become somber and slightly uncomfortable.

"I'm sorry," says Laurel. "I didn't mean to make you feel sad. I just . . . it's an odd little connection, that's all. Between you and me. And Ellie. I just wanted to understand it a bit more."

He nods. "I get that," he says. "I totally get it. And of course it's Poppy I feel bad for, being abandoned like that. No child wants to feel that they weren't wanted, even if they don't care much for the abandoner. But"—he brightens slightly—"now Poppy has you. And you are quite a tonic. For us all. Cheers." He tilts his glass toward hers and their glasses meet and so do their gazes.

She returns her focus to the meat on her plate, to the pink-gray flesh of the slayed baby calf. She cuts into it and a rivulet of wine-colored juices run across the plate.

She finds she has lost her appetite, but she doesn't know why.

26

The following day, Laurel parks her car in a multistory car park in Kings Cross and heads to St. Martin's school of art in Granary Square. Floyd had told her that SJ was working there today when she'd asked nonchalantly over breakfast.

It's a bland day, newspaper gray, lifted by the Christmas lights and decorations in every window. Granary Square is wide and quiet as she approaches it, a scattering of pigeons across its surface, a few people braving the cold outside to smoke a cigarette with their morning coffee.

At reception she asks for Sara-Jade Virtue. She's told that Sara is working until lunchtime, so she sits in the restaurant next door and she eats a second breakfast and drinks two coffees and a peppermint tea before returning at twelve thirty and waiting for her outside.

Sara-Jade finally appears at ten past one. She's wearing a huge pink fake-fur coat and boots that look far too big for her. She starts when she sees Laurel.

"Oh," she says. "Hi."

"Hi! Sorry for, you know, turning up unannounced. I was just . . . Are you hungry? Can I take you for lunch?"

SJ looks at her wrist and then up at the sky. "I was supposed to . . ." but she trails off. "Sure," she says. "Fine. Thank you."

They go to the pub across the way. It's brand new with plate-glass windows on every side giving views all across the

square and the canal. It's buzzing with business suits and students. They both order fishcakes and fizzy water and pick at the
bread basket halfheartedly.

"How are you?" says Laurel.

"I'm OK."

"How was work?"

"Yeah, it was OK. Bit cold."

"Yes, I don't suppose this is a great time of year for nude
modeling."

"Life modeling."

"Yes. Sorry. How many students are there? Drawing you?"

"About twelve today. But sometimes it can be thirty or forty."

"And what do you think about? All those hours, in one position?"

SJ shrugs. "Nothing, really. Just what I need to do when I
get home. Things I've done, places I've been. I do this thing
sometimes where I let my head just sort of bounce around
from place to place; I find myself in places I haven't thought
about in years, like a bar near my old college, or a restaurant in
Prague I went to when I was eighteen, or a railway track I used
to walk down when I visited my grandparents and the smell of
cow parsley there . . ." She tugs off a small piece of bread and
puts it in her mouth. "Those birds, what are they called? Wood
pigeons. That noise they make." She smiles. "It's kind of fun."

"And then you suddenly remember that you're naked in
front of a group of strangers?"

SJ throws her a look of incomprehension. Her mouth opens
as though trying to form a response but then closes again. Laurel remembers what Poppy said about her being humorless.

"So, did you see him today? Simon?"

SJ looks nervously from left to right and raises a hand warn-
ingly.

"Sorry," says Laurel, "indiscreet. And, to be honest, not why I came here to see you. I just . . ." She recrosses her legs. "What we were talking about the other night. About Ellie . . ."

"Yeah. I'm really sorry about that. It was a bit insensitive of me. I can be a bit like that."

"No. Really. I didn't mind. I don't mind. It's not anything I haven't thought about before. There's not one aspect of the whole thing I haven't thought about a million times already, I promise you. Including the rucksack. But you were about to say something, the other night, something about Poppy's mum. About Noelle."

SJ looks up at her through her thick eyelashes and then down again. "Oh yeah," she says.

"So?" Laurel encourages her. "What was it? What were you going to say?"

"Oh, nothing much. Just that she was a bit strange. A bit freaky."

"You know," Laurel says, "I read Ellie's old diaries last night. And she wrote about Poppy's mum. She called her a 'bunny boiler.' And she also wrote that Noelle used to bring her gifts and call her her best student. And it all just struck me as a bit . . ." She struggles for the next thread of her commentary. "Did you have much to do with her?"

"No, not really. I used to come and stay with Dad quite a lot when I was small and sometimes she'd be here, but not always and she acted like she hated me."

"In what way?"

"Oh, you know, cutting remarks about my behavior. That I was out of control. That in her family she'd have been belted black and blue for such cheek. And the minute my dad left the room she'd just ignore me, act like I wasn't there. She called me 'the girl.' You know, 'Will the girl be there?' 'When is the girl going home?' That kind of thing. She was fucking vile."

"Oh Lord, how horrible. You must have been horrified when she got pregnant."

"I cried."

"I'm not surprised."

They move apart for a moment to allow the waiter to put down their dishes. They thank him and then they glance at each other, significantly.

"How did you feel about Poppy when she was born?"

Sara-Jade picks up her cutlery and slices through the middle of her fishcake. Steam blooms from it for a second or two. She puts the cutlery down again and shrugs. "It was, I don't know . . . whatever. I was twelve. She was a baby."

"But as she grew, became a little person? Did you feel close to her?"

"I guess. Sort of. I didn't see her all that much at first because . . . well, basically because I didn't want to."

"Oh," says Laurel. "Was that because you were jealous?"

"No," she says firmly. "No, I was too old to be jealous. I didn't want to see her because I didn't believe . . . I didn't believe she was real."

Laurel looks at her questioningly.

"It's hard to explain, but I thought she was like a robot baby. Or an alien baby. I didn't believe that Noelle had really given birth to her. I was scared of her. Terrified of her."

"Wow," says Laurel, "that's a really strange reaction."

"Yes. Kind of freakish."

"Why do you think you felt like that?"

Sara-Jade picks up her knife and turns it between her fingertips. "There was a thing—" she begins, but then stops abruptly.

"A thing?"

"Yes. An event. A moment. And to this day I don't know if I imagined it or not. I was kind of a weird kid." She laughs wryly.

"Still am. I do know that. I had a special assistant at school for a while, because of emotional difficulties. I was prone to insane outbursts of anger. Tears sometimes. And this, this thing, it happened right at the height of all this, when things were peaking for me in so many ways. Puberty, hormones, social anxiety, I was still fucked up over my parents splitting up, all that shit. I wasn't a pretty sight. I wasn't an easy kid, either. I was a total nightmare, to be honest. And right in the middle of all this I thought I saw something." She places the knife gently down on the table and looks straight at Laurel. "I looked through the door of my dad's bedroom, when Noelle was about eight months pregnant. I looked in and . . ." She stops and her gaze drops to the table. "She was naked. And there was no bump. She was naked," she repeats. "And there was no bump.

"And I don't know what I really saw. I have never been able to process it. Never known if it was just me being a nutty little kid freaking out about a new baby or if it really happened. But when that baby was born three weeks later, I was terrified. I didn't see her until she was nearly one."

Laurel hasn't moved a muscle since SJ's pronouncement.

"Did you tell your dad?"

She shakes her head.

"Did you tell anyone?"

"I told my mum."

"What did she say?"

"She told me to stop being a crazy person."

"Where was the baby born?"

"I don't know. I never thought about it."

Laurel closes her eyes and suddenly the face of Noelle Donnelly flashes to the forefront of her consciousness, clear and precise as if she'd seen her only yesterday.

PART THREE

27

So, it's my turn, is it?

OK then. OK.

Shall we do it like an AA meeting? *My name is Noelle Donnelly and I did something bad.*

I'm not about to make excuses, but I had a tough time grow ing up. Two horrible brothers above me. Two below. And a sister who died when she was only eight. My mother and father were unforgiving of the limitations of children. They believed that a child should be a grown-up in every way apart from the way of having an opinion you could call your own. Not that religious, which was strange for the times and the place. Church on a Sunday was a good opportunity to find out that everyone else's children were doing better than their own. The Bible had some good quotes that could be used to sow a seed of terror here and there. We all believed in hell and heaven, even if we believed in nothing else. And sex was something that only disgusting people did, married or not. We never asked after our own provenance, imagined a kind of chaste communion across a brick wall somehow. Because they had separate bedrooms, my mother and father.

Home was a ten-bedroom villa on a hill, sheep all around, a mile and a half to school, downhill going there, uphill coming back. My parents took in orphans sometimes, in emergencies. They'd arrive bleary-eyed in the small hours, huge sets of siblings that they housed in the dormitory room in the attic. We called it "the orphan room" long after there'd been an orphan in it. So my parents can't have been all bad. But mainly, on the whole, yes they were.

We were known as the clever family. You know that family? We all know that family. Pianos all over the place. Books beyond belief. Grade As or you had *failed*. That was all we ever talked of. Academic success. My father was a maths teacher. My mother was a writer of books about medical history. We all went to the best schools and worked harder than everyone else and won all the awards and all the medals and all the scholarships and all the trophies going. I swear there was not a scrap of anything left for anyone else.

Well, I was clever enough to keep up, there was no doubt about that. But I was at a disadvantage for being (*a*) the middle child, (*b*) a girl, and (*c*) not the girl who had died. Michaela. That was who I was not. Michaela, who was bonnier than me and nicer than me and yes, naturally, cleverer than me. And also much less alive than me. You'd think, wouldn't you, that that would make me all the more precious to my mother and father. *Well, at least we still have our lovely Noelle.* But no.

Michaela died of cancer. We all thought it was a cold. We were wrong.

Anyway, that was me. The less bonny, less clever, less dead sister with the four horrible brothers and the mum and dad who judged more than they loved.

I did OK. I got into Trinity. I got a degree in mathematics, a PhD in applied mathematics. I moved to London shortly after I graduated and it was nice for a while just to be *clever Noelle*, not just *one of the Donnellys*. I tried my hand in the financial sector, thinking that I'd quite like to be very rich and have a performance car and an apartment with a balcony. But it really wasn't me and everyone there knew it wasn't me and so I left before I'd earned enough money for a scooter let alone a car.

You know, when I look back at this time, I'm amazed by myself, I really am. I was so young and so appallingly unsophisticated, didn't know a soul, yet there I was in the seething belly of the metropolis, had a room in a flat in Holland Park of all places. I had no idea then how high I was flying in that postcode; I thought everyone who came to London from Ireland lived in a road full of big wedding cake houses. I didn't know that Walthamstow existed. And I was cute, you know, looking back on it, had model looks, almost, in that bare-faced, hollow-chested sort of way, all legs and tangled hair and huge watery eyes. No one ever told me I was pretty, though, not once; I don't really know why.

I took a job at a posh magazine for a while. I was in the finance department and I was literally invisible for the full three years. Then I got made redundant and I had to give up my little room in lovely Holland Park, say goodbye to the wide avenue with the organic butcher before anyone knew what *organic* even meant, the food shop that sold lobster bisque in tins, the park itself with its orangery and its bowers. And that was when I discovered that Walthamstow existed: E11 with its little brown houses and its tired laundrettes, shuttered cab offices and boarded-up buildings.

I decided to retrain as a teacher.

I don't know what possessed me. I'd already proved to myself that I had no presence, that I was unable to draw any attention to myself whatsoever. How I thought I'd be able to engage a class of thirty slack-jawed teenagers on the principles of algebra I *do not know.*

I qualified but I never did teach my own class. I lost my nerve. It made me feel sick to my stomach just thinking about it. So at the age of thirty, I placed an ad in my local paper and I began tutoring. I was very good at it and all those smoothie-making mums spread the word, passed me around like a restaurant recommendation, and I made enough to move out of my little room in the little house in Walthamstow and buy myself a place in Stroud Green where the houses were slightly bigger, but not much. And that was that. That was that for a long time. And, oh—did I mention?—I was still a virgin at this point.

No, seriously, I was.

I'd had a boyfriend for a while back in Ireland, from age fourteen to fifteen. Tony. So I'd got all the kissing stuff out of the way, thought the rest would come later. Well, it never did.

And then I read in the *Times Educational Supplement (TES)* about a book. It was aimed at people who thought they "couldn't do maths," and believe me the world is full of people who think they can't do maths, which I have to try very hard to understand, because truly, I don't. How can people understand how to walk into a room full of people and find something to talk about but they can't understand how numbers work? It makes no sense to me. Anyway, I can't remember the name of the book now. It might even have been called *Bad at Maths*. Yes, that's right, it was. *Bad at Maths*. I bought it and I read it. It opened my eyes to things I'd never thought about before. But more than that, it made me laugh. I wasn't one for reading books, generally, and I only read this because it was in the *TES*, and so I hadn't been expecting such humor in a book about maths. But there it was. Humor. Bags of it. And a photo on the inside cover of a lovely man with a smiling face and a thatch of dark hair.

It was a photo of you.

I'd never been a fan of anything much before I read your

book. There were TV shows I enjoyed, *Brookside* being a particular favorite; I watched that up to the last episode. And I always perked up if *Take That* came on the radio, although on the whole I was more of a classical fan. And *of course* I'd had crushes across the years. Loads of them. But this was different.

You were different.

Do you remember, the first time we met? I know you do. You were signing books on your publisher's stand at the Education Show at the NEC. I go every year. Tutoring is a lonely world and you have to plug yourself into the mains every now and then and get a fix of what everyone else is getting. You can't be yesterday's flavor of the month when it comes to these north London mummies. You have to keep on top of things.

But mainly I was there because I knew you were going to be there. I'd made an extra-special effort: I had on a skirt and tights and a lipstick the color of toffee apples that set fire to my hair and made my blue eyes shine. I was forty-one years old. The autumn of my youth. Christ, virtually the winter. And yes, I was still a virgin.

You sat on a high stool at a high table, a small pile of your books in front of you. There was no one there, no queue, only a small sign on the wall behind you that said "Author Floyd Dunn Will Be Signing Copies of His Book 'Bad at Maths' Today, 1 p.m. to 3 p.m." And next to it a photo, that photo of you, the same one from inside your book that I'd stared at for so many hours, memorizing the way your hair fell around your ears, the line your mouth made as it attempted a serious smile.

My eye went from the photo to you and back to the photo. You were thinner than I'd imagined. I'd expected a little belly, maybe. I don't know why.

"Hello!" you said at my approach, as though someone had just plugged you in and switched you on. "Hello!" You wouldn't have known how nervous I was. You wouldn't have guessed. I played it very, very cool.

"Hello," I replied, my hands tight around my dog-eared copy of your book. "I have my own copy. Would you mind signing it for me?"

I passed it across to you and you smiled that smile you have, the one that makes your eyes into fireworks that go *bang bang bang* in my soul.

"Well," you said, "that is a well-loved copy."

I could have told you I'd read it thirty times. I could have told you that your book made me laugh more in a week than I'd laughed in the year before I read it. I could have told you that I was completely in awe of you. But I wanted you to see me as an equal. So I simply said, "It has been a very useful tool. I'm a maths tutor."

"Well," you said, "I am very glad to hear that." You took the book from me and held your pen over the title page. "Shall I sign it to you?"

"Yes," I said. "Please. Noelle."

"Noelle," you said. "That's a lovely name. Were you a Christmas baby?"

"Yes. December the twenty-fourth."

"Best Christmas present ever, eh?"

"No," I replied, "apparently not. Apparently I ruined Christmas Day for everyone."

You laughed then; I hadn't imagined a laugh for you. In your photo you looked as if you might go so far as a chuckle, if tickled to the point of no return. But no, you had a proper laugh where your mouth opened wide and your head tipped back on your neck and a big thunderclap boom exploded from you. I liked it, very much.

You wrote something after my name, I wanted to see what it was, but I didn't want to look as though I cared.

"You're American," I said.

"To a certain extent," you said. "And you're Irish?"

"Yes. To the fullest possible extent."

You liked my little joke and you laughed again. It felt like someone massaging the inside of my stomach with velvet-gloved hands.

"Where are you from?"

"Near Dublin," I replied. "County Wicklow. Where all the sheep live."

You laughed for a third time and I felt emboldened in a way I'd never felt before in my life. I looked behind me to check that a queue hadn't built as we'd talked. But I still had you all to myself.

"Are you here again tomorrow?" I asked.

"No. No. They're putting me on a train back to London after this. Which leaves in, oh"—you looked at your watch—"approximately two hours. I should probably be wrapping this up soon."

"Have you signed many books?"

"Oh, yeah, hundreds and hundreds." You clicked the lid back on your pen and gave me a sideways smile. "Kidding," you said. "About twenty."

"Long way to come, to sign twenty books."

"I tend to agree with you."

You slid the pen into your jacket pocket and turned away from me, looking about for a person to whisk you away, no doubt.

"Well," I said. "I'll let you get away. I hope you have a safe journey back to London. Whereabouts do you live?"

"North London."

"Oh," I said, an Oscar-worthy moment of fakery, "snap. So do I."

"Oh!" you said. "Whereabouts?"

"Stroud Green."

"Well, well. What a coincidence. Me, too."

"What? You live in Stroud Green?" This I had not known. This I could never have believed to be possible.

"Yes! Latymer Road. Do you know it?"

"Yes," I said, joy virtually pouring out of my ears and my eyeballs and my nostrils. "Yes, I do know it. I'm just a few roads down from you."

"Well, well, well. Maybe our paths will cross again then?"

"Yes," I'd said, as though it would be no more than a fun coincidence if they did, not the culmination of all my hopes and worldly dreams. "Maybe they will."

Two weeks later, they did.

28

To say that I'd been stalking you would be an overstatement.
We lived but two hundred feet apart after all. It would be fair,
though, to say that I was going out a little more than I usually
tended to. Coming upon a nearly empty bottle of milk in the
fridge would fill me with delight. *Oh dear, I shall have to visit
the corner shop again.* And if I returned to the realization that I
should also have bought a newspaper while I was out, well, that
really wasn't the end of the world. On with the coat, back to
the high street, one eye open for you in one direction, another
eye open for you in the other. And anything that gave me cause
to pass the end of Latymer Road was a particular bonus.

And then one evening, there you were, in the convenience
store, in a blue anorak and jeans, a bottle of red wine hanging
from your fist, studying the breakfast cereals intently. I said,
"Floyd Dunn."

You turned and you remembered me immediately. I knew
you did. I hadn't expected that. No one ever remembered me
immediately. But you smiled and you said, "I know you. You
were at the NEC."

"Yes, I was indeed. Noelle."

I gave you my hand and you shook it.

"Noelle. Of course. The unwanted Christmas present. How
are you?"

"I'm truly grand, thank you. And you?"

"I am moderately grand, if that's possible."

"Oh yes," I said. "There are many shades of grand."

There was a small moment then, I recall. It was likely awkward, though I'd be hard-pressed to judge as my whole life until this point had been vaguely awkward. But you stepped into the moment and saved it and that was when I knew.

You said—and I shall never ever forget this because it was so remarkable to me—you said, "Rice Krispies or Mini Shredded Wheats?"

Which may not sound like much of anything, but it was what it *wasn't* that was so important to me. It wasn't a rebuttal. It wasn't a glance at your watch and an *oh, is that the time, I'd better get on*. It wasn't a suggestion that I was taking up too much of your life; that I was somehow blocking your view of better things. It was an invitation to banter.

So of course I seized it. "Rice Krispies," I said, "are delicious, but five minutes later you're hungry again. All that air . . ."

You smiled. I liked your crooked teeth.

"All that air," you repeated. "You are funny."

"No. I'm just Irish."

"True," he said. "You do have a natural inbuilt advantage when it comes to humor. So." You turned back to the breakfast cereals. "Seven-year-old girl. Mother is a health freak, so no sugary stuff. What would you choose?"

Seven-year-old girl? Well, there'd been no mention of a seven-year-old girl in your biography. I can't say I was too fond of small girls. "Is this your daughter we're talking about?"

"Yes. Sara. Her mother and I recently separated and now I'm a weekend dad. So I can't afford to make any mistakes. My wife already thinks I'm going to leave my daughter somewhere or let her put her hand in a food blender. That kind of thing."

"Weetabix then," I said. "It has the least sugar of all the cereals."

Your face softened and you smiled again. "See," you said, "I knew you'd know about things like that. I knew you would. Do you have children of your own?"

"No. Not even vaguely."

You looked at me then, and I could tell you were wondering whether or not to say something, something in particular.

I acted like I wasn't fussed and, whatever it was, you decided against saying it. I could see you swallowing the words back into yourself. "Well, you have been most helpful. Thank you, Noelle."

You picked up the Weetabix. And that was that.

But it was enough so that the next time I bumped into you, a week later, we had a little open-ended thing going on, a little rapport. We chatted about the weather a bit then. And the next time we chatted about some government scheme to ruin all the schools, which we'd both read about in the papers that morning. It was the fourth time, a month after the Education Show, that you said, "Have you ever tried that Eritrean place? By the tube?"

"As it happens, no I have not."

"Well, it is excellent. I've been going there for years. You should try it . . . In fact . . ."

And there it came, your invitation to dinner.

Yes, Floyd. *Your invitation to dinner.* I know you will try to twist this and rewrite it, like you try to twist and rewrite everything, but you know and I know that *you started this*. You saw me, Floyd. You saw me and you wanted me. You asked me to dinner. You turned up at that dinner on time and smartly dressed. You did not look at me and say, *This has been a terrible mistake,* and do a runner. You smiled when I walked in, you stood, you took my shoulders, and you pressed your face against my face. You said, "You look lovely." You waited until I'd sat down before you sat down. You maintained a steady line of eye contact.

You did. You totally, totally did.

And then it was *you*. You phoned me a few days later (just long enough to make me sweat, just long enough to make me think about calling you first but I did not. *I did not.*). And you invited me to your house.

Yes you did.

Your goal was clear that night. You wanted to fuck me. But that was OK because I wanted to be fucked by you. I didn't care that dinner was somewhat perfunctory—what was it now? Pasta, I think, with some kind of shop-bought sauce that must have taken you all of five minutes to throw together. But a nice bottle of wine, if I recall. And we ended up on your sofa an hour later and while you were pulling at my clothes and panting all over me I said, "Believe it or not, I am a virgin, possibly the last one in existence." And you were very kind about it. You didn't laugh or say, *You're taking the piss.* You didn't recoil or sigh or tell me to go home. You were kind. You touched me all over until I was a blob and then you were slow and patient. And it did hurt. Yes, it really did. But I'd been expecting that and frankly, you weren't the biggest boy in the class, if you know what I mean. A blessing really.

And I knew. I think I really did know from that point on that you and I were mainly about sex. And that was fine with me.

But I grew accustomed to you over the months, grew accustomed to your pillows and your cereal bowls, the smell of your scalp before you had a shower, the sight of your name on my phone when you called or texted. You inhabited a big chunk of my life: over 30 percent if we're going to talk in numbers. And probably 30 percent of that 30 percent was sex. The rest was just lying in your bed listening to you shower, waiting for your calls, watching you cook, watching you eat, sitting on your sofa watching TV with you, meals out from time to time, walks in the park from time to time, making arrangements to meet. That's a lot of shared existence for two people in a sex-based relationship, a lot of time not having sex. More than enough time for a bond to form. I never told you I loved you. You never told me you loved me. Some people would say that that was sufficient grounds to diminish everything else that happened between us. But I disagree.

I disagree very strongly.

29

I first met Sara-Jade when you and I had been together for a year. Up until then she'd only been spending every other weekend at yours and it was easy to keep us compartmentalized. But then your ex got a job and suddenly she was dropping Sara on your doorstep all the time, quite often at short notice, quite often when you'd already invited me over for the evening.

Well, you'd told me that she was a difficult girl; she'd responded badly to the split, so you said. And like I said, I'd never really liked little girls. They have a way of looking at you sometimes, as though their hearts are full of hate.

And Sara-Jade, she barely looked human. Skin so thin and pale you could see the veins of her. And this shock of *white* hair. Not blonde, no; white, like an old lady. She was tiny too, more like a five-year-old than an eight-year-old.

I tried to be nice. I really did. You know that. You were there, remember?

"Oh, so you must be Sara-Jade. It is a pleasure to meet you." I tried to shake her hand. I always do that with young children because you never know whether they're the kind to appreciate adult attention or not. Some children thrive on it; their eyes find you and they reel you in: *Look at me, find me impressive, tell me that I'm better than all the other children.* Others could not give a sideways shit and just want to get away from you as fast as they humanly can. So I find that a handshake is a good compromise between fussing over them and ignoring them, and sometimes you'll find you're the very first person to shake their hand and that's a nice thing however you look at it.

Sara-Jade did not take my hand. She turned and ran from the room sobbing.

Jesus Christ.

You ran after her and I heard your voices and stood there in your hallway, my hand hanging heavy at my side.

I felt like a monster. I remember looking at myself in the mirror that hung on your wall there, above the table by your door. I'd begun to look fondly upon myself at that point. I'd begun to focus on the positive rather than negative. If a man like you wanted to touch me, to behold me, then surely I could not be quite so bad? But the face in the mirror that day, as you soothed your sobbing girl behind a closed door somewhere, it was not a face I wanted to look at. I saw the darkness around my eyes, the pull of my skin away from my cheekbones and toward my chin, the hair that had dulled to rusty water and grown too long for my face. I was not pretty. I was not.

Your daughter reminded me of that.

After that, well, it was hard to like her.

After that, for quite some time, it was hard to like myself.

～

I should not have taken it personally, I can see that now. Sara-Jade was a highly strung child, scared of many things, not just the woman in her hallway. But I did take it personally and I could not bring myself to be kind to that child ever again. To be fair, you found her hard work yourself. She was an aloof child and prone to the most terrible, terrible tantrums. *Tantrums* is barely the word for it. If I'd been that way inclined, I might have theorized that she'd been possessed by the devil. She threw things, she broke things, she screamed that she wanted to kill you and stab you and cut off your head with a knife. She hated you; oh God, yes, she hated you. Other times she'd be regressive and needy, make you accompany her to the toilet because she was scared to go on her own, make you sit outside her room singing a particular song until she was asleep, sometimes for over half an hour.

We spoke about her a lot during those months, muttered softly across your pillows at night, wondered *what to do* and *how to deal with it*. I had nothing to offer. I knew nothing about small children. I had a thousand nieces and nephews back home, but I hadn't seen a one of them. Not even vaguely interested. But I made the right noises. "What about therapy?" I suggested. "Have you thought about that?"

But no, apparently *Kate*, perfect little Kate, the world's *most annoying ex-wife* (I'm sorry, Floyd, but she was and you know she was, with that breathy voice, her baby-doll eyes, the way her chin would drop when you told her about Sara-Jade's misdemeanors and she'd say, "Oh, Jadey-Wadey. Poor little sugar bum. Has Daddy been putting you to bed too late again?" Christ, I wanted to slice her in half, I really did), no, Kate wasn't having any of it. "Too much sugar." "Not enough sleep." "Hard week at school." Blah blah blah. She couldn't see that her own child was a virtual sociopath.

But I should have tried harder. I should have been nicer. And if there's any share of the blame that I'll take, it'll be that. I turned you against her. I did. We demonized her, the pair of us. We bonded over our mutual dismay, our mutual powerlessness. And the more you turned against her, the more you turned toward me. I became the *normal*. I became the *sane*. And I embraced the new dynamic. One hundred percent.

And now, Floyd Dunn, now look at me, look me in the eye

and tell me it wasn't you. Go on. I dare you. Tell me it wasn't you who said it first, who turned to me in the bed one night, after we'd made love, and took both of my hands inside yours, who kissed those hands hard and long and said, "Maybe if you and I had a child, maybe it would like me."

30

Laurel drives straight from King's Cross to Hanna's flat and she cleans her flat harder than she's ever cleaned it before. When there's nothing left to clean she goes into Hanna's horrible back garden with its stench of disappointing summers and she hacks everything off with a pair of pruning shears, leaving behind blackened arboreal skeletons and mud and a rusty barbecue that Hanna has never used. She doesn't wear gloves and afterward her hands are ripped and raw, but she doesn't care. She rubs some of Hanna's hand cream into her hands and enjoys the rasp of it as it seeps into her flesh.

There are no flowers today. But, frankly, Laurel no longer cares about her daughter's secret love life. Let her have a secret love life. Let her have a girlfriend, a boyfriend, an old man, a young woman, two young women and a dog for all she cares. Let her have whom she wants. Hanna will tell her when Hanna is ready.

All the things that had seemed important yesterday are important no longer. All that matters now is for Laurel to massage the essence out of the huge knot of new information that is currently blocking up her mind. It's all tangled together and she's sure it all means something but it's so unlikely and so bizarre that she cannot find the place to start.

She tucks Hanna's thirty pounds into her purse, locks Hanna's flat behind her, gets back into her car, and drives home fast.

◦◦◦

Typing *Noelle Donnelly* into Google doesn't offer her much to work with. The world is surprisingly full of Noelle Donnellys and Laurel is sure that if Noelle had deliberately disappeared and then come back to life as a physiotherapist in Chicago, she wouldn't be shouting to the world about it all over the Internet. She types in *Noelle Donnelly Maths Tutor*. This bears more fruit; a few listings on sites with names like FindMyTutor.com and MyPerfectTutor.com. But in all cases the listings have run dry and there are no new testimonials.

She tries *Noelle Donnelly Ireland*. There are many, but none of them are her Noelle. Finally she tries *Noelle Donnelly Disappearance*. The world, she concludes half an hour later, did not care much about the disappearance of Noelle Donnelly. No one seemed to notice. There is nothing.

She shuts down her laptop and scratches at her wrists. She tries to recall who recommended Noelle to her in the first place. It was a neighbor. She can see the woman's face. She can see her dogs, a pair of Irish setters, always jumping up at her, leaving muddy paw-prints on her jeans. But she cannot remember her name. She goes to the wardrobe in the spare room and she pulls out a box of things she still hasn't unpacked from the house move. In here, she hopes, is her old address book, a relic from the days when people had address books, when you wrote numbers down instead of typing them into a phone.

She finds it halfway and flicks through the pages feeling slightly appalled by the amount of people she once knew whom she now no longer thinks about.

It's Susie. Or Sally. Or Sandy. Something like that. She flicks faster and faster. And then she suddenly stops. A pink Post-it, clinging to the "S" page. Her own scratchy, hurried writing on it. And the words *Noelle Donnelly*. And a number. And then she remembers. Sally—yes, it was Sally—she remembers calling her one morning, saying, "Ellie wants a tutor. You had a good one, didn't you? Have you got her number?" Scribbling it down, pulling it off, sticking it down. "Thanks, Sal, you're a star. See you soon!" The sound of her dogs barking in the background.

She phones the number. Remarkably, someone answers. It's a young man with an Irish accent.

"Hello," says Laurel, "sorry to disturb you. But I'm looking for someone who used to be on this number? Noelle Donnelly?"

"Ah, right, yeah," says the young man. "Noelle's my aunty. But no one knows where she is."

Laurel is speechless for a second. She'd expected an unavailable tone. At the most she'd expected someone who'd never heard of Noelle Donnelly. But here was a blood relative.

"Oh," she says. "Right. Yes. She disappeared, didn't she?"

"So they say," says the boy. "So they say."

"I wondered . . ." Laurel begins. "I've become quite friendly with Noelle's daughter. And Noelle's ex. And there's . . ." How could she phrase this? "There's things I'm not sure about. About her leaving. Could I come and see you?"

"Who are you, did you say?"

"I'm a friend of Poppy's."

"Ah, right. The girl she had. My grandma talks about her sometimes."

There's a brief silence and Laurel wonders if he heard her asking to come over, but then he says, "Sure. Why not? It's number twelve Harlow Road. Just off Stroud Green Road."

"Now?" she confirms. "I can come now?"

"Sure," he says. "My name's Joshua, by the way. Joshua Donnelly."

"And I'm Laurel Mack," she says. "I'll be there in about half an hour."

⌐⌐⌐

Harlow Road is a turning off the high road, a section of the road that Laurel is more than familiar with after watching the CCTV footage from the day Ellie disappeared so many times on the news. It's exactly opposite the spot where the car had been parked, the one whose windows Ellie had checked her reflection in.

Number twelve is close to the turning. It's a tiny house, in a terrace of other tiny houses, with a small cherry tree in the front garden. The house is in a bad state. It looks almost as though nobody lives there.

Joshua Donnelly opens the door wide and steps aside. "Come in, Laura," he says. "Come in."

"It's Laurel," she says, "like the wreath."

"Oh, sure, like the wreath, yeah." He pulls the door closed behind her. He's small and bouncy in oversized jersey joggers and a red and white football shirt. His hair is cut very short and has a small line shaved into it from the hairline. He has an appealing face, almost pretty, and very long eyelashes.

"You'll have to excuse the state of the place," he says, leading her into the tiny front room. "It's just me and my brother here and we're not very domesticated."

The room is furnished with two brown leather sofas and lots of varnished pine furniture. On the walls are framed prints of modern art. Clothes are hanging to dry by the back door and over the backs of chairs. There are some mugs here and there and piles of what looks like college work. But it's not so bad, considering.

"So, you're the sons of Noelle's . . . ?"

"Younger brother. Yeah. There's four of them. Four brothers. And there were two girls but one of them died when she was tiny and the other one was Noelle and God knows what happened to her." He takes some textbooks off a sofa and brushes some crumbs onto the floor with the side of his hand, gesturing to Laurel to take a seat. "Can I get you anything? Tea? A Coke?"

She sits. "No, no, I'm fine, thank you."

"Are you sure? It's no bother."

"Honestly. Thank you."

He clears space for himself on the other sofa and sits down, his knees spread wide, one leg jigging up and down.

"Did you inherit this place from Noelle?" she asks.

"Well, no, I wouldn't say *inherited*. The family just kind of absorbed it, y'know? It's like our personal little hotel for anyone in the family who needs a place in London. And right now that's me and Sammy, my kid brother."

"How long have you been here?"

"Since October. I've just started on a degree at Goldsmiths. I'll be here for a few years yet. But there were others here before me. I mean, there are thirteen of us cousins. But we're not allowed to move anything or touch anything, you know what I mean? We have to keep it as she left it. More or less."

"In case she comes back?"

"Yeah, sure, in case she comes back. Exactly."

"And do you think she will?"

"Ah." He shrugs. "That's a question. You know, I never met her? None of us did, us cousins. She was like a ghost member of the family. We'd hear things about her, that she was buying herself a house, that she'd got together with a famous writer, that she was expecting a baby, all of that. But we never, ever met her. Isn't that crazy?"

He blinks at her, his mouth set into a wide smiling circle, and Laurel agrees. "Yes," she says, "yes, that is crazy."

She looks around the room at the pine shelves full of books and the sun-bleached prints on the walls. "So all this," she says, "the furniture, and the books, this is all Noelle's?"

"Yeah, yeah. All of it. I mean, upstairs, in the wardrobes, all her clothes are still there. Seriously. All her underwear and her bits and pieces."

"And no one ever packed anything away? It's all as she left it?"

"Yeah. Pretty much."

Laurel feels a shocking urge to run upstairs now and rifle through everything, to upend drawers and search through paperwork. *For what?* she wonders. What is it she thinks she will find?

"What do you think happened to your aunt?" she asks instead.

"I genuinely don't have a clue. I mean, she was supposed to be coming over to Ireland, that's what I was told. And she took her things: her passport, her cards; she packed a bag, some photos. She was clearly *going somewhere*. But wherever it was it looks like maybe she never got there? Her passport was never used. She hasn't used her cash card for years." He turns his hands palms upward and then places them on his knees. "Strange shit."

"You know," Laurel says lightly, "my daughter disappeared."

"Oh yeah?" Joshua sits forward, his interest piqued.

"She disappeared in 2005. And the last place my daughter was seen alive was there." She points toward Stroud Green Road. "Just there. Opposite the Red Cross shop. On CCTV."

He narrows his eyes at her and they sit in silence for a moment.

Laurel wonders how far she can push this personable young

man before he goes on the defense. "Poppy," she says, "your cousin. Have you met her?"

"No, none of us has. She's the only cousin we haven't met. And it's a shame because I have another cousin about her age, Clara—she's a laugh, she really is, such a character—and maybe they could have been friends. But that guy, the writer guy . . ."

"Floyd?"

"Yeah, that's the guy. He keeps himself to himself and he keeps her close to home. He didn't want to know when we suggested we could help him out with her care. I think one of my uncles went round there, you know, about a year after Noelle disappeared, tried to make a friendship." He shakes his head. "Apparently he was quite sharp with him, made it clear that we weren't wanted."

Laurel wonders if Poppy even knows about her Irish family.

"How do you know them then, Poppy and Floyd?" asks Joshua.

"I'm . . . well, I'm in a relationship with Floyd, actually. He's my boyfriend."

"Oh." He raises his brow. "Right."

"And funnily enough, Noelle used to tutor my daughter, Ellie. In fact, she was tutoring her in the weeks before she disappeared."

"What—here?" He points at the floor.

"No. Noelle came to my house. About half a mile from here."

"Right," he says. "Right."

Laurel gazes at him for a moment, willing him to provide her with the strand that will unfurl the knot of threads in her head.

"So, are you saying that something untoward happened?" he says eventually. "Is that what you're saying?"

"I don't know," Laurel says. "I really don't know."

"It does sound a bit odd," he says. "I'll grant you that." He puts his elbows on his knees and stares at the floor for a moment. "You've got me thinking now, got my brain ticking over." He circles his temple with his fingertip. "You have a mystery, and I have a mystery, and you think that maybe the two mysteries are connected?"

"Have you ever been through Noelle's things?" she asks. "Her private things? Diaries or such?"

"No. I never did. But there was . . . " He pauses. "There was one thing. A really strange thing. We could never quite fathom it." He looks toward the door and then back again. He sighs. "Shall I show you?"

"What?"

"You'll have to trust me, because I'm a stranger to you and I could be anyone."

"What do you mean?"

"Well, it's in the basement."

"What is?"

"The strange thing. The thing we found. In the basement."

Laurel feels a surge of adrenaline. She looks at the boy with the sweet face sitting opposite her.

"I'd totally understand if you don't want to go down. I wouldn't if I were you. Probably seen too many scary movies— you know, the ones where you go *don't go down into the basement, you bloody idiot!*"

He smiles and he couldn't look more like a nice young man over from Ireland to do a degree.

"I could just describe it if you like. Or I can go down and take a photo on my phone for you? Would that be a better idea?"

She smiles. "It's fine. I'll go and have a look."

"Text someone," he says, still looking anxiously at her. "Text someone to say where you are. That's what I would do."

She laughs. "Just show me," she says.

The door to the basement is in the kitchen. Joshua takes a torch from a drawer and leads her down a set of wooden steps. At the bottom is a door. He pushes it open into a small square room, completely clad in the same heavily varnished pine as the living room and the kitchen. There's a small window set high into the wall that frames the thin bare branches of the cherry tree in the front garden. There's a small sofa pulled out into a bed, a TV set, and a chair. And there's a series of what looks like hamster cages piled up one on top of the other on a table against the far wall.

Joshua sweeps the torchlight across them. "There were, like, twenty-odd hamsters in those when my uncles came. And they were all dead, you know, on their backs with their little legs in the air." He mimes a dead hamster lying on its back with its legs in the air. "Some of them had eaten each other apparently. We couldn't work it out *at all*. We thought maybe she'd been breeding them, y'know? Selling them to kids? But we couldn't find any evidence of that. It's just, like, why would you have all those animals? In your basement? And then just leave them to die?"

Laurel looks at the cages and shudders. Then she looks around again. In spite of the honey-colored cladding, the room feels bare and cold. And there's something else, something chilling and unnerving in the very air of the room.

"What do you think this room was for?" she asks, turning to examine the locks on the door, three of them in total, then turning again to look at the high window, the bare branches of the tree, the open sofa bed, the TV.

"A guest room, I suppose."

"It's not very homey, is it?"

"No. I don't suppose she had many guests. From all accounts she was a bit antisocial."

"So why would she have kept a sofa bed down here? And the TV? And all the animals that she left to die?"

"I told you, didn't I? I told you it was weird. To be honest, I think my aunty Noelle was probably all round weird, full stop. We think losing her sister at such a young age damaged her, y'know."

Laurel shivers again. She thinks of Hanna losing Ellie. She thinks of Hanna's dark, soulless flat. She thinks of her humorless persona, her awkward hugs. She feels a surge of panic that her daughter might end up like Noelle Donnelly, hoarding hamsters and then disappearing, leaving behind nothing but shadows in her wake. And as she thinks all this her eye is caught by something poking out from under the sofa bed. Something small and plasticky. She reaches down to pick it up. It's a lip balm in a bright pink and green casing. It's watermelon-flavored.

She turns it over in the palm of her hand and then she puts it into her pocket. For some reason she feels that it belongs to her.

⌁

Laurel's hands shake against the steering wheel as she drives home. She can still smell the basement room at Noelle Donnelly's house, the damp wood, the rotting carpet. Every time she closes her eyes she sees the ugly sofa bed, the piles of hamster cages, the dirty window set high in the wall.

When she gets home she goes to her spare room and pulls out Ellie's box from under the bed once again. She rakes through pens and badges and rings and hair clips. Ellie's toothbrush is in the box, and Ellie's hairbrush, along with tangles of elastic bands and key rings and face creams. And there, in the mix, is a selection of lip balms. Three of them. One is papaya-flavored, one is mango-flavored, and the other is honeydew melon. She pulls the watermelon lip balm from Noelle's basement from the pocket of her coat and lines it up with the others.

It forms a set.

31

Yes, it's true that I told you I'd gone on the pill when that wasn't strictly the case. In all honesty I thought I was too old anyway and did not expect to get pregnant literally two months after we stopped using condoms. It was all over the papers at the time how your eggs all dried up and fell out on your thirty-fifth birthday and—genuinely—when my period was late I thought that was it, thought I'd had my menopause. It wasn't until my jeans started getting a little tight that it occurred to me to check. So I bought a test and got the little pink lines and sat there on the toilet in my house rocking back and forth and having a little cry because suddenly I thought I didn't really want a baby after all. Suddenly I realized I'd been an idiot and a fool. How could I raise a child, me with no maternal instincts, me with my baby-scaring face? And how did I know that you'd even want it? Yes, you'd said the thing that you said but I had no idea how you'd react. Not really.

But when I told you, you were happy. At least, you weren't *unhappy*.

"Well, well," you said, "that's a curveball." And then you said, "Do you want to keep it?" as though it was a necklace I'd bought myself that I might just take back to the shop. I said, "Well, of course I want to keep it. It's ours." And you nodded. And that was that. Except you also said, "I can't ask you to live with me, you know that?"

That hurt me, but I didn't show it. I just said, "No. Of course not." As though the thought had never occurred to me. And to be truthful I did think you'd change your mind once you met the baby. So I never said what I really thought, which was that I couldn't possibly raise a baby by myself.

I'd missed two periods but wasn't sure how far along I might be. You came with me for my scan. I remember that day; it was a nice day. You held my hand in the waiting room. We were both a little giddy, with nerves, no doubt, but also I think with excitement. It felt like one of those days that you have sometimes in life, where you feel like you've reached a branch in the road, that you're setting off on a new journey, suitcases packed, full of trepidation and anticipation. The day felt clean and new, disconnected to the days that had come before and to the days that would follow. I have never felt as close to another human being as I felt to you that day, Floyd. Never.

And then there was the screen, with the tadpole, and I felt your hand tighten around mine and you were thrilled, I know you were. There was your child, inside me, a human being who would come into our lives and who would never tell you that they hated you. A chance to start again. A chance to get it all right. You were happy in that moment. You were, Floyd. *You were.*

But there was no noise. No noise. I had never been pregnant before. I thought maybe the heart hadn't been formed yet. Or that maybe it was my heartbeat that kept the tadpole alive. I didn't know that even at this size—ten weeks along, the clinician said—there should be a heartbeat. *How was I supposed to know?* But you looked at the clinician as she moved the monitor around my belly, the smile fading from her face, and you said,

"Is there a problem?" And she said, "I'm having a little trouble locating a heartbeat."

And then I knew, too. I knew that there should have been a noise and that there wasn't.

Your hand came away from my hand.

You sighed.

And it wasn't a sigh of sadness. It wasn't even a sigh of disappointment. It was a sigh of annoyance. A sigh that said, *You couldn't even do this properly, could you?*

More even than the lost baby, that sigh virtually killed me.

⌒

After that you made it clear that this could be our chance to walk away from each other, no hard feelings. But you weren't strong-minded enough just to end it and I took advantage of that. I lingered on, yes, I'll admit that. I overstayed my welcome. I reverted 100 percent to the person I'd been before I was pregnant. I came to your house at your command for sex. I even moved in for a few months when they were doing the damp in my house. I knew you didn't really want me there. "Have they said how much longer?" you'd ask. "The builders. Do you have a date yet?"

So I knew nothing had really changed and I didn't pretend to lay any special claim to you and your time just because my womb had once hosted your tadpole.

And there was your terrible child, Sara-Jade, hating you and needing you in equal measure, confusing you and upsetting you, hitting you and spitting at you, then refusing to get off your lap for half an hour when you had things you needed to do. And there was my womb, touched so briefly by unexpected life, echoing with the unheard heartbeat of our dead baby. And I couldn't make sense of it all.

You'd gone back to the condoms as I was clearly not to be trusted. So there would not be a baby for you and me, and I needed to accept that.

I tried really hard to accept it, Floyd. Really hard. I tried for two years. I turned forty-three. And then I turned forty-four. And then you started taking chances, thinking, probably, that I was all out of eggs, and one night you ran out of condoms and said, "Never mind, I'll just pull out."

Well, clearly you did not pull out fast enough or early enough and it happened all over again. I missed a period. I took a test. Two pink lines appeared. For three days I felt like I was sitting on the crest of a wave, the sun shining on my face, the wind in my hair, angels playing on harps wherever I went. I booked a scan, but this time I didn't tell you: I could not have born the quiet room, the sigh of annoyance, the dropped hand. But before I could even make it to the clinic your baby had died and fallen out of me. A small bleed. I'd have thought it was a heavy period if I hadn't taken the test.

I canceled the appointment.

I never told you about the second tadpole.

And it was that day, Floyd, it was that very day that I first went to the home of Ellie Mack. The same day your baby died inside me. I had to slap on a smile and a friendly disposition and sit in a room with a spoiled pretty girl and a hairy cat, surrounded by the paraphernalia of family life: the photos and the kicked-off shoes, the trashy paperbacks and the furniture all from Habitat no doubt, and I had to teach this spoiled pretty girl with a brain too big for her own good who already knew everything she needed to know when what I really wanted to do was sob and say, *Today I lost another baby!*

But I did not. No. I drank her mother's lovely tea from a mug with the words "Keep Calm and Clean My Kitchen" on it. I ate her nice chocolate-chip biscuits made by Prince Charles himself. I taught her daughter a good lesson. I worked hard for my thirty-five pounds.

I felt calm when I left Ellie Mack's house that evening. I walked the half-mile home and it was a cold, sharp evening, with drops of ice in the air that stung the backs of my hands. I walked slowly, relishing the darkness and the pain. And as I walked I felt this certainty build within me, a certainty that somehow it was all connected, the gone baby and the spoiled girl, that there was a conflation, that maybe one thing balanced out the other.

I got home and I didn't call you or look at my phone to see if you had called me. I watched a TV show and I cut my toenails. I drank a glass of wine. I had a long, long bath. I let the water rush up between my legs, washing away the last traces of your baby.

And I thought of the girl called Ellie Mack, of her big brain and her perfect features, the honey of her hair tied so carelessly into a topknot, the socked feet tucked beneath her and elegant hands folded into her sleeves, the smell of her—of apples and toothpaste, of clean hair and girl—the keenness to learn, her gentleness, her perfection. She had a glow about her, a circle of light. I bet she never told her parents she hated them. I bet she never spat at them or pinched them or threw her food across the room.

She was quite, quite lovely and quite, quite brilliant.

And I have to confess, I became more than a little obsessed.

32

Later that day Laurel visits her mother, Ruby.

"Still here?" she asks, placing her handbag on the floor and slipping off her coat.

Ruby tuts and sighs. "L-L-L-Looks like it."

Laurel smiles and takes her hand. "We drank a toast to you on Friday," she says, "at the birthday party. We all missed you very much."

Ruby rolls her eyes as if to say *sure you did.*

"We really did. And guess what? I met Bonny!"

Ruby's eyes open wide and she puts her fingertips to her mouth. "W-Wow!"

"Yes. Wow. She's nice. I knew she would be. Cuddly."

"F-F-Fat?"

Laurel laughs. "No. Not fat. Just bosomy."

Ruby looks down at her own flat chest, the same flat chest that she bequeathed to her daughter and they both laugh.

"Boyf-f-friend? All happy?"

"Yes!" she replies with more positivity than she's feeling. Her mother has extended her miserable existence beyond the point of comfort to see her daughter happy. "Really happy. It's going really well!"

She sees a question pass across her mother's eyes and

she moves the conversation along quickly, asks after her health, her appetite, if she's heard anything from her hopeless brother, who moved to Dubai the same day Ruby moved into the home.

"I won't see you again," her mother says as Laurel puts on her coat.

Laurel looks at her, looks deep into her eyes. Then she leans down and holds her in her arms, puts her mouth to her ear and says, "I will see you next week, Mum. And if I don't, then I want you to know that you have been the best and most amazing mother in the world and I have been extraordinarily lucky to have you for so long. And that I adore you. And that we all do. And that you could not have been any better than you were. OK?"

She feels her mother's head nodding against hers, the soft puff of her hair like a breath against her cheek. "Yes," says her mother, "yes. Yes. Yes."

Laurel wipes tears from her cheek and puts on a smile before pulling away from her mother.

"Bye, Mum," she says. "I love you."

"I l-l-love you, t-t-too."

Laurel stops in the doorway for a second and looks at her mother, absorbs the shape of her and the exquisite feeling of her existence in the world. Then she sits in her car for a moment afterward, in the car park. She allows herself to cry for about thirty seconds and then talks herself out of it. Wanting to die and dying are generally unrelated. But this felt like more than her mother simply wanting to die. This seemed to come from inside her, from the inexplicable place that thinks about an old friend moments before bumping into them, that can sense the approach of a thunderstorm before it's broken, the place that sends dogs to dark corners of the house to die.

She picks her phone from her bag and stares at it for a while. She wants to talk to someone. Someone who knows her better than anyone.

She nearly calls Paul. But she doesn't.

33

I'd had crushes on girls before. There were girls at the posh magazine where I used to work. Posh, posh, posh girls. I hated them all, really. But at the same time I yearned for them, particularly the fun ones, the friendly ones. The ones with sticks up their arses I could take or leave; they were just me, with better genes. But the fun girls, the lovely girls, the ones who thanked me if I held a door for them or made goofy faces if there was a problem with their expenses, God, I wanted them. Not in a sexual way, of course. But I wanted to know what it felt like to be them, to walk down the street with everything in exactly the right place, the sun shining down on their honey-colored heads, doors opening as they passed, men turning, parties starting at the precise moment that they arrived.

I was protective of my antisocial persona in many ways. It felt safe to be invisible. No one had any expectations of me, and after eighteen years living in my parents' house it was liberating not to be expected to do anything or be anything. So it was ambiguous, this feeling. On the one hand I wanted to be like these golden girls. On the other I felt far superior to them.

And Ellie Mack was possibly the most golden girl I had ever encountered.

It turned out that she was in love. She had this boy, Theo. I met him once. He was pretty golden, too. The sweetest, sweetest thing, he was, and handsome right off the handsome scale.

He shook my hand and he made proper eye contact and he was clever, clever, clever and I found myself thinking, Just imagine the babies that these two lovebirds could make, would they not be just *spectacular*.

That might well have been the root of it, thinking about it now.

But it was your fault as well: you with the dropped hand and the sigh of annoyance. You and your *I can't ask you to live with me, you know that?* You with your small girl sitting on your lap, an arm hooked around your neck, staring at me with her pale horror-film eyes as though she was a ghost and I was the one who'd murdered her.

And there was Ellie Mack, the highlight of my thankless weeks. I brought her gifts. I told her she was marvelous. I shared little snippets from my life and she shared little snippets from hers. The mother was a pleasant woman. I thought she liked me. I got my tea in the same mug every week. I came to think of it as *my* mug. The biscuits were always, always good.

It was a sort of cocoon at Ellie's house: dark outside, cozy inside; me, Ellie, the cat, the sounds of her family all around, the tea, the biscuits, the reassuring solidity of the numbers on the pages between us. I liked our Tuesday afternoons. For those few weeks they were all that stood between me and myself. And I think I already knew even then that *myself* was not a place where I should be spending too much time.

I'd seen Ellie and me as riding a train together toward her GCSEs, toward triumph. I'd pictured myself on her doorstep in August with a small bottle of champagne and possibly a shiny balloon, her arms thrown around my neck, her pleasant mother standing behind smiling beneficently, waiting her turn to hug me too, words of thanks and gratitude, *Oh, Noelle, we could not have done this without you. Come in, come in, let's drink a toast together.*

And then came that phone call. The pleasant mother being not quite so pleasant. Christ, you know, I can barely remember what she said now. I wasn't really listening. All I could think was no, no, no. Not my Tuesdays. Not my Tuesdays. So I was curt, verging on rude, most likely. I told her that it was a *great inconvenience*. When it was nothing of the sort. It was a *fucking travesty*, that's what it was. A fucking travesty.

I dropped the phone afterward and I screamed out loud.

I fixated on all the nice things I'd done for Ellie. The gifts I'd bought her. The special papers I'd found for her, printed off for her. The extra ten minutes I'd sometimes tag on to the end of our lesson if we were *in the zone* as I called it. I bubbled and fermented with resentment.

That phase went on for a week or two and then I entered the nostalgia phase. Everything had been *better* then, I told myself, when I'd spent Tuesday afternoons with Ellie Mack. My relationship with you had been better, my teaching had been better, my life had been better. And I thought, Well, maybe if I could just see her, just see her face, maybe I'd feel a bit like I'd felt then.

There's a word to describe what I did next. And that word is *stalking*. I knew where Ellie was at school, of course I did; not too far from my home, as it happened, so it was easy to pass by at 9 a.m., at 3:30, to watch her coming and going, the boy with his arm slung around her shoulders, the glow coming off the two of them so fucking bright and golden it's a wonder they could see where they were going. They were the culmination of every teen romance movie ever filmed, right there, in real life.

Then came the half-term and I no longer knew where she

was going to be. So I had to become a little sneaky. It was tricky because obviously I was working all the hours with my other students, and seeing you too, servicing your sexual requirements like a good girl. But I worked out that she was at the library a lot, and that she passed my road on her way there and that if I put myself in the window of the café on my street corner I'd be able to see her when she passed by. So whenever I wasn't teaching I'd be there, in the café on the corner, looking for a glimpse of that waterfall of gold hair. And you know, Floyd, I swear that was all I wanted. I just wanted to see her.

But for some reason that day, I found myself rising from my chair. There she was standing between two parked cars, waiting to cross the road. Her blonde hair was tied back and hidden somehow inside her hood or the back of her jacket and I wanted . . . I swear, I just wanted her to see me, to acknowledge me in some way. And I approached her and there it was, like a punch to the gut: *Jesus Christ, she doesn't know me.* Not for the first second or two. I watched the memory slot into place like a slide in one of those carousels from the olden days and then of course she was all smiles and kindness. But it was too late. She had completely failed to verify my existence.

If only she had known, Floyd, if only she had known how much I'd needed her to do that, then maybe none of it would have happened. Maybe Ellie Mack would have gone to the library, got to sit all her GCSEs, got to marry Theo, got to live her life.

But, unfortunately, that's not the way it worked out.

34

Poppy serves dinner for Floyd and Laurel on Friday night. She lights candles, wraps a bottle of wine in a linen napkin, and pours it from the base, like a sommelier. She doesn't eat with them because that would ruin the role play, merely hovers at a discreet distance, clears the table between courses, asks how their food is. Her hair, Laurel notices, is in a topknot, rather than the more formal hairdos she normally favors, and she has a tea towel tied around her waist in an approximation of a waiter's apron. She looks very grown up. Very pretty. More like Ellie than ever. Laurel can barely tear her eyes from her.

She makes love to Floyd that night.

She is wrong, she concludes, lying in his arms afterward. She is wrong about it all. The lip balm means nothing. Maybe Noelle bought herself fruity lip balms. Maybe her whole house was full of fruity lip balms. The fact that Poppy looked like Ellie was also neither here nor there. People looked like people. That was a simple matter of fact. And maybe SJ had imagined Noelle's flat stomach.

And this man, this man right here with his lovely jumpers and his gentle touch, this man who sends her smiley-face emojis and cannot live without her, why would he have invited her into his life if he was somehow involved in Ellie's disappearance? It makes no sense at all.

She falls asleep in the crook of his arm, her hands entwined with his, feeling safe.

"I love you, Laurel Mack," she thinks she hears him whisper in the middle of the night. "I love you so much."

∼

The uncertainty returns the following morning. She is the first up and the house ticks and creaks as all Victorian houses tick and creak. The kitchen is filled with cold white morning light and last night's candles and background music are a distant memory. She quickly makes two cups of coffee and takes them upstairs to the warm cocoon of Floyd's bedroom.

"I have to go somewhere today," he says.

"Somewhere?" she says. "That sounds mysterious."

He smiles and pulls her to him. They sit up side by side in the bed, their feet and ankles entwined. "Not really," he says. "I'm meeting my financial advisor."

"On a Saturday?"

He shrugs. "I always see him on a Saturday. I don't know why. But I'll only be a couple of hours. I wondered if maybe you'd be able to stay here and sit with Poppy? While I'm gone?"

"I'd love to," she says and they drink their coffee. From upstairs they hear the sound of Poppy rising. They hear her footsteps on the stairs and then her knocking on the bedroom door. Laurel pulls Floyd's dressing gown tighter across her breasts and Floyd calls out for her to come in. Poppy runs in and throws herself between them, right onto the sex-scorched bedsheets, against the pillows that Laurel had gripped last night and buried her face into.

Poppy rests her head against Floyd's shoulder and then she finds Laurel's hand and grabs it and Laurel feels oddly wrong, braless and unwashed, holding the hand of a young girl inside this nest of adult yearnings.

"I'm popping out later. Laurel's going to stay with you," says Floyd.

"Yay!" says Poppy. "Let's go somewhere."

She presses her face against Laurel's shoulder now and Laurel nods and smiles and says, "Yes, that would be lovely."

And as she says it she drops a kiss onto the top of Poppy's head, the way she used to do with all her children when they were small. And there's a smell about her scalp, her hair, a smell that sends her reeling back in time: the smell of Ellie.

"We'll go out for cake," she says, a particular café coming immediately to mind. "We'll have fun."

～

The café is on the corner of Noelle's road. Laurel noticed it when she was here on Thursday. It's called the Corner Café and it's been there forever; she's sure she once took the children there for tea when they were tiny after a swimming lesson or a visit to the dentist.

Poppy has a pecan and maple twist. Laurel has a granola bar. They share a pot of tea. Laurel glances at Poppy nervously. She's aware that she's horribly overstepping the boundaries of her relationship with Floyd by asking his daughter to collude with her behind his back like this, but her need to answer questions outweighs her sense of loyalty to Floyd.

"Have you ever been here before?" Laurel opens.

Poppy looks around her over the rim of her oversized teacup. "Don't think so."

"You know," Laurel says cautiously, "you used to live on that street?" She points over her shoulder.

"Did I?"

"Yes. With your mum."

Poppy glances up at her. "How do you know?"

Laurel smiles tentatively. "It's a very long story. How's your pastry?"

"It's totally fantastic," Poppy says. "Want to try some?"

"Yeah," says Laurel, "why not. Thank you." She accepts the piece that Poppy tears off and passes her. "You know," she continues carefully, "I went in there the other day." She nods in the direction of Noelle's house.

"Where?"

"To the house where you used to live. To talk to your"—she drums her fingertips on the underneath of her chin and pretends to think hard—"well, I suppose he's your cousin."

"My *cousin*? I don't have any cousins."

"Well, yes, actually, you do. You have tons of them. Most of them live in Ireland."

"No they don't." She looks defiantly at Laurel. "I promise you, I do not have any cousins."

"That's definitely not true," says Laurel. "There's two living in your mum's house, just there. Joshua and Sam. They're in their early twenties. Joshua's at university studying history. He's really lovely. You'd like him."

Poppy glares at her. "Why have you been talking to them?"

"Oh, just one of those things. One of those great coincidences in life. Because it turns out that"—Laurel draws in her breath and forces a smile—"I used to know your mum, a long, long time ago. And when your dad told me that she'd disappeared, well, I was a bit curious. So I called her up on her old phone number and this lovely boy answered the phone and he invited me for tea. He doesn't know where your mum went either. He's just looking after her house for her until she comes back."

Poppy shudders. "I don't want her to come back."

"No," says Laurel. "No. I know you don't. But Joshua said"— she turns her smile up a few degrees—"that there's another cousin your age. Called Clara. He said she's really funny and clever. He said you'd like her."

"Clara?" says Poppy, her eyes brightening. "She's my cousin?"

"Apparently," says Laurel. "And your mum's family all agree with you, that your mother was a bit strange. But apparently she had a sister who died when she was little. It sent her a little loopy. But it sounds like the rest of the family are really normal."

"Her sister died?" Poppy repeats pensively. "That's really sad."

"I know," Laurel replies. "It is really sad."

"But no excuse for being a horrible mum."

"No," she agrees. "No excuse at all."

Laurel allows a silence to fall, giving Poppy a chance to absorb it all.

"What did you say he was called?"

"Joshua."

"That's a nice name."

"Yes. It's a very nice name."

Another silence follows. Laurel makes a great pretense of being absorbed by her granola bar while her heart races with nerves about what she's about to do. "I've got his number," she says after a moment. "I could call? See if he's about? Go and say hello?"

Poppy looks up at her and says, "Do you think Dad would mind?"

"I don't know," she replies. "Do *you* think he'll mind?"

Poppy shrugs. "He might. But then . . ." Her face is set with a slightly staged resolve. ". . . I don't have to tell him, do I? It's not like he tells me everything he does."

"I don't want to be responsible for you lying to your father, Poppy."

"But I wouldn't be lying, would I? I'll just tell him we went for tea. And that is true."

"Yes. That is true."

"And it's not as if he'll say *and did you do anything else?* Is it?"

"It's unlikely."

"And he might not even be there. My cousin."

"No. He might not. But I could give him a call. Just in case. Would you like me to do that?"

Poppy nods, once.

Laurel taps in his number and presses call.

❧

Poppy's steps slow as they turn onto the front path.

"Maybe we shouldn't," she says.

"We don't have to. It's fine."

But before they have a chance to change their minds, the front door is pulled open and Joshua is standing there in a hoodie and jeans, another young man standing just behind in a fluorescent green T-shirt and they're both saying, "Oh my God. Poppy! Poppy! Come in! Come in out of the cold. My God, if it isn't little Poppy!" and things of that ilk and Poppy turns briefly to Laurel, who smiles encouragingly at her, and they are both swept into the house on a wave of slightly manic hospitality and delight.

"So," says Joshua, his hands in his pockets, bouncing up and down and beaming, "so you're Poppy. Wow! Sit down, Poppy. And Laurel. Sit down. Please. Tea? Coffee? Anything?"

Poppy sits primly and shakes her head. "No thank you," she says. "We just had tea and cake," and Sam and Joshua look at each other and hoot and Joshua says:

"An English cousin! We finally have an English cousin. We already have a Canadian cousin, two American cousins, and a German cousin. And now we finally have an English one. Wow. And look at you. I can see my grandmother in you, so I can."

Poppy smiles grimly, slightly overwhelmed.

"So, this used to be your house? Is that right?"

"Maybe," she replies, looking around herself. "I can't re-member."

"We should give you a tour, wouldn't you say? What do you think?"

Poppy glances again at Laurel, who nods, and they follow Joshua and Sam through the house. Poppy is uncharacteristi-cally quiet at first, peering nervously around doorways.

Joshua pushes a door at the top of the landing, "This must have been your room. Look, it still has the wallpaper."

Poppy falters for a moment on the threshold and then she steps in, her eyes wide, her hands running across the wall-paper. It's pale gray with a repeated pattern of pink rabbits and green tortoises on it, engaged in a running competition. The tortoises are all wearing sweatbands and the rabbits have on running shoes.

"I remember this wallpaper," she says breathlessly. "The hares. And the tortoises. I used to see them running in the night. I'd stare at them and then I'd shut my eyes and they'd be running. Hundreds of them. Through my dreams. I remember it. I really do."

"You want to see some more?" says Joshua, giving Laurel a knowing look. "There's another room downstairs. I wonder if you'll remember that, too?"

Quietly they descend back to the ground floor, through the kitchen and then down into the basement.

Poppy stops once more on the threshold, grips the outside

of the door with her fingertips. She gasps and says, "I don't want to go in there."

"Oh, but it's fine," says Joshua. "It's just a room."

"But . . . but . . ." Her eyes are wide and her breathing is audible. "I'm not allowed in there. My mum told me never to go in there."

Laurel touches her shoulder softly. "Wow, that's an interesting memory. Why do you think that was?"

"I don't know," says Poppy, sounding vaguely tearful. "I don't know. I just remember thinking there was a monster down there. A big, scary monster. But that's just silly, isn't it? There was no monster down there, was there?"

"Did you have pets?" asks Laurel. "When you were tiny? Do you remember having some hamsters?"

Poppy shakes her head slowly and walks out of the kitchen and toward the front door.

35

Laurel takes Poppy home after their visit to Noelle's house. They walk in silence for a while. Laurel has never known Poppy to be so quiet.

"Are you OK?" she asks as they wait at a crossroads for the lights to change.

"No," she says. "I feel all weird."

"Why do you think that is?"

"I don't know." She shrugs. "Just remembering things I haven't remembered before. Thinking about my mum when I haven't thought about her for so long. Meeting cousins I didn't know I had. It's been a bit overwhelming."

"Yes," says Laurel, cupping the crown of Poppy's head with her hand. "Yes. I bet it has."

Laurel swallows away the lump in her throat. She needs to stay focused. She cannot jump to fantastical conclusions. In the scheme of things it is far more likely that the monster in Noelle's basement was actually twenty dead hamsters, not Ellie. She needs to assume that this was the case and then find the evidence that it was not. She needs to stay sane.

Floyd is there when they get back. Poppy starts to babble immediately about cake and tea and then disappears very quickly to her room before, she assumes, Floyd can ask her anything else.

Laurel watches Floyd unpacking carrier bags of shopping.

For a moment, as he reaches for a tall cupboard to slide in a box of teabags, his shirt slips from the moorings of his waistband, flashing a slice of pale flesh, and she feels herself sliding back through time again, as she'd felt in Nando's the week before last with Poppy. She's back in her own kitchen in Stroud Green. In front of her is Paul. He's wearing the same shirt, it tugs itself briefly from his waistband, he slides the teabags into the cupboard, he turns to face her. He smiles. For a second the two moments blend in her mind, the two men merge into one.

"Are you OK?" Floyd asks.

She shakes her head once, to dislodge the glitch. "Yes," she says. "I am. I am fine."

"You looked like you were miles away."

She smiles as widely as she can, but she suspects it is not wide at all. She knows she should say something about her visit to Noelle's house with Poppy but she can't. And she can't ask him any of the questions she wants to ask him—*Did you know that Sara-Jade claims to have seen Noelle at eight months pregnant without a bump? Do you never want to find out what happened to Noelle? Would you not like to find her? Do you never ask yourself questions about the strangeness of everything?*—because then everything about them, about Floyd and Laurel, all of it would be squashed and remade, like a clay pot on a wheel. And it's such a lovely pot and she's worked so hard on it and so much depends on it staying exactly as it is.

"Tell me," she says, turning the conversation round 180 degrees, back to a place that nurtures intimacy and growth. "Tell me about your first marriage. How was it? How did you and Kate meet?"

He smiles as she'd known he would and tells her a story about a beautiful young girl at a bus stop, totally out of his league in every way, a charmingly gauche conversation and an invitation to a party that turned out to be a rave in an abandoned car park, a lost night of neon lights and recreational drugs, a full moon, a fur coat. And at some point Laurel zones out of the detail and fixates instead on the feeling of jealousy that seeps out from deep inside her, the dark, bleak stab of pain that for a short while at least overpowers her creeping sense of unease, that stops her asking questions.

Laurel leaves the next morning. Floyd tries to persuade her to stay, tempts her with suggestions of gastro-pub Sunday lunches and riverside walks, but her mind is elsewhere; she can no longer force herself to stay focused on their romance; she needs to be alone.

She'd parked her car in the next road down the day before because there was no space on Floyd's street. To get to it she has to loop back onto the high street and then left again. Her eye is caught by a man standing outside the small branch of Tesco on the corner. He has a little black dog on a lead. He's tall; in his midtwenties, Laurel guesses. He's wearing a huge parka with a fur-trimmed hood and dark jeans with trainers. He's extremely good-looking, rangy and eye-catching. But as she glances at him Laurel realizes that it's not his good looks that have caught her eye. She realizes that she recognizes him and it takes a moment for the details to slot into place and form a solid memory before it hits her. It's Theo. Theo Goodman. Ellie's boyfriend.

She'd seen him briefly at Ellie's funeral back in October. He'd been somewhere toward the rear, talking with Ellie's old school friends. He'd looked sallow and hollowed out with grief. She remembered feeling surprised that he hadn't come to her during that day, that he hadn't offered his condolences, that he'd simply disappeared into the ether.

She toys with the idea of crossing the street to say hello, but her head can't deal with small talk right now and she decides to keep walking. She is about to turn away when a woman comes out of Tesco holding two canvas bags full of groceries; she's a tall blonde woman in a similar parka, baggy joggers, and black Ugg boots, a green bobble hat on her head and a wide smile on her face. She hands one bag to Theo and then stops to pet the small dog, who seems overjoyed to see her. Then they go on their way, the lovely young couple and their dog. And it is only then that Laurel really registers what she has just seen.

It was the smile that threw her.

She hasn't seen Hanna smile for so long she'd forgotten what it looked like.

PART FOUR

36

THEN

Noelle Donnelly's house was small and tidy and smelled exactly like Noelle Donnelly.

"Let me get you a squash," said Noelle in the hallway. "You go and sit down." She gestured into the small front room.

Ellie peered through the door into the room and then smiled politely. "I think I'd better not stay," she said. "I've got loads and loads of work to do."

"Nonsense," said Noelle. "You can spare two minutes. Besides, it'll take me that long to unearth the thing. You might as well take a seat and have a drink. Orange or elderflower?"

Ellie smiled stiffly. She was in a corner. "Elderflower," she said. "Please. Thank you."

Noelle smiled at her strangely. "Yes," she said, "elderflower. Of course. I'll be one minute. You sit down."

Ellie sidled into the living room and perched herself on the farthest edge of a brown leather sofa. The room was filled to its limits with houseplants and smelled earthy and slightly sour. The wall around the fireplace was bare brick and the hearth filled with sprays of dried flowers and some terra-cotta animals that looked as though Noelle might have made them herself. Overhead was a bulb in a globular paper shade and the windows were obscured by wooden Venetian blinds, one slat of which was missing, allowing a reassuring view of a strip of cherry blossom and sunshine. Ellie stared through the gap in the blinds, imagining the world beyond Noelle Donnelly's front room.

"There you are," said Noelle, placing a glass of squash in front of her.

The squash looked nice. It was in a pretty glass, clear with green polka dots. She was thirsty. Noelle watched her as she lifted the glass and began to drink from it. "Thank you," she said, putting down the almost empty glass.

Noelle glanced at the glass and then at Ellie. "Oh, lovely girl, you are welcome. Now, you wait there and I will get the papers and be back in a short minute."

She left the room and Ellie heard her heavy steps ascending the stairs. *Like a baby elephant*, as Ellie's mum would have said.

Stamp stamp stamp stamp . . .

She was unconscious before Noelle had made it to the landing.

◦◦

Ellie heard a sound, a tiny woody squeak. A chair, moving. Then she heard a breath.

"You're awake now, are you?" said Noelle from somewhere in the dark. "Now, listen. I really want to apologize to you. This is a terrible thing. A terrible thing I've done to you. Unforgivable really. But I hope you'll see why, in time. I hope you'll understand."

In time.

Ellie struggled against the glue. Nothing moved.

"The effects will wear off soon. Or, well"—Noelle laughed—"at least I *hope* they do. It said on the Internet three to twelve hours. And you've been out for twelve. So." She laughed again and Ellie thought, It's 11 p.m. I've been away from home since ten o'clock this morning. My mum.

Her eyes had started to lose their heaviness and she could make out parts of the room now. The cool glow of moonlight through a narrow window set high in a wood-clad wall, a toilet and sink in a recess behind a curtain, empty shelves on a wall, a small wardrobe. And there, in front of a closed door, the outline of Noelle Donnelly, legs crossed, hands in her lap.

Ellie tried again to lift her head and this time managed to move it a millimeter or two.

"Oh, there you go," said Noelle. "You're coming through it now. That's great. I'll just sit here with you for a while longer and then when you're sitting up I'll get you something to eat. You missed your lunch and your dinner and you must be ravenous. What would you like? Maybe just a sandwich? I have some good ham. I'll do that for you."

She stood then and picked up a cup from the table by the bed. "Here." She angled a bendy straw toward Ellie's mouth. "Drink some water. You must be parched."

Ellie sucked at the straw and felt the tepid water spread across the dry towel of her tongue and the papery roof of her mouth.

"My mum," she croaked, "my mum."

"Ah, now, don't you worry about your mum. She probably just thinks you're off canoodling somewhere with that boy of yours. It's a lovely evening. Just like last night. Summery, you know, the sort of evening you want to go on for longer."

"No," Ellie said through a parchment throat, "she'll be scared. My mum."

And she felt it then, like a needle in her heart, the love her mother always talked about. "You won't understand how much I love you until you're a mother yourself."

But she felt it now and all the pain in her heart was for her mother, her mother who she knew would be crying and worrying and feeling the meaning of her life slipping away from her. She couldn't bear it. She truly couldn't bear it.

"Of course she won't be scared. Don't be daft. Now, let's see if we can sit you up. Can you move your fingers now? Your toes? Your arms? Ah, yes, there you go. Good girl. That's great, that really is."

And then Noelle Donnelly's arms were around her waist and she was being pulled gently up the bed and she could see more now, she could see that she was in a room lower than ground level, walls clad with dirty gold pine.

"Where am I?"

"In the basement. Which makes it sound worse than it is. It's my guest room, really. Not that I ever have any guests. But I used to keep all my overspill in here, you know, bric-a-brac, but knowing you were coming I had a good clear-out. Took it all to the Red Cross shop. So now we're very *minimal*. There now." She adjusted the pillow behind Ellie's head. "All comfy. I'll go and get you that sandwich. You just rest a bit. But don't try and get up. You might fall out of the bed and hurt yourself, being a bit woozy as you are."

She smiled at her indulgently, like a kindly nurse. "Good girl," she said, running her hand down Ellie's hair. "Good girl."

Then she turned and left the room.

Ellie heard one lock click into place. And then she heard another. And then one more.

☙

Ellie didn't eat her sandwich. Despite the pain of an empty stomach, she wasn't at all hungry. Noelle silently removed it and said, "Ah, well, I'm sure you'll be hungry in the morning. We'll try again then, eh?"

Then she looked fondly at Ellie and said, "Oh, it is a treat to have you here, it really is. Now you sleep tight and I'll see you bright and early."

"I want to go home!" Ellie yelled out at Noelle's back. "I really really want to go home!"

Noelle didn't reply. The three locks clicked into place. The room turned black.

37

The sun came up early. Ellie took the chair that Noelle had sat on the night before and pulled it across to the window. She climbed onto it and peered through the grimy glass. She saw a tangle of undergrowth, a brick wall painted cream, a water pipe streaked green. If she peered upward, she saw the pink clouds of the cherry blossom tree, the blue sky, nothing more. She realized immediately that the only way anyone would see her in here would be if they were looking for her and she wrote the words "help" and "Ellie" into the dirt. She stood on the chair for more than an hour, her face pressed up against the glass. Because people must be looking for her. They must be.

She jumped down from the chair at the sound of the locks being turned on the door and she picked it up with both hands. At the sight of Noelle in a green polo neck and faded jeans a surge of horror and anger coursed through her and she grabbed the chair hard and swung it at Noelle. It glanced off the side of Noelle's head, but she caught it before Ellie was able to properly hurt her with it, caught it and threw it across the room. Ellie jumped on her then, jumped on her back, her arms around Noelle's throat as she tried to bash her head against the wooden wall. But Noelle proved herself to be stronger than she looked and manhandled Ellie backward and against the wall where she strangled the breath out of her, strangled her to the point of light-headedness and stars and then let her fall to the floor.

"You cannot be doing things like that," Noelle said afterward, dropping Ellie on the sofa bed upside down, locking her ankles together with a plastic tie. "We're in this together, you and me. We have to work as a team. I do not want to have to tie you up like a criminal. I really do not. I have treats in mind for you, lots of lovely things I want to do for you, to make this nicer. And I won't be able to give you the treats if you behave like this."

Ellie struggled against the cuffs around her ankles, pounded her feet against the end of the bed. She roared and thrashed, and Noelle stood and watched her, her arms folded, shaking her head slowly. "Now, now, now," she said. "This isn't going to work. The longer you behave like this, the worse it will be and the longer you'll be here."

Ellie stilled at those words. So, there was an end. Noelle had an end. Her muscles softened and her breathing steadied.

"Good girl," Noelle said. "Good girl. If you can behave like this for the rest of the day, I'll bring you your first treat. How about that?"

Ellie nodded, tears rolling down her cheeks.

The treat was a chocolate bar. A big one. She ate it in five minutes.

༄

Ellie thought of before; she thought of eating toast and jam, calling Hanna a cow because she'd taken the last bag of salt and vinegar crisps that Ellie had mentally put aside for herself. She thought of filling her bag with books, a packet of ready salted crisps and a banana. She thought of her dad off work with a summer cold, in his dressing gown, sticking his head down the stairs and saying, "I'll go through that maths with you later on if you like?" And her smiling at her dad and saying, "Cool! See you later!"

She thought of leaving the house without turning back to look at it.

She thought of her house.

She cried.

38

Another night passed. It was Saturday morning and Ellie had just remembered that her period was due tomorrow.

"Good morning, dear girl," said Noelle, quickly relocking the door behind her and standing with her hands on her hips, appraising Ellie with an unsettling smile.

Ellie jumped to her feet and Noelle backed away slightly, crossing her arms in front of her. "Now," she said. "Now. Remember what we said yesterday. I want no trouble from you."

"I'm not going to do anything," Ellie said. "I just needed to tell you something. Something important. I'm going to need some towels. Or something. My period is due to start tomorrow."

"Tomorrow?" Noelle narrowed her eyes.

"Yes. And I have really heavy periods. Really heavy. I'll need loads."

Noelle tutted and sighed as though Ellie had somehow deliberately arranged to have a heavy period while being held prisoner in her cellar. "Do you have a preferred brand?"

"No," said Ellie, "anything will do as long as it's extra-absorbent."

"Fine," she said. "I'll bring you some. And I suppose you'll be needing new underwear. Deodorant. That kind of thing."

"Yes," said Ellie. "That would be good." And then she sat on her bed, on her hands, and she looked up at Noelle and asked, "Why am I here?"

Noelle smiled. "Well, as it happens," she said. "I have a plan. A fabulous plan. I'm just waiting for a couple of things to slot into place." She mimed an object slotting into place and laughed. "So, you just be patient and all will be revealed." Her eyes twinkled as she spoke. Ellie wanted to bite her.

"Is it on the news?" she asked.

"Oh, I dare say it is. I can't say that I've been looking." She shrugged dismissively as though the world taking an interest in a missing teenage girl was all a lot of silliness. "Anyway, I suppose I should be getting off to the shops, stock up on all your bits and pieces. Christ, you're going to bankrupt me, young lady, you really are!"

She turned to leave. Before she turned the handle she looked back at Ellie and said, "I've got a lovely surprise for you. Later on. A really lovely surprise. Just you wait. You're going to *love me*."

She left with a lighthearted flourish.

Ellie stared at the back of the door, listened to the three locks, heard Noelle's baby elephant footsteps up the stairs, *stamp stamp stamp.*

She took the chair to the window and stood on it, balanced on her tiptoes.

She waited until she heard the front door slam shut and then she began pounding at the glass, pounding so hard that her hands hurt. She pounded and she pounded and she screamed, "Help me, help me, help me!" Then she pounded on the walls on either side of the room, the walls that must surely divide her from neighbors, neighbors who might, right now, be in their cellars, searching for batteries, maybe, or a bottle of wine.

Ellie pounded on the walls and the windowpane for over an hour. By the time she heard Noelle return from the shops the sides of her hands were black and purple.

～

"Are you ready?"

Ellie sat up straight at the sound of her captor's voice behind the locked door.

"Yes," she replied.

"Are you sitting on the bed? Like a good girl?"

"Yes."

"OK, then! I'm coming in and my goodness me do I have the best surprise for you! You are going to *love* me!"

Ellie sat on her hands and watched the door with held breath.

"Ta-da!"

It took a moment for Ellie to fully understand what she was looking at. A small plastic box with metal bars, pink on the bottom, white on the top, a handle. In Noelle's other hand was a cardboard box, the type you might be given to take away a salad from a health-food shop.

Noelle took the plastic box to the table across the room and then returned with the cardboard box. She sat next to Ellie on the bed and she pulled open the lid of the box and there was a sudden blast of farm smell, of warm manure and damp straw. Noelle parted the straw with her long fingers and said, "Look at the little souls. Just look at them!"

And there, peering up at Ellie, were two small animals with honey-colored fur, black beads of eyes, two pairs of nervously twitching whiskers.

"Hamsters!" said Noelle triumphantly. "Look! You said you always wanted hamsters! Remember? So I got you some. Aren't they just the dearest little things you ever saw? Look at their sweet little noses. Look!"

Ellie nodded. She had no idea how to react. None whatsoever. She had not said she wanted hamsters. She had in fact said that she had not ever wanted hamsters. She did not understand why Noelle had bought her hamsters.

"Look," said Noelle, taking the box to the cage on the table and carefully unlocking the door. "Let's put them in here. They must be fed up being scrunched up together in that box. And my *goodness*, they're not a cheap undertaking, these things. The animals themselves are virtually given away for free. But all the kit and caboodle. My word."

She picked one from the box and carefully freed it into the cage. Then she did the same with the other. "Now you must name them, Ellie. Come. Come and have a look at them and find them some nice names. Though I'm not sure how you'll tell one from the other, to be honest. They're identical. Come here, come."

Ellie shrugged.

"Oh, come along now, Ellie," Noelle chided. "You don't seem terribly excited. I thought you'd be jumping up and down at the sight of them."

"How can you expect me to be excited about anything when you're doing what you're doing?"

Noelle appraised her coolly. "Oh, now, it's not so bad. You know, Ellie, it could be so much worse. I could be a man. I could be a big sweaty man coming in here to do God knows what to you at all hours. I could keep you tied up all day. Or in a box under my bed. Christ, I read a book once about that. A married couple. Stole a girl from the side of the road and kept her under their bed for twenty years. Sweet Jesus. Just imagine." She clasped her throat gently. "No, you've got it good here, missy. And now"— she turned to the hamster cage—"you have it even better. Now come along, let's name these little monsters. *Come along.*"

Her voice had lost its singsong tone and was hard and immovable.

Ellie peered into the cage and stared at the two dots of fur. She did not care. Name them One and Two for all she cared. Name them A and B.

"Come on. Two nice names for girls, or I'll be taking them away and flushing them down the toilet."

Ellie felt her breathing pitch and stall, a wash of light-headedness. She let her thoughts loop violently back and forth inside her head, rush headlong into moments from the past, and grab blindly at things they found there. Her thoughts found a doll. It had pink hair and a gingham dress and huge pink cloth boots.

"Trudy," she said.

"Ha!" said Noelle, tossing back her head. "I *love it*."

Then there was a girl at nursery school, so, so pretty. All the girls used to circle her and try to touch her ice-blonde hair, try to be her friend. Ellie had not thought of her in years. She was called Amy.

"Amy," she said, breathlessly.

Noelle beamed. "Oh, oh, that is *superb*. Trudy and Amy. Just perfect. Good girl! So, I'll keep you supplied with everything you need, all the straw and toys and nibbles and what have you. Your job will be to *nurture* them. You will need to keep them clean and loved and fed." She laughed. "A little like I do for you. Do you see? I keep you clean and fed. You keep them clean and fed. A lovely little circle of caring we have here."

She put her hand to Ellie's crown and caressed it. "Oh dear," she said, quickly removing her hand. "You're getting a little grim up the top here. You'll be needing a shampoo, I suppose." She sighed. "I think I have one of those attachment things somewhere, those things you put over the taps with a little showerhead. I'll see if I can find it."

"You know, Noelle, I'm missing my GCSEs."

Noelle tutted sympathetically. "I know, lovely girl, I know. Terrible timing for you, and I'm sorry for that. But you know, there's always next year."

Next year. Ellie grabbed on to the concept. She saw herself, next year, at home, legs crossed, sitting on her bed, notebooks spread around her, the sounds of her family floating through the walls and the floors, the sun picking out the sequins on her favorite cushion. She would be one year older. But she would be home.

"You know," Noelle was saying, "I did see a little story in the papers today. About you. And you know what they're saying, Ellie?" She looked at Ellie, sadly. "They're saying that you've run away. That you couldn't face the possibility of failing your exams because you are an *overachiever*. They're saying that you ran away from home because you were stressed, having a breakdown."

Ellie felt a huge wash of anger pulse through her, and then crash to the pit of her stomach when she thought of the implications. No one had seen her walk down Stroud Green Road with Noelle Donnelly. No one was following any Noelle Donnelly–related leads. Everyone was flailing around with nonsense theories because they had nothing else to go on. "But . . ." she began. "But that's not true! I was *enjoying* my exams. I wasn't stressed about them at all!"

"I know, love, I know. I know what a tremendous student you are. But clearly other people don't know you as well as I know you."

"Who said it? Who said I was stressed?"

"Well, it was your mother, I think. Yes. It was your mother."

Ellie felt a wail of fury and injustice and grief building inside the walls of her chest. How could her mother think she'd run away? Her own mother? Her mother who knew her better, loved her better than anyone? How could she just have given up on her like this?

"Don't give it too much thought, dear girl. Just you focus on these two." She gestured at the hamster cage. "Dear little Trudy and Amy. They'll take your mind off it all, I guarantee you."

Noelle left then, on the hunt for the shower attachment, and the room fell silent as her footsteps receded up the stairs. A moment later the silence was broken by the metallic, round-and-round creak of the wheel turning in the hamsters' cage. Ellie threw herself onto her bed and clamped her hands over her ears.

39

Well, *obviously* I had to plan it a little bit. There were certain things I had to think of in advance. I cleared that room for a start. Had to make sure it was safe for her: no sharp objects, that kind of thing. And I bought in some nice juice for her because I knew what sort of family they were, I knew they were all organic this and that, I knew she'd expect something nice or she'd probably just take a sip and then leave the rest. Just like your Sara-Jade. Generation Fussy. So I bought in the nice elder-flower stuff for her. Then of course there was the drug; that was easy-peasy. I've been prescribed the sleeping stuff before. I just needed to show up at the GP's looking dreadful and waffle on about insomnia. Thank you very much, Dr. Khan.

So, you know, there was planning involved. But honestly, when I look back on it, I can't quite believe I did it, can't quite believe what I was capable of. Especially the violence. Oh my goodness, the violence! I throttled that poor girl, stood with my hands to her throat and squeezed and squeezed. I mean, she might have died!

But on the whole, as the time passed by, I think we rubbed along together OK, me and Ellie, once she realized that we were a team, once she knew that I did not want to hurt her, that she was safe with me.

And giving her those animals was a masterstroke, I think. Oh my word, how she loved those animals. They gave her a purpose. Something to focus on. She was lovely with them, maternal and caring, just as I'd known she would be. It warmed my heart to watch her. What were they called now, those first ones? I can't remember. But it turned out they weren't a pair of girls after all. No, they were not. So many came afterward, so many that it was impossible to keep track of them all. *She* knew their names, though. Even when there were cages full of them. She knew each and every one by name. She was amazing like that. Is it any wonder I was obsessed with her? Is it any wonder I did what I did?

And yes, *clearly* I knew what I was doing. Of course there was a bigger picture. Of course there was. I had a truly audacious plan.

And my goodness me if I didn't go and pull it off.

40

THEN

The days had lost their structure, their edges, their middles. At first she'd been aware of the passing of time, had distinctly felt the shape of the hours and days moving by. Friday had felt like Friday. Saturday like Saturday. Monday had felt like the day she would be sitting her history and Spanish GCSEs. Tuesday had been the day she should have been taking her first maths paper. The weekend after had come and gone and she'd still had a grip on it. It was next Monday. She'd been here for eleven days. Then twelve days. Then thirteen. It was her sixteenth birthday. She didn't tell Noelle.

After fourteen days, though, she lost count. She asked Noelle, "What day is it today?" And Noelle said, "It's Friday."

"What's the date?"

"It's the tenth. I think. Although it might be the ninth. And it might be Thursday. Me and my daft, fuzzy head."

It all spiraled away from her then, her peg in the map of time was irretrievably lost.

⌒

Noelle still brought her gifts. Fruit pastilles. A sugar-topped doughnut. A packet of tiny pencil erasers in the shapes of animals. Lipstick with glitter in it.

She brought her things for the hamsters, too. Bags of straw and little toys and chews and biscuits. "The babies," she called them. "How are the babies today?" Then she'd take one out of its cage and hold it in the cylinder of her hand and stroke its tiny skull with a fingertip and make kissy noises at it and say, "Well you are the prettiest little thing I ever did see, you truly are," and then sing it a song.

Still, though, Noelle Donnelly would not tell Ellie why she was here or when she would be leaving. Still she'd tantalize and tease and talk about her *amazing plan* and how everything was going to be *just woopitydoo, just you wait and see.*

Ellie still carried around the raw wound in the pit of her belly, the place where her mother lived. Constantly, she pictured her mother alone at home, touching Ellie's things, lying down with her face pressed against Ellie's pillow, circling an empty trolley around the supermarket, black-faced and wondering why why why her perfect girl—because Laurel had always made it abundantly clear to Ellie that she perceived her as such—had gone and left them.

She'd picture Hanna, too, her infuriating big sister, always trying to pinch brownie points from her, always snatching back little chunks of Ellie's glory with barbed comments that she didn't even mean. How would she be feeling now, now that Ellie was gone and she had no one left to play out her childish power struggle with? She would be hurting. She would be blaming herself. Ellie wanted to reach through the walls of this house and into hers, place her arms around her sister's body and hold her tight and say, *I know you love me. I know you do. Please don't blame yourself.*

And her father? She couldn't think about her father. Every time he came to mind she saw him in his bathrobe, with bed hair. She saw the softness of his morning stubble, his bare feet, his hand reaching up to pluck the coffee jug from the shelf in the kitchen. That was how her father existed now to her, trapped in an amber tomb in his bathrobe. And Jake—she saw Jake as a free spirit; she saw him when he was a young boy, in the garden, playing football, slouching to school in his oversized blazer, a weighty school bag slung across his small boy body, picking up his pace at the sight of his friends up ahead.

And it was surprising to Ellie how little she thought about Theo during those first few days of captivity. Before Noelle had taken her she'd thought about him virtually every living moment of every living day. But now her family had taken center stage. She missed Theo but she needed her family. Ached for them. Curled herself into a ball with her hands pressed hard into her stomach and cried for them.

Ellie's days were longer than twenty-four hours. Each *hour* felt like twenty-four hours. Each minute felt like thirty. Dark came late at this time of year and the sun rose early and the time in between was spent in a violent swirl of dreams and nightmares, twisted bedsheets and sweat-drenched pillows.

"I want to go home," she said to Noelle one morning when she came to deliver her breakfast.

"I know you do. I know." Noelle squeezed Ellie's shoulder. "And I'm sorry about all this. I truly am. I'm trying to make this as nice for you as I possibly can. You can see, can't you, you can see the effort I'm making? The money I'm spending? You know, I'm going without myself to pay for you."

"But if you let me go home, you wouldn't have to pay for me. You could just go somewhere and I'd never tell anyone it was you. I'd just be so happy to be home, that's all I'd care about. I wouldn't tell the police, I wouldn't . . ."

And then *crash*. The back of Noelle's hand hard and sharp across Ellie's cheek.

"Enough," she said, her voice still and hard. "*Enough*. There'll be no going home until I say. You need to *stop* with your talk of *going home*. Do you understand?"

Ellie held the back of her hand to her cheek, rolled the cool flesh across the red sting of Noelle's knuckles. She nodded.

"Good girl."

⌒

Noelle went out that night and Ellie awoke in the dark, confused by the sound of heavy footsteps down the basement stairs.

"Ah, did I wake you?"

Noelle was in the room. She swayed slightly in the doorway, before clicking it shut behind her and locking it.

Ellie sat up straight, clutched her racing heart. Noelle looked strange. She was wearing an awful lot of makeup, some of which had been rubbed away. One eye had more eye shadow than the other. There was a black smudge by her cheekbone. And she was dressed very smartly: a shiny black blouse with fitted black trousers and some high-heeled shoes. She had a single gold hoop in one earlobe.

"I'm sorry," she said, edging toward Ellie. "I didn't realize how late it was. I've had a bit to drink and you know how the time just rolls itself up when you've had a few jars."

Ellie shook her head.

"No," said Noelle, perching herself on the side of Ellie's bed. "Of course you don't. You're just a girl."

She smiled and Ellie could see a blackish stain on her teeth.

"So," she said. "Aren't you going to ask me where I've been?"

Ellie shrugged.

"I've been to my boyfriend's flat," she said. "Did I tell you I have a boyfriend?"

"No."

"I bet you can't believe it, can you? Boring old Noelle the tutor. Having a boyfriend. I mean, he's not a patch on your fella. Obviously not. But he's a god to me. Cleverest human being I've ever met. No idea what he sees in me, of course."

"You look very nice tonight," said Ellie, obsequious in the wake of Noelle's slap to her cheek earlier on.

Noelle glanced at her. "Oh, you little sweetie. I *do not*. But thank you."

Ellie smiled tightly.

"Anyway, how has your evening been?"

Ellie shrugged and said, "OK."

Noelle glanced around the room then and sighed. "I was thinking maybe I could fix you up with a TV and a DVD player. You can get one of those little all-in-one things for next to nothing these days. It might mean less treats and what have you for a while. But better than staring at these four walls for hours on end. What do you think?"

Ellie blinked. A DVD player. Movies. Documentaries. "Yes, please, thank you, yes."

"And some books, too? Would you like some books to read?"

"Yes. I would. I'd love some books."

Noelle smiled fondly at her. "Books then," she said. "I'll pick some up from the Red Cross shop. And some DVDs. We'll make it nice in here for you. We'll make it as good as home."

She got to her feet then and looked down at Ellie and said, "It's all coming together now. I can feel it. It's all coming together. Just you wait."

Ellie watched her fiddle clumsily with the key in the lock. She sensed a moment of vulnerability. She played with the idea of ambushing her. Throwing herself upon her, slamming her drunken, makeup-smeared face into the wall, once, twice, three times, grabbing the key from her, shoving it hard into the lock, turning, opening, running, running, running. But even as the thought showed itself to her, the door clicked open and Noelle Donnelly was passing through it and then slamming it shut behind her and then she was gone.

"Mummy," Ellie whispered into the palms of her hands. "Mummy."

⌘

Ellie would never really know what happened the following night. She could guess, because of what happened afterward, but the actual facts, the details, only one person knew, and she would never tell her.

Noelle came down with her supper at six o'clock. It was chicken nuggets and chips with a perfunctory spoonful of mixed peas and sweet corn on the side. There was a big cream bun on the tray, a small bowl of jelly beans, and a glass of Coke with a slice of lemon in it. Noelle cooked for her as though she was five years old. Ellie ached for a bit of sushi, or some garlic prawns and rice from the posh Chinese up the road.

Noelle stayed a while that evening. She'd brought Ellie a new book and some fancy shampoo. She seemed to be in a sparkling mood.

"How's the dinner?" she asked.

"It's nice, thank you."

"You're so lucky," she said. "At your age you can eat and eat and eat and never gain an ounce."

"But you're very slim."

"Well, yes, but that is purely because I barely eat. When I turned forty, oh"—she made a circle of her mouth—"what a shock that was. No more cream buns for me. And the older you get, the worse it gets. I'll be living on water and air by the time I'm fifty at this rate."

"How old are you?"

"Too old," she said. "Far too old. I'm forty-five. What a silly-sounding age that is, to be sure."

"It's not that old."

"Well, love you for saying that, but all the same it *is* that old. Particularly when it comes to certain things."

Ellie nodded. She didn't know what the *certain things* were and she certainly wasn't going to ask.

"So, it's a joy to have a young person to cook for. I can buy all the yummy things in the shops instead of just looking at them." She smiled and there were the tiny teeth that chilled Ellie's soul.

And that was that.

The edges of Noelle Donnelly began to blur and shiver, the walls of the room turned black and bled into everything and for a small second there were just Noelle's teeth, suspended alone in a sea of blackness, like a UFO in the night sky.

And after that it was the morning. And even though everything felt normal, Ellie knew it wasn't normal, that something had happened.

41

The summer slowly died away and nothing changed. The nights became longer; the temperature dropped five degrees. Noelle bought Ellie a fleece-lined hoodie and some warm pajamas. The foliage around the basement window was still green. It was, Ellie imagined, September. Maybe early October. Noelle wouldn't tell her.

"Oh, sweet girl, you do not need to know. It's of no use to you to know. No use at all."

And then, one morning, lying on her bed, Ellie felt something very strange. A small judder, like a *pop* going through her middle section, as though a person living under her mattress had just nudged her in the back. For a terrible moment Ellie thought she was lying on a hamster and quickly jumped to her feet to check. But no, there was nothing there.

She sat gingerly on the edge of the bed, waiting to see if the sensation returned. But it didn't so she lay back down on the bed. As she lay down it happened again. This time she could place it. It was coming from within her. Bubbles popping inside her stomach. She rubbed and rubbed at her stomach, trying to ease the bubbles away. Eventually the pops dissipated and the inside of her own body stopped doing surprising things; by the evening of that same day Ellie had forgotten entirely about the otherworldly feeling, the sense of being occupied, the sense of no longer being alone.

42

You may recall the exact night of conception. It was the night after I came over to yours all dressed to the nines in my satin blouse and my high heels, the night we drank two bottles of champagne and had sex three times.

I'd thought it would be a long-term project. I had more plastic pots waiting in the freezer, let's put it that way. But it turned out I didn't need them. I'd been charting Ellie's ovulation for a couple of months, making sure to dole out the pads and tampons on a day-by-day basis so I'd know exactly when she was bleeding and how much. And I hit the jackpot the first time. I stood by with the tampons and the towels, waiting for Ellie to ask me for them. But two weeks passed, three weeks, then four. And then she started to be sick every morning and I knew.

I waited until Ellie was about four or five months along before I told you about the baby. I put it off for as long as possible so the period of subterfuge would be as short as possible, because of course if it was to be your baby, then you needed to think I was pregnant. And in order for you to think I was pregnant, I needed to look pregnant. And if I was going to fake a pregnancy, then that was the end of our sex life. So I told you the doctor had said the placenta was low-lying and so there was to be NO SEX. So, there was no sex, but as you probably recall we did plenty of other things because of course I had to keep you, more than ever then, I had to keep you.

I said I'd been to the scan alone, really hammed it up, do you remember? "Oh, I couldn't take it if the baby was gone again. I couldn't bear to let you down again." You were sweet about it, but I could tell your heart wasn't in it. I could tell that without the sex, without the intimacy of sharing a bed with me, of passing your hands around my body, of the shared bottles of wine and the lie-ins on a Saturday morning, that I really wasn't a good fit for your life. The baby was neither here nor there to you. I could tell. I felt, in a way, that you were hoping I'd take the baby as a consolation prize and disappear somewhere with it, like a low-ranking lion taking a scrap of old skin from a kill and slinking away with her tail between her legs. We'd never been close, not in the way that other people see as close, and the little that had held us together all those years was starting to crumble, like mortar between bricks. I could feel us coming loose from each other and I didn't have a clue what to do about it.

The only hope I had was that when the baby came you'd fall in love with it, that you wouldn't be able to live without it and that we'd be inextricably linked. Forever.

43

THEN

Her stomach was stretched as taut as a spacehopper, laced with bluish veins and dissected by a long, brown line. She could sometimes see the vivid outline of a small foot pressing at the paper-thin skin, elbows and knees; once she even saw the delicate pencil shading of an ear. The person inside her rolled and roiled and danced and kicked. The person inside her pressed hard against her lungs and her esophagus, then the person turned over and pressed hard against her bladder and her bowels.

Noelle bought her pregnancy books to read and medicine to counteract the indigestion and the constipation and the backache. She bought her a special pillow, shaped like a banana, to keep her knees apart at night. Ellie liked the pillow: it felt like a person; sometimes she spooned herself against it, laid her cheek upon it. Noelle bought a book of baby names and she'd sit and read them out to her. She bought a doctor's stethoscope and together they listened to the baby's heartbeat. Noelle would run her hands around the bump and talk about what she could feel. "Ah, yes, that baby's on the move," she'd say. "It's turning beautifully. It'll be engaged before we know it."

Ellie had suspected she was not fat but pregnant a few weeks after she'd first felt the baby moving. She couldn't pinpoint the precise moment; it just became increasingly obvious, day by day. She'd stared at Noelle one afternoon, trying to think of a way to ask the question while simultaneously not wanting to know the answer. Eventually she'd said, "Something's moving inside my stomach. I'm scared."

Noelle had put down her cup of tea and smiled at her. "You have nothing to be scared of, sweet thing. No, no, no. You just have a little baby in there, that is all."

Ellie gazed down at her belly and stroked it absentmindedly. "That's what I thought," she said. "But how could it be?"

"It's a miracle, that's what it is, Ellie. And now you know. Now you know why I chose you. Because I couldn't have a baby of my own and I asked God to find me a baby and God told me that it was you! That you were special! That you were to have my baby!" Noelle looked rapturous, elated, her hands clasped together in front of her heart. "And look," she said. "Look at you now. An immaculate conception. A baby sent from the Holy Father. A miracle."

"But you don't believe in God."

Noelle moved fast and Ellie was too big to move swiftly enough to get out of her way.

Whack. Noelle's hand hard across the back of her head.

Then Noelle was gone from the room, turning the locks hard behind her.

⌒

Noelle refused to countenance any questions about the provenance of the baby inside Ellie over the following weeks. All Noelle did was smile and talk about "our miracle" and swan into Ellie's room clutching tiny sleep-suits from Asda and little knitted slippers from the Red Cross shop, a wickerwork sleep basket with a tiny white mattress and a gingham shade, a little book made of cotton that squeaked and crinkled and jingled when you touched the pages. She brought lovely cream for Ellie's swollen feet, and sang lullabies to the bump.

And then one day, in very early spring, Ellie awoke in a strange mood. She had slept badly, been unable to find a position in which the baby wasn't squashing some part of her insides. And in the moments that she had slept, she'd dreamed vividly and shockingly. In her dreams she gave birth to a puppy, hairless and tiny. The puppy had quickly grown into an adult dog, a hound from hell with bared teeth and red eyes. The dog had hated her, it had skulked outside the door to her room, growling and slavering, waiting for Noelle to unlock the door so that it could come in and attack her. She awoke from this dream three times, sweating and hyperventilating. But each time she fell back into sleep the dog would be there, outside her door.

She was keen to see Noelle that morning. The night had felt long, virtually endless. She wanted a human being to break the strange spell she'd cast herself under. But Noelle didn't come at breakfast time and she didn't come at lunchtime. With every passing minute Ellie became more and more anxious, more and more scared. When she finally heard the sound of Noelle's key in the lock in the early evening she was ready to throw herself at her and sling her arms around her neck.

But when the door opened and she saw Noelle's expression, Ellie immediately recoiled into the soft cocoon of her bed.

"Here," said Noelle, slamming a bowl of Coco Pops, a bag of Wotsits, and half a packet of Oreos on the bedside table. "I haven't had time to cook."

Ellie sat cross-legged, her arms wrapped around her bump, looking at Noelle in surprise and fear.

"Oh, stop with the big brown eyes. I'm not in the mood for it. Just eat your food."

"It's not very nutritious," she ventured quietly. Noelle had been making a big effort to give Ellie vegetables and fruit since she'd become pregnant.

"Oh, for fuck's sake," she muttered. "One shit meal's not going to kill you or the baby." She sat heavily on the chair, radiating fury.

Ellie waited a few minutes before speaking again. "Where've you been?" she asked, pulling apart the packet of Wotsits.

"That's none of your affair."

"I was worried," she ventured. "I mean, it made me think, what would happen if something happened to you while you were gone? Like, maybe you were in an accident or you got ill. What would happen to me?"

"Nothing's going to happen to me, don't be stupid."

"No, but it might. You might get a concussion and forget your address. And I'd be locked here with a baby in my tummy and no one would know we were here and we'd both die."

"Look," said Noelle, exasperated. "I am not going to get a concussion. And if anything else happened, I'd tell someone you were here. OK?"

Ellie saw that Noelle was losing patience, that she should drop the conversation right now and eat in silence, but what she'd just said, that she would *tell someone she was here*, this was new and transcendental and extraordinary and thrilling. This couldn't be ignored.

"Would you really?" she asked, slightly breathless.

"Of course I would. You think I'd just leave you here to die?"

"But what about . . ." She picked her next words carefully. "Wouldn't you be worried? That the police would come? That you'd be arrested or something?"

"Oh, for crying out loud, child. Will you *stop*. Stop with all this nonsense. I've had enough filthy shit today already to last me a fucking lifetime. I do not need any more from you. All I do is spoil you and care for you, and all you do is sit on your huge fat arse thinking up stupid things to worry about. I have put my life on *hold* for you and that baby. Now just stop whining and let me deal with everything. For God's sake."

Ellie nodded and stared into the orange rubble of the crisp packet, her eyes filling with tears.

"Those animals *stink*, by the way," Noelle growled, tossing her head in the direction of the hamster cages. "Get them cleaned out or they're going down the toilet."

And then she was gone, and Ellie was alone. Outside the high window a sharp wind threw the tangles of the leafless foliage around like tossed hair while Ellie ate her Wotsits and prayed for a bus to bang into Noelle Donnelly next time she went to the shops, prayed for her to be hospitalized for long enough to have to tell someone about the girl in her basement with a miracle baby growing in her tummy.

Noelle didn't seem to be excited about the baby anymore. The bigger Ellie got, the more disinterested Noelle became. The gifts stopped, the baby names stopped, there were no more little sleep-suits to admire or gentle palpations of the bump to see what position the baby was in. Noelle still came three times a day to visit Ellie, to bring her food—no longer the healthy, good-for-the-baby meals of the early months, no more boil-in-the-bag vegetables and uninspired arrangements of tomato and cucumber, just fried food in varying shades of white, pale brown, and occasionally orange—and often she stayed to talk.

Sometimes these chats were mundane, sometimes they bore precious nuggets of information—the weather outside, for example, with its suggestion of the changing seasons, or the increase in her business as children in the world outside began their GCSE studies with its suggestion of the time of year. Other times these chats were a kind of catharsis for Noelle, an unburdening of herself. Ellie had found these mood swings terrifying at first, had never been quite prepared for whichever version of Noelle might come through her door that day. But as the time passed she started to get an instinct for Noelle's psychology, started to sense immediately what their chat would be like before Noelle had opened the door, just by the rhythm of the fall of her feet on the wooden staircase outside, the sound of the key in the lock, the speed with which it opened, the angle of her hair across her face, the sound of her breath as she drew it in to form her words of greeting.

Today she knew immediately that Noelle was in a self-pitying mood.

Flop flop flop came her size-eight-and-a-half feet down the stairs.

Sigh before she put the key in the lock.

Creak as the door opened slowly.

And *sigh* again as she closed the door behind her.

"Here," she said, presenting Ellie with her lunch: two slices of white toast cowering under the contents of a can of Heinz beans with minisausages, a film-wrapped pancake filled with chocolate spread and rolled into a flattened tube, a can of Lucozade, and a bowl of jelly beans.

Ellie sat straight and took the tray from Noelle. "Thank you."

She began to eat in silence, aware of Noelle brewing and cogitating beside her.

Finally she heard Noelle take a deep breath and mutter, "I'm wondering, Ellie, what the heck this is all about. Aren't you?"

Ellie peered at her and then moved her gaze back to her

beans on toast. She knew better than to offer any input when Noelle was like this. Her role was simply to be a human sounding board.

"Everything we do, every day. The effort it takes just to get out of your fecking bed every morning. Doing the same goddam things every day. Switch on the kettle . . ." She mimed switching on a kettle. "Brush your teeth." She mimed this, too. "Choose your clothes, comb your hair, cook your food, clear up your food, take out the rubbish, buy more food, answer the phone, wash your clothes, dry your clothes, fold your clothes, put your clothes away, smile at all the cock-sucking bastards out there, every day, over and over and over and there's no opt-out. I mean, you can see why some people take to the street, can't you? I see them sometimes, the homeless, lying there on their cardboard mattress, dirty old blanket, can of something strong, and I envy them, I do. No responsibility to anyone, for anything.

"And you know, I must have been mad thinking I could do this." She gestured around the bedroom, at Ellie and her bump and the hamsters in their cages. "More mouths to feed, more drudgery to add to the workload, more money to find to pay for more things that will need to be washed and cooked and folded and put away. I don't know what I was thinking. I really don't."

She sighed deeply and then got to her feet. She was about to leave but then she turned and glanced at Ellie curiously. "Are you OK?" The question was an afterthought. Noelle didn't really want an answer. She didn't want to hear that Ellie had barely slept in days because she was too uncomfortable at night. She didn't want to know about Ellie's sore tooth or the fact that she'd run out of clean underwear and was washing her pants by hand in the basin or that she needed a new bra as her breasts were now the size of watermelons or that she missed her mum so much, her insides burned with it, and that she could smell summer approaching and could feel the days growing longer and that she cried when she thought about the smell of fresh grass and barbecues in the back garden and Jake on the trampoline and Teddy Bear the cat stretched out in the pools of light that fell upon the wooden floorboards. She didn't want to know that Ellie no longer knew what Ellie was, let alone *how* she was, that she had bled into herself, become a puddle, a pool, plasmatic in form. That sometimes she felt as though she loved Noelle. Sometimes she wanted Noelle to hold her in her arms and rock her slowly like a baby, and other times she wanted to slit Noelle's throat and stand and watch as the blood spouted out, slowly, magnificently, running through Noelle's fingers, the collapse of her, then the death of her.

Ellie knew what Stockholm syndrome was. They'd studied it at school. She'd read about the Patty Hearst case. She knew what could happen to people kept in captivity for prolonged periods of time. She knew that her feelings were normal. But she also knew that she must not let those feelings of affection—those moments when she yearned for Noelle's attention or for her approval—she mustn't allow them to dominate. She needed to hold on to the parts of her that wanted Noelle dead. Those were the strong, healthy parts of her. Those were the parts that would one day get her out of here.

44

Ellie was eight months pregnant when you ended it. Or in other words, *I* was eight months pregnant.

I just feel for the sake of the baby, we should draw a line in the sand now.

You fucking bastard. You said that the relationship had run its course and that you wanted to play a part in the baby's life but that you thought it was for the best if we went our separate ways as a couple. That we should work out "how to be apart" before the baby came.

How to be apart. Ha! What does that even *mean*, Floyd?

I don't think you really knew, to be honest. I think you were just sick of not getting any sex, I think you wanted to be able to go off and screw someone else. That's what I think.

I managed not to beg. I managed not to plead. And I still had my trump card. The baby. I was very calm, remember? I went up to your room to pack up the belongings that had migrated there over the years. My toothbrush, my deodorant, my hairbrush, spare pants. That kind of thing. I dropped them all into a carrier bag; they made a sad sight when I peered in at them. I was wearing a top of yours, an oversized T-shirt that skimmed my fake bump. I thought about stealing it but then I thought it would have more poignancy if I left it draped across your bed for you to come upon that evening as you climbed into bed, for you to maybe think, *Oh Noelle, what have I done?* When I left the room, your horrible daughter was standing there on the landing, looking at me as she did with those horror-movie eyes. Fuck you, I thought as I swanned past her. Fuck you.

Because I knew what I had in my basement. And I knew that it was better than her. And if it was better than her, then it could still bring us back together.

I had not lost hope.

45

Well, I wouldn't say it was a textbook birth. No. I wouldn't. I'd read everything there was to read on the subject of home birth and there was no eventuality I wasn't prepared for. Apart from the really, really awful ones that would have taken us to a hospital, I suppose (I had my story all lined up: a desperate niece, too ashamed to tell her family back in Ireland—well, you can guess the rest). But it didn't come to that. I got that baby out of her without any medical intervention. I'm not saying it was pleasant. It was far from pleasant, but out that baby came, alive and breathing. And that was all that mattered at the end of the day.

She was a sweet baby. Full head of brown hair. Little red mouth. I let the girl choose a name for her. It was the least I could do after what she'd been through.

Poppy, she said.

I'd have preferred something a bit more classical. Helen, maybe, or Louise. But there you go. You can't have everything your own way.

I left the baby with the girl those first few days. Well, there was not much I could be doing now really, was there? And then when the baby was two weeks old, I took her to the baby clinic to get her weighed and checked, get her on the system so that she would be a real person and not just a tiny ghost in my basement.

I had to answer lots of awkward questions but I had my

spiel sorted: Didn't know I was pregnant, thought it was my menopause, hardly changed shape, gave birth at home with my partner, all happened really fast, no time to call for an ambulance, wham bam there was the baby, so no, we never went to the hospital. No, the baby was not given an Apgar score. I told them that I'd been too nervous to bring the baby out of the house before now, that I thought it was OK as long as the baby seemed OK. I sat and took their telling off, let them slap my wrists good and proper. Oh, I said, I'm really, really sorry. But you know, I was a virgin until a few months ago (I used my strongest Irish accent for this), I've led a sheltered life, I don't really know much about anything.

They sighed and looked appalled and made notes about me no doubt: "potential loony, keep an eye on this one." But they gave me all the papers I needed to register the baby at the town hall and made me an appointment to come in five weeks later for my postnatal exam (I didn't go, of course, but had I done, I think they'd have been very impressed with the pristine condition of my underneaths) and told me a midwife would be coming to interview me later that week. I just pretended I was out when she came and hid in the back room while she rattled my letterbox. She came again a few days later and she called me about a hundred times, but she gave up in the end. I duly took the baby to all the appointments at the clinic; she got her shots, she was weighed and measured. I did the bare minimum to keep them off the scent. But in social worker parlance, we slipped through the net. Worrying, really, when you think about it.

But the girl meanwhile . . . Well, I thought I'd done my best by her. I really did, but she didn't seem well. It was one thing after another really. First an infection down below. That seemed to heal of its own accord but then she got an infection in one of her breasts, or at least that was my theory. I read up about it on the Internet. I told her she must feed the baby from that one breast, feed and feed and feed. She was very hot, then very cold. I gave her over-the-counter remedies but they didn't work. She lost interest in the baby and I had to take over feeding her. Then she stopped eating. She called for her mother *all the time*. Incessant it was. All hours of the day and night. I couldn't bear it for another moment.

Then one day, when the baby was about five months old, I shut the door to that room, and for a very long time I did not go back.

46

Joshua had given Laurel his grandparents' phone number in Dublin. Henry and Breda Donnelly. They were both alive and both still working.

"They're amazing," Joshua had said. "Like really amazing. Scary as shit—you don't want to cross them. But incredible people. Forces of nature, the pair of them."

Laurel calls them on Sunday when she gets back from Floyd's house.

A woman picks up the phone and says "hello" so loudly that Laurel jumps.

"Hello. Is that Mrs. Donnelly?"

"Speaking."

"Breda Donnelly?"

"Yes. This is she."

"Sorry to bother you on a Sunday, you're not eating, are you?"

"No, no. We're not. But thank you for asking. What can I do for you?"

"I've just met up with your grandson, Joshua."

"Ah, yes, young Josh. And how is he these days?"

"He's great. Really great. I went to visit him at your daughter's house. Noelle's house."

There's a brief silence on the line and then Breda Donnelly says, "Who is this, please? You haven't said."

"Sorry. Yes. My name's Laurel Mack. My daughter used to be one of Noelle's students. About ten years ago. And as a weird coincidence, my current boyfriend is Noelle's ex-partner. Floyd Dunn? The father of Poppy?"

There's another silence and Laurel holds her breath.

Eventually Breda says, "Ye-es," pulling out the vowel to suggest that she needs much more information before she'll offer any herself.

Laurel sighs. "Look," she says, "I don't really know why I'm calling, except that my daughter disappeared shortly after she finished her tutoring with Noelle. And she disappeared right next to Noelle's house. And then Noelle herself also disappeared, a few years later."

"And?"

"I suppose I just wanted to ask you about Noelle, about what you think happened to her."

Breda Donnelly sighs. "Are you sure you're not from the papers?"

"Honestly. I swear. You can google me if you like. Laurel Mack. Or google my daughter. Ellie Mack. It's all there. I promise."

"She was supposed to be coming home."

Laurel blinks. "What?"

"Noelle. That week. She was coming home. With her little girl."

"Oh," she says. "I didn't realize. Floyd just said that she disappeared. He didn't mention that she was supposed to be going back to Ireland."

"Well, maybe she didn't tell him that. But she was. And the papers barely cared. The police barely cared. A middle-aged woman. A bit of a loner. An ex-partner who said she was mentally unstable. I told them she was coming home but they didn't think it was relevant. And maybe it wasn't."

"And she said she was coming with her daughter?"

"Yes. She was coming with her daughter. With Poppy. And that they would be staying here. At the house. And we were all ready for her, we were. Beds all made up. We'd bought the child a big bear. Yogurts and juices. Then suddenly she's given the child to the father, packed a bag, and disappeared. I suppose we weren't surprised. It always did strike us as faintly unbelievable that she'd had a baby in the first place, let alone that she was able to raise it on her own."

"So you think she changed her mind? That she was going to start a new life, with you and Poppy, and then freaked out at the last minute?"

"Well, yes, it certainly seemed that way."

"And where do you think she is, Mrs. Donnelly? If you don't mind me asking?"

"Oh, God, I suppose, if I'm honest, I would say she's dead."

Laurel pauses to absorb the impact of Breda's words.

"When did you last see Noelle, Mrs. Donnelly?"

"Nineteen eighty-four."

Laurel falls silent again.

"She came home for a few weeks after her PhD. Then she went to London. That was the last time we saw her. Her brothers tried to visit when they came to London but she always kept them at arm's length. Always made excuses. We had no Christmas cards from her, no birthday cards. We'd send news on to her: new nephews and nieces, degrees and what have you. But there was never a reply. She genuinely, genuinely didn't care about us. Not about any of us. And in the end I'd say we'd stopped caring about her, too."

47

I first brought the baby to see you when she was about six months old. I dressed her up in the most spectacular outfit: a cardigan with a fur collar of all the things. It was in the sales at Monsoon. And a tutu. And shoes! For a baby! Quite ridiculous. But this baby was the prettiest thing you've ever seen and I wanted her to really dazzle the life out of you.

The day I brought her to meet you I had the butterflies. I'd called you to warn you that I was coming. I wanted us to be made welcome, for a friendly cup of tea to be poured for me, for you to be ready.

It was a sunny morning, a hopeful day, I felt. You answered the door in a horrible jumper. I'm sorry, but it really was. You never were the snappiest dresser, we had that much in common, but really, this was off the scale. A Christmas present from your horrible daughter, no doubt.

You didn't look at me. Your eyes went straight to the baby in the car seat that I was holding. I watched your face, I saw you absorb her, this fat-limbed, tawny-skinned, dark-haired plum of a child, so different from that scrawny, miserable thing your wife had made you. You smiled. And then, God bless that bonny child, she smiled right back at you. She kicked her little satin-shod feet. She gurgled at you. It was almost as though she knew. As though she knew that everything hinged on this one moment.

You ushered us in. I put the car seat down on the floor in your lovely kitchen and looked around, enveloped immediately by the sanctity and niceness of being back in your personal space. And strangely I felt more like I belonged there in that moment than I ever had when I was your girlfriend. You made me the cup of tea that I'd dreamed of you making for me. You passed it to me and then you crouched down by the car seat, looked up at me, and said, "May I?"

I said, "Please, go ahead. She's your daughter, after all."

You unclipped her straps and she kicked those little feet of hers and held her arms aloft for you. You plucked her out softly but securely and you brought her to your shoulder. I think maybe you thought she was younger than she was, because you hadn't seen her when she was a newborn. But she showed you that she was a bigger girl than that and turned herself around in your arms, held her hand against your cheek, tugged at the straggles of beard on your face. You made faces at her. She laughed.

"Wow," you said. "She's lovely, isn't she?"

"Well, I'm a bit biased of course . . ."

"And she's six months, yes?"

"Yes. Six months on Tuesday."

"Poppy. It's a pretty name."

"Isn't it?" I said. "And it suits her, I think."

"Yes," you agreed. "It really does."

You blew a raspberry at her then and she looked at you in utter delight.

"And how's it been?" you asked. "How's it been for you?"

"It's been . . ." I plastered a stupid smile on my face and didn't mention the endless, nightmarish nights when I'd be in her room two, three, four times with endless bottles of milk. I didn't mention how sometimes I'd put her in her cot for an hour and sit in my kitchen with the radio turned right up so I couldn't hear her crying. And I certainly didn't mention the time I seriously toyed with the idea of leaving her on the steps of the hospital just like your own parents had done to you. "It's been amazing," I gushed. "She's a real dream. She sleeps all night. And she smiles. And she eats. And, honestly, Floyd, I can't think why I didn't do this a long time ago. I really can't."

You really liked this response, I could tell. Probably in your head you'd had me painted as a terrible, sexless aging crone that you were best shot of. And suddenly here I was in your kitchen, looking well (I'd been to the hairdresser's and made them take my hair back to its original copper. It was the first time I'd been to a hairdresser for anything other than a trim in about twenty years) and with this drop-dead *gorgeous* baby that I was *clearly* in love with, like any *normal* woman would be. And I could feel you then, I really could, reevaluating me, reconfiguring your prejudices. I could feel that we still had a chance.

I stayed for an hour and a half and when I left (at my behest, off to a fictional friend's for supper), you came out of the house with me, holding the baby in her chair. You insisted on strapping the chair into the backseat. I watched you adjust the straps on the seat, making sure they weren't too tight around her fat little arms.

"Bye bye, gorgeous Poppy," you said, kissing your fingertips and placing them against her cheek. "I hope I see you again really, really soon."

I smiled inscrutably and then drove away, leaving you there on the pavement not knowing where you stood with anything.

And that was exactly where I wanted you.

48

Bonny calls Laurel at work on Monday. Laurel recognizes her been-around-the-block voice immediately.

"We've been talking," she begins, "about Christmas."

Laurel stops herself groaning. She cannot possibly bring herself to think about Christmas even though it's less than a week away and the world is full of lights and music and even the plumbing supplies shop has baubles in its windows. She's not ready for it.

"Now, unfortunately we're at my stepmother's on Christmas Day itself, she's eighty-four, far too frail to make it down to London, so we'll be heading up to Oxford. So what I thought is that we could do a big Christmas Eve bash here. We can do gifts and games and cocktails and what have you. And I have space for thousands, so all the children, partners, etc. And you can absolutely bring your gorgeous man and his lovely daughter." She pauses for breath; Laurel can hear the rattle of a cough in the bass of her breathing. "What do you think?"

Laurel fingers the pendant at her collarbone.

"Have you asked Jake?" she asks after another pause.

"Yes. Yes I have." There's a finality to this that tells Laurel immediately that Paul and Bonny are now aware of the current impasse.

"And is he coming?"

"He says he thinks so."

"And what about Hanna?"

"She said yes. She'll be coming."

Laurel's stomach lurches. Hanna has completely transmogrified in her mind from an ice princess destined never to thaw to a scarlet woman throwing herself at other people's boyfriends with no thought for anyone but herself. Laurel no longer knows what to think about her daughter.

"Well," she says after a significant pause, "that does sound lovely. I'll ask Floyd. He did say that he and Poppy usually stay in on Christmas Eve, but I'm sure they could be persuaded. Can I get back to you?"

"Yes, of course! Please do. But sooner rather than later, if you don't mind. I'll have to get my Waitrose order in by tomorrow at the very latest."

Waitrose orders. Laurel cannot imagine that she ever had a life that involved Waitrose orders.

She puts down her phone and sighs.

⌇

At Floyd's that night Laurel asks him how Poppy had reacted when Noelle dropped her on his doorstep and disappeared into thin air. "Was she happy?" she says. "Was she sad? Did she miss her mum? What was it like?"

"Well, first off," he replies, "she looked awful. She was overweight, refused to let anyone brush her hair, bathe her, brush her teeth. So she was a mess. And that was basically why Noelle left her with me. She'd had this perfect little baby and she'd totally fucked her up because she did not know how to parent and she'd ended up four years later with a monster.

"And no, Poppy wasn't sad. Poppy loved being here with me. When she was with me she behaved. She didn't have tantrums. She didn't demand chocolate spread on everything. She sat

and we talked and she learned and she read and when Noelle
left her here she was happy. Really happy. And of course"—he
shrugs—"neither of us had any idea that we would never see
her again after she dumped her with me. We thought she'd be
back. And by the time it was clear that she wasn't coming back,
Poppy and I were a team. I genuinely don't think she's suffering
because of not having Noelle in her life. I think . . ." He glances
up at her. "I think it was a blessing."

Laurel's eyes flick to Floyd's and then away again. A thought
passes through her head, so fast and so unpalatable that she is
unable to keep hold of it.

～

Poppy stands at the top of the stairs. She hangs off the banister,
her head tilting at an angle, her hair swinging back and forth.

"Laurel," she says in a stage whisper. "Quick. Come up!"

Laurel looks at her quizzically and then says, "OK."

"Come in here. Quickly!" Poppy pulls her by the hand into
her bedroom.

Laurel has never been into Poppy's bedroom before.

It's a small square room overlooking the garden. She has a
four-poster bed with white muslin curtains and the walls are
painted white. Her duvet cover is white and her curtains are
white with a fine gray stripe. There's a chrome lamp on her
white bedside table and white bookshelves are filled with novels.

"Wow," says Laurel, stepping in, "your room is very minimal."

"Yes," she replies. "I like keeping it all simple. Sit," she says,
pulling out a white wooden desk chair. "Look. My Christmas
present for Dad arrived. Tell me what you think?"

She opens the door of a white wardrobe and pulls out an
Amazon delivery box.

Then she pulls out a large mug with the words "UNBEAR-ABLE COFFEE SNOB" written on it.

"Oh!" says Laurel. "That's fabulous! He'll love it!"

"Because, he is, isn't he? He's ridiculous about coffee. You know that stuff he has to have otherwise he says he'd rather drink water. Grown in Ethiopia with water from angels' tears . . ."

Laurel smiles and says yes, lots of people are a bit weird about coffee these days and she really can't tell the difference and she's the same with wine, it all tastes the same to her unless it's bad and as she's talking her eyes pass across the detail of Poppy's room and she stops and clasps her chest.

"Poppy," she says, getting to her feet, taking a few steps across the room, "where did you get those candlesticks?"

Poppy glances up at the top shelf of her bookshelves where a pair of chunky geometric silver candlesticks are displayed.

"I don't know," she says, "they've always been there."

Laurel reaches to pick one up. It's hugely heavy in her hand, as she'd known it would be. Because they are her candlesticks, the candlesticks taken in the burglary four years after Ellie disappeared, the candlesticks she's always been certain Ellie took.

"I don't really like them," says Poppy. "I think they were Mum's. You can have them if you like."

"No," says Laurel, putting it back on the shelf, her stomach churning over and over. "No. They're yours. You keep them."

49

THEN

Ellie lay on the bed. The moon shone down on her, waxy blue; the foliage outside rustled in a sharp breeze, crackling and popping like distant fireworks. She tried to swing her legs off the bed, but they were too weak. She couldn't remember the last time she'd eaten. Six days ago? Maybe seven?

She was partway to delirium, but still aware on some subliminal, terrifying level that she had been abandoned. She could hear her baby crying upstairs from time to time and an ache would emanate from her heart to every point on her body. But she had no voice to call with and no will to live. Her head was pulsing, aching, sending her strange pictures, flashes of imagery, like scenery lit up at night by strikes of lightning. She saw her mother, stirring a teabag in a mug. She saw her father, zipping up his jacket. She saw Theo, throwing a ball for his little white dog. She saw Noelle, turning over her homework, sliding her glasses up her nose. She saw a house they'd rented in the Isle of Wight one summer. She saw the pale brown pony that stood in a field at the bottom of the garden, eating apples from their hands. She saw Poppy, lying on her back on Ellie's bed, making Os with her tiny red mouth. She saw Hanna, twirling her head around and around, her waist-length ponytail spinning above her head like a propeller. She saw her own funeral. She saw her mother crying. Her father crying. She saw the corpses of her dead hamsters sprinkled on top of her coffin like sods of earth.

She saw herself floating above her coffin.

She saw herself floating higher and higher. Below her she saw her room. Her sofa bed. The grimy, unwashed bedsheets, the tangled knot of duvet. The plastic cages filled with death. The bin overflowing with empty crisp packets. The blocked toilet bowl streaked brown with rust and bacteria.

She crossed her arms across her chest.

She closed her eyes.

She let herself float higher and higher until she could feel the clouds against her skin, until she could feel her mother's arms tight around her, her breath against her cheek.

50

When Poppy was around two or three years old I decided to put my house on the market. You were giving me a little money here and there for her upkeep but I was too proud to ask you for more and, besides, it had never been about money, none of it. But I was poor then, Floyd. Like properly poor. I could only work when Poppy was with you and she was only with you half the time. So I decided to release some equity. We didn't need a big house on three floors. We'd make do in a small flat.

But then of course I remembered the spanner in the works. That girl. That bloody girl.

She'd passed over at some point. I don't know when exactly. It was for the best, I'd say. Yes, it was for the best. According to the papers they'd scaled back the search for her. That to me said they had her as a runaway. So I decided to make it look that way.

⁓

I'd kept the bag she'd been carrying when she first arrived. Which shows, doesn't it, that I'd been half intending to let her go at some point, that I wasn't entirely bad. I took the keys from her bag and when I saw the mother leaving the house with her swimming kit I let myself in through her back door and I took some things that I thought the girl would have taken if she was heading out of the country: a scruffy old laptop, some cash, a pair of candlesticks that she might have wanted to sell. I'd always liked those candlesticks—they'd sat on top of the piano by the table where we worked. I'd admired them once and the girl had said something about taking them on to the *Antiques Roadshow* one day to find out how much they were worth.

I also took a cake. I was reminded when I saw it there of a day when the pleasant mother had brought us two slices of still-warm chocolate cake instead of the posh biscuits and the girl had said, "Is it one of Hanna's?" and the mother had said, "Yes. Freshly baked." And the girl had turned to me and said, "My sister makes the best cakes in the world. You will never eat a better chocolate cake than this." I can't say I can particularly recall the cake or whether or not it was the best in the world, but I do remember the girl's face when she told me that, the anticipation shining in her eyes, the unabashed pleasure she took in the eating of it.

It's odd, you know, because when I look back to those days when I was her tutor I feel sure I must have dreamed the whole thing, because by the end I swear I had no idea what I'd ever seen in her. No idea at all.

She was, after all, just a girl.

⋅◇⋅

I looked everywhere for her passport. The passport was the key to everything. But it could not be found for love or money. And then I had the most brilliant idea. I'd seen her sister when I'd been watching the house and the two girls were very similar to look at. So I went to the sister's bedroom and found her passport in under a minute. I slipped it in the big bag with the computer and the candlesticks and the cake in its Tupperware box and ten minutes later I was home.

It's hard to talk about what came next, because it did require a certain level of barbarity, I must be honest. A few years earlier, when the smell from the basement had become problematic (I had a visit from the next-door neighbors shortly after she passed, asking after it. I told them it was the drains), I'd moved the girl to a blanket box in the attic. So while Poppy stayed the night at yours I took her from there (well, I say "her"; I think "it" would be more accurate by this stage) and I dropped her into the boot of my car along with her rucksack, which I'd packed with the old clothes and the passport, and I drove through the dark of night to Dover. Then I found a quiet lane deep, deep in the middle of nowhere, and I laid some of her bones down in the road and drove my car over them and then I dropped them into a ditch, dropped her rucksack at her side, kicked over some leaves and mud and left, pretty sharpish The rest of her bones I took to a municipal dump a few miles down the road.

I thought she would be found almost immediately. I'd made hardly any effort to hide her. I wanted her found. Wanted it over. Wanted, on some subconscious level, to be caught out. I'd barely given a thought to the forensic aspect of the thing, after all, hadn't thought about the fibers and the tire marks and the like. But months and months passed by and it was as though it had never happened. It seemed I'd got away with it, completely.

Then the London housing market slowed down and I decided against selling my house. Life, as it was, went back to normal.

～

Well, I say normal, but sweet Jesus, what was normal about living with a toddler? And this toddler was a law unto herself. A monster. All she wanted, morning, noon, and night, was sugar. Sugar on her cereal, sugar on her fruit, Nutella on everything;

otherwise she wouldn't eat it. She would not go to sleep at night, and at nursery she was mean to the other children, she'd wallop them and trip them up; I was forever being called in. And then I'd bring her to your house for her weekly stays and she'd be, oh, the perfect little angel. All, Daddy this and Daddy that and at first of course I loved it because she was my route back to you and in that respect it had worked. But then I could see the two of you forming a kind of breakaway team. It was like you and SJ all over again. She'd sit on your lap and she'd twirl your hair and she'd look across at me as if I was *nothing* to her. Less than nothing.

I'd come to collect her from your house sometimes after you'd spent a day together and she'd hide behind your legs. Or hide herself in a room somewhere in the house and refuse to come out.

"I'm not going!" she'd say. "I'm staying here!"

And sometimes I'd think, *fuck it, fuck you both*, and I'd leave and there'd be the two of you, closing the door behind me, going back into your lovely cozy house to do lovely things together. And she ate what you gave her. She'd come home and tell me about stir-fries and crispy prawns and stews from African restaurants. There was no sugar in your house, no junk food, no CBeebies, no cheap electronic toys that made noises that imprinted themselves onto your psyche forevermore. None of the stuff I'd given her to shut her up. Just books and music and trips to the park.

Then one day, and you'll remember this day, Floyd, it was pretty significant, you told me you were thinking about home-schooling Poppy. I'd just filled in the forms on the Internet for a place at our local primary school. But that wasn't good enough apparently: oh no, nothing was good enough for your precious Poppy. Only you, Floyd. Only you.

"My mini-me."

That's what you used to call her.

As though I literally had *nothing whatsoever* to do with the child. And as though only a child who mirrored you in every single respect could possibly be worth loving.

Anyway, you said, "She's very bright. Really very bright. I wouldn't be surprised if she was Mensa level. I don't think a mainstream school is going to know what to do with her. And if I'm going to home-school her, it makes sense for her to come and live with me permanently."

And you know, I think you thought I'd be relieved. I think you thought I'd say, *OK, fabulous, well, that's a weight off my mind.* You knew how hard I found her at home. You knew how much we clashed. And you knew, deep down, that I wasn't a natural-born mother, that I wasn't a nurturer.

But what you didn't know was what I'd done to get that child for you. You had no idea. You had no idea that my life was not a life, not in any real sense of the word, and that the only thing that lit the path for me was you, Floyd. And if you had full custody of Poppy, then, really, what was the use of me? You'd have no reason to see me anymore. You'd have no reason to keep me on the side.

I couldn't let you take Poppy. She was my ticket to you.

We started that conversation like adults and finished it in a red heat.

I knew then that you wouldn't let it go. And a few weeks later you found your moment and you pounced.

༄

I couldn't bear to leave the house with that child half the time. She was a liability in public places. In shops she wanted me to buy her everything. And I mean *everything.* There was no shop that didn't sell something she wanted. And if I didn't get it for her, then I was "mean" and I was "horrible," and she'd scream the place down. So I learned to do all my errands when she was at the nursery. But that afternoon I remembered that I needed ketchup—not for me, mind, oh no, I could live without ketchup without having an epileptic fit, but Madam couldn't. So I left her. I was gone for ten minutes. Possibly fifteen.

She had climbed up onto the work surface in the kitchen, looking for food—*of course*, because she might die if she didn't eat something for ten minutes—and she'd fallen and bashed her head against the corner of the unit and there was a cut and there was some blood and I called the 111 number and they told me what to look out for and when to bring her in if necessary and I *did everything right, Floyd, everything*. I behaved like a proper decent parent. But of course the next time she saw you she had a huge black eye and she was all wan and bruised and oh, Mummy went out and left me and I was hungry and I just wanted some cereal, that was all, and blah blah blah. And you turned to me and you said, "That's it, Noelle. That is it."

And I knew what you meant and I knew it was going to happen. So that was when I decided. Me and Poppy. We were going away. And if you wanted us back, you'd have to come and find us.

⁓

I had it all planned out. I would take my bonny, brown-eyed girl back to Ireland! My mother and father would be *captivated*! All my brothers would say, *Well, look at the child, sure if she isn't the prettiest Donnelly in a generation*. And after a few weeks I'd phone you to tell you where we were and you would get on the first plane into Dublin and you'd see me there in the bold green light of the Emerald Isle, in the bosom of my family, our child with cheeks like rose blossoms, and I'd take you to see the perfect little village school where we went ourselves when we were small and you'd meet my mother and father, the cleverest people I know, and my brothers with their huge brains, and you'd see the shelves in their big Victorian villa heaving with the books and the trophies and the shields and you'd know that I'd done the best for my child, that she was in the best place and that you could not take her, not now that she was so happy and so settled, cousins all around, the sheep and the sea and the sweet meadow air.

In this fantasy, you would decide to stay. You'd rent a small windswept cottage and eventually, because we were all so happy and everything was so perfect, you'd ask us to move in with you. And that was how we'd end our days. The three of us together. The perfect family.

51

"Where did Poppy get those candlesticks? The silver ones in her bedroom?"

Floyd looks up at Laurel from the newspaper. It's Tuesday morning and they're having breakfast. Laurel nearly didn't stay last night. She'd nearly said she had a headache and wanted to sleep in her own bed. But something kept her here: the promise of a shared bottle of wine, the proximity to Poppy, unanswered questions.

"The art deco ones?"

"Yes. On her bookshelves."

"Oh, I found those at Noelle's when I went to collect Poppy's things. Lovely, aren't they?"

She draws in her breath and smiles tightly. "I used to have a pair," she says, "just like that."

"I did wonder if they might be worth something. That's why I took them. And it was strange because Noelle literally had *nothing*. All her stuff, all of it, just tat. Yet she had those. Genuine art deco I'd say they were. I meant to get them valued, but I never got around to it."

Laurel keeps smiling. "The pair I had were definitely worth a fair bit. Some friends bought them for us, for a wedding present, said they'd got them at an auction. These friends were incredibly wealthy and they suggested that we should get them insured, but we never did."

She leaves that there, between them, waiting to see what Floyd does with it.

"Well, there you go then," he says, smiling tightly. "Maybe Noelle did manage to leave Poppy something worth having after all."

"But, what about her house? Doesn't that belong to Poppy? Technically?"

"Noelle's house? No, she didn't own her house. It was rented."

"Was it? I thought . . ." Laurel stops herself. She's not supposed to know anything about Noelle's house. "I don't know, I just assumed she would have owned it. And what about Noelle's family? Did you ever meet them? Did they ever meet Poppy?"

"No," says Floyd. "Noelle didn't have much of a family. Or at least not one she told me about. It's possible they were estranged. It's possible they were dead. She might have had a dozen brothers and sisters for all I know." He sighs. "Nothing would surprise me about that woman. Nothing."

She nods, slowly digesting Floyd's lie. "And when you went to her house to get Poppy's things, what was it like? Was it nice?"

Floyd shudders slightly. "Grim," he says. "Really grim. Cold and bare and uncomfortable. Poppy's room looked like a room in a Romanian orphanage. It had this really weird wallpaper. Everything was painted Pepto-Bismol pink. And my God, Laurel, the worst thing, the worst thing of all . . ."

His eyes find hers and he licks his lips. "I've never told anyone this before because it was so bleak and so sick and so . . ."—he shudders again—". . . *depraved*. But in her cellar she had been hoarding hamsters or gerbils or something. God knows what. Mice maybe. In cages stacked one on top of the other. Must have been about twenty of them. And a dozen in each cage. And all of them were dead. The *smell*. Jesus Christ." He blinks away the memory. "I mean, seriously, what sort of woman, what sort of *human* . . . ?"

Laurel shakes her head, widening her eyes in faux wonder. "That's horrible," she says, "that really is."

Floyd sighs. "Poor sick woman," he says. "Poor, poor individual."

"Sounds like the only good thing she ever did was to give birth to Poppy."

He glances at her and then down at his lap. His eyes are dark and haunted. "Yes," he says. "I suppose it was."

52

I kept you very sweet in those days after our big contretemps. I made all the right noises about Poppy coming to live with you, pretended I was "giving it some thought," said that I could "see the advantages." But all the while I was painstakingly planning our escape.

It was your turn to have her overnight and I'd packed all our bags ready for our journey to Dublin, filled the car with petrol so we wouldn't have to stop. My mother was expecting us on the 9 a.m. ferry the following day. I thought I was so clever, I really did.

But I'd underestimated you. You'd worked out what was going on. Poppy wasn't there when I came for her that evening. You'd taken her to stay at someone's house. You were ready for me.

"Come in," you said, "please. We need to talk."

Were there ever four more terrifying words in the English language?

You sat me down in the kitchen. I sat in the same chair I'd used that perfect day when I first brought Poppy to meet you. I remembered how your kitchen had swallowed me up like a womb then. But that afternoon, your kitchen broke my heart. I knew what you were going to say. I knew it.

"I've been thinking," you said, "about Poppy. About arrangements. Going forward. And it can't go on like this. And to be horribly, horribly frank with you, Noelle, I fear for her, living with you. I think . . ."

Here it came. Here it came.

"I think you're toxic."

Toxic.

Dear Jesus.

"And this is about much more than home-schooling, Noelle. This is about everything. Did you know that Poppy hates you? She's told me that. Not just once. Not just when she's cross with you. But often. She's scared of you. She doesn't . . ." You looked up at me, eyes full of cool guilt. "She doesn't like the way you smell. She's said that to me. And that . . . that's not normal, Noelle. A child should not be able to differentiate between their own smell and the smell of their mother at this stage. That, to me, suggests a terrible, fundamental disconnect between you both; it suggests a failure to bond. And I've been talking to a social worker about what my options are and she said that I should take Poppy out of the picture for now, just while we thrash this out, so she's gone to stay with a friend. Just for a few days . . ."

"Friend?" I said cynically. "What friend? You don't have any friends."

"It doesn't matter what friend. But we really need to reach an agreement on this, civilly, before Poppy comes home. So I'm asking you, Noelle, as Poppy's mother, could you . . ."

You struggled for the words here, I recall.

"Could you let her go? Please? You could still see her. Of course you could. But it would have to be under supervision. It would have to be here. And it would have to fit in with Poppy's education."

I struggled for words then, too. It wasn't so much what you were saying—though that was bad enough—as the tone in which you were saying it. There was no *oh, I'm terribly sorry, Noelle, but I've passed your child onto strangers and now I want you to fuck off away from us.* There was no sense in the tone of your voice that what you were saying was anything other than entirely reasonable.

Finally I said, "No. No, Floyd. I won't allow it. I want my child back. And I want her back right now. You have *no right*. No right whatsoever. She's my child and—"

You put your hand up then. You said, "Yes. I know that. But, Noelle, you have to accept the fact that you're not strong enough to be a parent. The way you're raising her, the junk food and the TV on all day and the lack of physical affection. Not to mention leaving her alone in the house, Noelle. It's verging on abuse, and that's exactly how a team of social workers would see it. Poppy's teeth are appalling. She has nits half the time that you simply don't deal with. You're not well. In the head, Noelle. You're *not well*. And you're not fit to be a parent."

And there. There it was. The defining moment of all the defining moments.

Everything in my head splintered. I saw that girl's bones laid out in front of me on a dark road in Dover, my headlights shining over the bumps of them, my foot against the gas pedal. I thought of what I'd allowed myself to become, for you. I never wanted that bloody child. I only wanted you. And I looked at you then, so calm and reasonable, and I knew you hated me and you wanted me gone and I wanted to hurt you, I wanted to really hurt you so I said to you, "What makes you so sure she's your child, Floyd? Did you never wonder why she looks so little like either of us?"

Your face was worth the horror of me showing myself to you, it really was.

"She doesn't belong to either of us, Floyd," I said, feeling the twist of my words into your heart. "I made her for you, with another woman's womb and another man's sperm."

The words were falling from me uncontrollably. I'd nothing left to lose. "She's a Frankenstein's monster, Floyd, that child you so adore. She's barely human, in fact."

"Noelle, I don't—"

I spoke over you, desperate to answer your questions before you asked them, desperate to take control. "A girl called Ellie had that baby for me. I was never pregnant, you dumb idiot. How could you have thought I was, you with your big, *brilliant* brain? Ellie had that baby. She was the mother. And the father was some stranger on the Internet selling his sperm for fifty pounds a shot."

Oh come on now, Floyd. You didn't honestly think that child could be yours, did you? That glorious golden thing? That she could be formed from your tired old genes? Really? Didn't you wonder? Didn't you think? No, Floyd. Poppy's father was a young, young man, a PhD student. The website I bought his sperm from said he was under thirty, that he was six foot one with green eyes and dark hair. I pictured Ellie's boyfriend when I picked him out. I pictured Theo. And then I came to you in my satin shirt and high heels and seduced you in a way that you'd be sure to remember. The whole thing was a total scam, Floyd. And you fell for it, you feckless, bollockless, soulless shit. You totally fell for it.

"Well, you can keep her, you scumbag. Keep her and pay for her and know for the rest of your life every time you look at her that she's nothing but a big bag of cells and other people's DNA. Good luck to you both."

I had my handbag by its strap. I was done. It was over. The splinters in my head were spinning so fast and so wildly I could barely remember my own name. But I felt euphoric.

And then I watched your face turn to stormy skies, saw your skin color change from gray to seething purple. You leaped to your feet; then you threw yourself bodily across the table at me. You had your hands at my throat and my chair tumbled backward with me still in it; my head hit the floor and by God I thought you meant to kill me, by God, I really, really did.

53

Laurel drives past Hanna's flat on her way from Floyd's to work that morning. She's hoping for a sneaky glimpse of Theo and Hanna leaving for work together. But it's dark and quiet and at least now Laurel can picture where her daughter has been. She has been in Theo Goodman's bed.

Theo is a schoolteacher now. Hanna had told her that, funnily enough, about a year ago. Said she'd bumped into him somewhere or other. Laurel couldn't really remember the details. That must have been when it started, she supposed.

Laurel is unfairly horrified by this twist in the fabric of things.

Theo was Ellie's. He'd belonged to her and she'd belonged to him. They'd inhabited each other completely, like a pair of gloves folded into itself. And now she is cross with Hanna. Cross enough to wonder what Theo even sees in Hanna, in comparison to Ellie. She imagines, in the warped threads of her irrational thought processes, that Theo chose Hanna as a consolation prize.

But then she remembers seeing that blonde girl coming out of the supermarket on Sunday morning, that smiling, golden girl who looked nothing like the sour-faced girl who greets Laurel at her door from time to time, the pinched child who never laughs at her jokes, the tired-looking woman who sighs down the phone at the sound of her mother's voice.

And it occurs to her for the very first time that maybe Hanna isn't intrinsically unhappy.

That maybe she just doesn't like her.

◇

She calls Paul later that afternoon. He's at work and she can hear the warm rumble of normality in the background.

"Listen," she says, "can I ask you something? About Hanna?"

There's a beat of silence before Paul says, "Yes."

He knows, thinks Laurel, he already knows.

"Has she said anything to you about a boyfriend?"

There's another silence. "Yes, she has."

She exhales. "How long have you known?"

"A few months," he replies.

"And you know—you know who it is?"

"Yes. Yes, I do."

Laurel closes her eyes. "And she told you not to tell me?"

"Yes. Something like that."

Now Laurel pauses. "Paul," she says after a moment, "do you think that Hanna hates me?"

"*What?* No. Of course she doesn't hate you. Hanna doesn't hate anyone. Why would you say that?"

"It's just, whenever we're together she's so . . . spiky. And cold. And I've always put it down to arrested development— you know, losing Ellie when she was just on the cusp of adult life. But I saw her the other day, with Theo. And she was so bright and so happy. She looked like a completely different person."

"Well, yes, she is madly in love, by all accounts."

"But when she's with you, and Bonny, what's she like then? Is she lighthearted? Is she fun?"

"Yes. I'd say she is. On the whole."

"So, I'm right, you see. It *is* me. She can't stand being with me."

"I'm sure that's not true."

"It is true, Paul. You've never seen it. You've never seen what she's like with me when it's just the two of us. She's like a . . . a *void*. There's nothing there. Just this blank stare. What did I do, Paul? What did I do wrong?"

She hears Paul take a breath. "Nothing," he says. "You did nothing wrong. But I'd say, well, it wasn't just Ellie she lost, was it? It was you, too."

"Me?"

"Yes. You. You went kind of—off radar. You stopped cooking. You stopped—you stopped being a parent."

"I know, Paul! I know I did! And I've apologized to Hanna a million times for the way I was then. Why do you think I go to her house every week and clean it for her? I try so hard with her, Paul. I try all the time and it makes no difference."

"Laurel," he says carefully, "I think what Hanna really needs from you is your forgiveness."

"Forgiveness?" she echoes. "Forgiveness for what?"

There is a long moment of silence as Paul forms his response.

"Forgiveness . . ." he says finally, "for not being Ellie."

❧

Paul's words have unfurled a whole roll of thoughts and feelings that Laurel hadn't known were so tightly wound inside her and she is plunged straight back into the minutes and hours following Ellie's disappearance, recalling the sour resentment at being left with Hanna, denying her the lasagna that Ellie had staked her claim on, as Ellie had staked her claim on so much in their family. Everyone had fought for Ellie's attention, for a blast of her golden light. Then the light had gone and they'd dissipated like death stars falling away from the sun.

And yes, Laurel had never accepted Hanna as a consolation prize. She really hadn't. And as a result she'd got the relationship with her daughter that she deserved. Well, now she knows this, she can work on it and make things better.

Laurel calls Hanna. It goes through to voicemail, as she'd known it would. But this can't wait another moment. She needs to say it right now.

"Darling," she says, "I just wanted to say, I am so proud of you. You are the most extraordinary girl in the world and I am so lucky to have you in my life. And I also wanted to say that I'm sorry, so sorry if anything I've ever done has made you feel like less than the center of my world. Because you are, you are absolutely the center of my world and I could not live without you. And"—she draws in her breath slightly—"I wanted to say that I saw you the other day, I saw you with Theo, and I think it's wonderful and I think he's a very, very lucky man. A very lucky man indeed. Anyway, that's what I wanted to say and I'm sorry I haven't said it before and I love you and I'll see you on Christmas Eve. I love you. Bye."

She turns off her phone and she rests it on the kitchen counter and feels a wave of relief and weightlessness pass through her. She is unburdened of something she hadn't even known she was carrying.

54

When Laurel arrives at Floyd's house that evening she feels lighter, more present, in the moment. And she notices for the first time that although there are only three days till Christmas, there is no tree in the house. In fact, there are no decorations of any kind.

"Do you not do Christmas trees?" she asks as Floyd helps her off with her coat in the hallway.

"*Do* Christmas trees?"

"Yes, do you not put one up?"

"No," he says. "Well, we used to, but we haven't for years. But we can if you want one. Do you want one? I'll go and get one now."

She laughs. "I was thinking more of Poppy," she says.

"Pops!" he calls up the stairs. "Would you like a Christmas tree?"

They hear her footsteps, loud and fast. She appears at the top of the stairs and says, "Yes! Yes please!"

"Right then," says Floyd. "That's settled then. I will go out now, like a proper father, and I will bring home the mother of all Christmas trees. Want to come with me, Pops?"

"Yes! Let me just get my shoes on."

"We'll need fairy lights," says Laurel, "and baubles. Have you got any?"

"Yes, yes, we do. In the attic. We always had a tree when

Kate and Sara lived here. There's boxes of the stuff up there. Let me go and get it."

He bounds up the stairs two at a time and returns a few minutes later with two large paper shopping bags full of tree decorations. Then he and Poppy get into the car and disappear into the dark night together and Laurel looks around and realizes that she is alone in Floyd's house for the very first time.

She turns on the TV and finds a satellite channel that is playing Christmas songs. Then she pulls some things from the bags; *random* is the word she'd use to describe them. Scuffed plastic balls, a knitted reindeer with three legs, a huge spiky snowflake that snags a hole in her jumper, stern-faced wooden soldiers, and a group of slightly alternative-looking wood nymphs in pointy hats with curled toes on their shoes.

She leaves them in the bag and takes out the fairy lights. There are two sets: one multicolored and the other white. The white ones work when she plugs them in at the wall. The multicolored ones don't.

She goes through some of the drawers in the kitchen, looking for a spare fuse. She looks in the drawers in the console table in the hallway. Takeaway menus, parking permits, spare keys, a roll of garden refuse bags. But no fuses.

Then she looks at the door to Floyd's study. This is where he and Poppy do their home-learning together, where he writes his books and his papers. In her own version of this house, they'd knocked through from the front to the back to make a double reception. But Floyd has left the two rooms separate, as they would have been in Victorian times. She hasn't been in Floyd's study yet, just viewed it fleetingly as he's walked in or out. She feels, quite strongly, although she's not sure why, that Floyd would not want her in his study without his permission, so she stands for a moment or two, her hand on the doorknob, persuading herself that it is just another room in the house, that Floyd cannot live without her, that of course she can go into his study to look for fuses.

She turns the handle.

The door opens.

Floyd's study is well furnished and cozy. The floorboards are covered over with threadbare kilims. The furniture is solid and old; there are two chrome table lamps with arced necks, one with a green glass shade, the other white. A laptop is open on his desk showing a screen saver of changing landscapes. She quickly starts to sift through his drawers.

Pens, notebooks, foreign coins, computer disks, CDs, memory sticks, everything organized in internal compartments. She goes to another desk, one that sits by the back window overlooking the garden. Here the drawers are locked. She sighs and absentmindedly riffles through the piles of paper that sit on top of the desk. She is no longer looking for a fuse, she knows that. She's looking for something to snap her out of the strange fug she's been trapped in for the past few days.

And suddenly she has it in her hands. A pile of newspaper cuttings, all from around the time of the *Crimewatch* appeal on May 26. There's her face, there's Paul, and there's Ellie. There's the interview she did for the *Guardian* and the interview she and Paul did together in the local paper. She remembers Floyd in his kitchen coyly confessing to having googled her after their first date. Yet six months earlier, before he'd even met her, he'd been tearing out and collecting newspaper cuttings about Ellie's disappearance. She slots the cuttings back into the pile of paperwork at the sound of a car door closing on the street outside and quickly leaves Floyd's study.

Floyd and Poppy return a moment later. The have bought an eight-foot tree.

"Well," says Floyd, his cheeks flushed pink with the effort of getting it into the house, balancing it on its stump briefly so that Laurel can appreciate its great height. "Will this fulfill the brief?"

"Wow," says Laurel, pressing herself against the wall so that Floyd can negotiate it through the hallway and into the sitting room. "That is a tree and a half. We're going to need more lights!"

"Ta-da!" Poppy appears behind him, clutching bags from a DIY store full of fairy lights.

"Brilliant," says Laurel. "You thought of everything."

The TV is still tuned into Christmas songs; "Stop the Cavalry" by Jona Lewie is playing.

Floyd cuts the netting around the tree and they all watch as the branches spring free. Floyd is strangely overexcited about the tree. "Hey," he says, turning to Poppy and Laurel, "it's a good one, huh? I got a good one?"

They both assure him that it is a good one. Then Poppy and Laurel begin to dress the tree while Floyd goes to the kitchen to prepare supper.

"So, you don't normally bother with a tree?" Laurel asks.

"No," says Poppy. "I don't really know why. We're just not a Christmassy kind of family, I guess."

"But Sara-Jade and her mum? They do a tree?"

"Yes!" Poppy's eyes light up. "Kate is *mad* about Christmas. Totally nuts about it. Their house looks like a Christmas card." She catches herself. "It's a bit much, really," she finishes.

"Sounds lovely to me."

Poppy smiles then and says, "Will there be a tree at Bonny's house? On Christmas Eve?"

"Oh, God, yes. I'm sure there will be. Definitely. A big one probably."

Poppy smiles broadly. "I can't wait," she says. "It'll be nice to have a proper Christmas for a change."

"What do you normally do on Christmas Day?"

"Nothing much, really. Have lunch. Swap presents. Watch a movie."

"Just the two of you?"

Poppy nods.

"You don't see family?"

"I haven't got a family."

"You've got SJ."

"Yes, but she's just one person. I mean like a whole big family. Like yours. I sometimes wish . . ." She glances toward the sitting-room door and then lowers her voice. "I love being with Dad. But I sometimes wish there was more."

"More what?"

Poppy shrugs. "More people, I suppose. More noise."

They take a step back from the tree a while later, just as "Fairytale of New York" comes on the TV. The tree is fully dressed and Laurel has switched on the fairy lights.

Floyd comes in and gasps. "Ladies," he says, putting an arm around each of their shoulders, "that is a *triumph*. An absolute triumph." He turns off the overhead lights and then turns back to the tree. "Wow! Just look at it!"

The three of them stand like that for a moment or two, the Pogues playing in the background, the lights on the tree flashing on and off; Floyd's arm is heavy across Laurel's shoulders and she feels him tremble slightly. She looks up at him and sees that he is crying. A single tear rolls down his cheek, a thousand tiny Christmas lights refracted through it. He wipes it away and then smiles down at Laurel.

"Thank you," he said. "I didn't know how much I wanted a Christmas tree this year." He leans down and kisses the crown of her head. "You," he said, "have made everything perfect. I love you, Laurel. I really do."

She stares at him in surprise. Not that he has said it, but that he has said it in front of Poppy.

She glances quickly at Poppy to gauge her reaction. She is smiling at Laurel, willing her to complete the moment. She has no idea how hard this is for Laurel. But they are both gazing at her, waiting for her to give them something, and it is Christmas and it is dark and for some reason Laurel feels that she must do this, that it is hugely important in some strangely sinister way she can't quite define, and so she smiles and says, "And I love you both, too."

Poppy pulls Laurel into a hug. Floyd follows suit. They hold each other for a moment or two, the three of them, the heat of their combined breath meeting in the heart of the embrace. Eventually they pull apart and Floyd smiles at Laurel and says, "That's all I want for Christmas. That's all I want. Full stop."

Laurel smiles tightly. She thinks of the press cuttings on Floyd's desk. She thinks of the carrot cake they'd shared in that café near her hairdresser, the overpowering certainty of him as he'd walked in the door and found his way to her. And then she thinks of the phone call from Blue.

Your boyfriend. His aura is all wrong. It's dark.

And she feels it, right there and then. Stark and obvious. Something askew. Something awry.

You're not who you say you are, she suddenly thinks, *you're a fake.*

55

Laurel's mother is still alive when Laurel pops in to see her the next day on her way to work.

"Still here then?" she asks, pulling her chair closer to her mother's.

Ruby rolls her eyes.

"You know it's Christmas Day on Friday," she says. "You can't go and die before Christmas and ruin it for everyone. You do know that? If you were going to do it, you should have done it last week."

Ruby chuckles and says, "Next week?"

"Yes," says Laurel, smiling. "Next week is fine. It's always a quiet time."

She takes her mother's hands and says, "We're having a big Christmas Eve do. At Paul and Bonny's. Hanna will be there. Jake. My new boyfriend. His daughter. I wish you could come."

"No thank you," says Ruby, and Laurel laughs.

"No," she says. "I don't blame you."

"How is n-n-new b-boyfriend?"

The smile freezes on Laurel's face. She doesn't know how to answer the question so she smiles and says, "He's wonderful. It's all good."

But as the words leave her mouth, she can feel the heavy lie of them.

Her mother feels it, too. "Good?" she repeats, concernedly.

"Yes," she says. "Good."

Her mother nods, just once.

"If you say so," she says. "If you say so."

◌◌

Laurel calls Jake when she leaves her mother's care home.

He picks up the call within two ringtones. "Mum," he says, a note of concern in his voice.

"Everything's fine," she says. "Not an emergency. I just wanted to say hello."

"I'm really sorry, Mum," he starts immediately. "I'm really sorry about me and Blue and what we said to you the other day. It was out of order."

"No, Jake, honestly. It's fine. I'm sorry I overreacted. I think I was just so shocked to find myself in a relationship after so long I was a bit raw. Just wanted everything to be perfect. You know. And of course nothing's perfect, is it?"

"No," says Jake in a voice full of things he'd like to say but can't. "No. That's true."

"Am I seeing you tomorrow?" she says. "At Bonny's?"

"Yes," he replies. "We'll be there."

"You know Floyd will be there too? Will that be a problem?"

"No," he says, overly assured, she feels. "No. It will be fine."

She takes a breath, ready to get to the point of her call. "Is Blue there?" she says. "I wondered if we could have a word?"

"Yeah," says Jake. "Yeah. She's here. You're not going to . . . ?"

"No. I told you, Jake. Water under the bridge. I just want to ask her something."

"OK."

She hears him call out to Blue, who comes to the phone and says, "Hi, Laurel. How are you?"

"I'm good, thank you, Blue. I'm fine. How are you?"

"Oh, you know. Busy, busy. As always."

There's a pause and then Laurel says, "Listen, Blue, I wanted to apologize for the way I reacted last time we spoke. I think I may have been a little over the top."

She can almost hear Blue shrug. "Don't worry about it."

"No, really. I'm sorry. And I just . . . I've been . . . I don't know. I suppose I just wanted to know more about why you thought what you thought when you met him."

"You feel it, too."

Laurel blanches and brings her hand to her throat. She feels horribly caught out. "No," she says, "no. It's —I just want to know what you think, that's all."

Blue sighs and continues. "Floyd has a dark aspect. Very dark. Dangerous, almost. But the discrepancy between his true self and the way he presents himself is striking. It's like he's taking cues from people. Working out how to be. And then there's the way he is with his daughter. It's not quite right. He watches her all the time, did you know that? You can almost see him prompting her under his breath. Like she's acting, too, and he's there to stop her making a mistake, to stop her exposing him for what he is. I don't think . . ." She pauses. "I don't think he really loves her. Not in the normal sense of the word. I think it's more that he needs her, because she makes him human. She's like a cloak."

Laurel nods and makes an affirmative noise, although she is still processing what Blue has said.

"But what you just said, about him being dangerous. What do you mean by that?"

"I mean," says Blue, "that a man who can't love but desperately needs to be loved is a dangerous thing indeed. And I think Floyd is dangerous because he's pretending to be someone he's not in order to get you to love him."

Laurel shudders at Blue's words. They chime so completely with her own feelings yesterday standing by the Christmas tree.

"What about Poppy?" she says. "What did you make of Poppy?"

"Poppy is like a rainbow. Poppy is everything. But she needs to get away from her father before he starts taking her colors away."

There is a long pause. Then Laurel says, "Thank you, Blue. Thank you for your time." She slowly slides her phone into her handbag and drives to work feeling slightly numb.

56

When Laurel gets to the office she finds she's the only one not wearing a Christmas jumper.

"Was there a memo?" she asks Helen.

"Yes," says Helen, who is wearing a jumper with flashing fairy lights somehow built into it and has red baubles hanging from her earrings. "Last week. It should be in your inbox."

Laurel sighs. She's sure it was. She's sure she must have read it. And then edited it out somewhere in the tangles of her life.

"Here." Helen throws her a piece of tinsel. "Put this in your hair."

Laurel twists the tinsel into her hair and smiles. "Thank you."

There are carolers in the shopping center today; she can hear them from her desk. They're singing "Good King Wenceslas." The management have invested in a job lot of mince pies from Waitrose and at 5 p.m. there'll be Secret Santa and sherry.

She can't wait to get home.

She goes into Waitrose on her way to her car that night, buys two bottles of champagne, two scented candles, and two boxes of chocolates. She'll work out what to give to whom tonight when she's wrapping them.

Everywhere she goes that day she hears Blue's words of doom echoing portentously around her head. When she'd been talking to Blue this morning she'd fully believed all she'd said. Yes, she'd thought, yes, this all makes perfect sense. Of course Floyd has a dark aspect. Of course he's pretending to be someone he's not.

But as the hours pass and Floyd sends her silly, festive text messages adorned with Santa Claus emojis and bunches of holly, as the carolers' repertoire sinks into her psyche and the sherry softens the edges of her consciousness, her fingers push the blades of the scissors back and forth through the shiny paper on her living-room floor, and the lights of the neighbors' Christmas trees flash their reflections on to her windows, it starts to seem bizarre and dreadful.

What a strange girl Blue is, she thinks to herself, turning off her lights, slipping off her clothes, untwirling the tinsel from her hair. What a very strange girl indeed.

57

Laurel rises late on Christmas Eve. She has two text messages from Floyd, one asking what to bring for Paul and Bonny, the other asking what to wear. She types in a reply: *Bring them cheese. The smellier the better. And wear a nice jumper and a festive persona. I'm wearing green.*

He replies immediately: *So, green cheese and a smelly jumper. I'm on it* ☺.

Silly bugger, she replies.

And then she has a shower.

When she gets out of the shower there is another message from him. *Could you come here first do you think? I have a gift for you, but it's too big to bring to the party.*

She feels a blade of dread pass through her. She's unsettled by his excitement about his gift to her. She's never been a fan of grand gestures. But more than that, she feels strange about this last-minute change of plans. Blue's words come back to her again: "A man who can't love but desperately needs to be loved is a dangerous thing indeed." She remembers Floyd's lies about Noelle Donnelly's house, about her family. She thinks of Noelle's flat stomach at eight months pregnant and she thinks of the lip balm in Noelle Donnelly's basement. And then she thinks of the press cuttings in Floyd's study and the candlesticks in Poppy's bedroom and she knows, she knows without a doubt that Floyd is bringing her to his house for some ulterior purpose.

She texts Paul and she texts Hanna.

I'm going to Floyd's on my way to Bonny's but I won't be late. If I am late please call me immediately. If I don't answer my phone please send someone to come for me. I'll be at 18 Latymer Road N4. I'll explain everything later.

Then she flicks back to Floyd's text.

OK, she types back. *No problem. I'll come over when I'm ready.*

Fantastic, he replies. *See you soon!*

She loads her car with wrapped gifts and champagne and leaves for Floyd's house at 11 a.m.

A text arrives from Hanna.

Mum?

She doesn't reply.

The roads are busy and slow. People pour out of the cinema at High Barnet, the high street is packed with shoppers, and there is a long-suffering reindeer in Highgate being petted by a crowd of children while a glowering Father Christmas tries to control them.

As she approaches Stroud Green Laurel feels a lump form in the back of her throat. Every street corner, shop front, and side road here holds a memory of Christmases past. The annual pilgrimage for pizzas on Christmas Eve, where they pre-booked the same table every year. The last-minute run down to the pound shop on the high street for extra wrapping paper. The little park at the bottom of the road where they used to take the children after lunch to let off steam. The neighbors' doors that Laurel and the children would post cards through on Christmas morning.

All of those messy Christmases, each a perfect gem, all gone, all turned to ash.

She pulls into Floyd's road and turns off her ignition.

And then she stops for a moment, sits in her car, feeling the air chill as the heater dies down, watching the wind whip the bare branches of the trees overhead, waiting to feel ready to face Floyd.

Five minutes later she takes a deep breath, and heads toward his front door.

PART FIVE

58

Laurel Mack.

My God, what a woman.

Dazzling.

I could not believe that this woman was allowing me to put my hands upon her. That she was in my house. In my bed

She smelled like five star hotels. Her hair, under my fingertips, was like a satin sheet. Her skin was smooth and gleamed under the light. She tasted of icy winter mornings when my mouth was on hers. She held the back of my head hard against hers, those pretty hands entwined in my hair. She laughed when I joked. She smiled when I called her name. She spent an entire weekend in my home. And then another. She told her dying mother about me. She let me join her for a family birthday celebration. She sought their approval and she got it. She took my daughter shopping. She cupped my buttocks as she passed me on the stairs. She woke up with her head on my chest and she changed into my clothes and walked barefoot through my house and drank coffee out of my mugs and parked her car on my street and kept coming back and coming back and every time she came back she was better than I remembered and every time I saw her she was more beautiful than I remembered and I spent every waking hour in a state of raw disbelief that a woman like her would want to be with a man like me.

But now it is Christmas Eve and I am sitting in my living room trussed up in a Paul Smith jumper and a pair of trousers that are slightly too tight on me. Poppy is in her room wrapping gifts and choosing clothes. And Laurel is parked in her car on the street outside and I can see the serious set of her face from my front window; I can see the way her jaw sits a millimeter offset, the slow blink of her eyelids as she finds the strength to come into my home. Because I know and now she knows it, too.

I am not the man she thought I was.

The doorbell rings and I go to my door.

59

Floyd greets Laurel with a kiss on each cheek. She smiles brightly and says, "You look lovely. Really Christmassy."

And he does. He looks handsome and jolly. The holly green of his jumper suits him. But under her chest her heart races, her breath comes tight and hard.

"And you look beautiful as ever. I love your jacket."

"Thank you." Laurel runs her hands down the silk velvet and forces another smile. "Where's Poppy?"

"Upstairs," says Floyd. "Wrapping your gift."

"Oh, bless her."

"Come in." He ushers her into the kitchen. "Come. I've got a bottle of champagne chilling. Can I interest you in a Buck's Fizz?"

Laurel nods. A small drink will calm her nerves.

Floyd seems tense, too, she notices, not his usual effortless self. She watches him closely as he pours her drink, checks that the glass is fresh from the cupboard, that he doesn't hide it from view as he pours in first the champagne and then the orange juice.

He raises a toast.

"To you," says Floyd. "To wonderful extraordinary you. You are the most remarkable person, I think, that I have ever known. I am honored to call you a friend. Cheers, Laurel Mack. Cheers."

Laurel smiles tightly. She feels that she should reciprocate in some way. But all she can think of to say is, "Cheers. You're pretty fab, too." Which sounds utterly pathetic.

She glances upward to the ceiling. "Is Poppy coming down?" she says, her voice catching nervously on the last word.

Floyd smiles at her. "Should be," he replies simply. "Should be."

"Here." She hands him the bag with his gift in it. "You may as well have this now. Save taking it to Bonny's."

He opens the shaving mirror and he makes all the right noises and all the right gestures. And then he comes toward her with his arms outstretched and she flinches as he hugs her, feels her breath catch, adrenaline pulsing through her. She is ready to push him from her, ready to escape. She can't imagine that she'd ever found this man's touch pleasing. She can't imagine she'd ever found this man anything other than terrifying.

"Here," he says, handing her an envelope. "Open that first. I'm just popping out to my car to get your other gift."

"Oh," she says, "OK."

He stops in the doorway and looks at her. A small smile plays on his lips.

"Good-bye," he says.

She hears the front door open and close.

⌘

The house, now that Floyd has gone, is completely silent.

She glances down at the card in front of her and she opens it.

It has a picture on the front of a dove in flight. It is strangely un-Christmassy.

Inside the card is a letter. She begins to read:

Laurel,

I sense that you are tiring of me. I sense that you have worked out what a hundred women before you have worked out. That I'm not the man for them.

That is fine. Because I have worked out that I am not worthy
of you. And that I must let you go. And before I let you go, I must
also unburden myself of an appalling, unthinkable truth. I have
something of yours. It was not given to me; rather, bequeathed to
me in a terrible sequence of events. I need you to know that when I
first came into possession of this precious thing, it had been horribly
abused by another person and for five years I have tended and cared
for this possession. I have polished it and nurtured it.

And now it is time to return it to you. I am glad we had this time
together. Time for you to see me not as a monster but as a normal
man. A man worthy of your affections. If only for a few short weeks.
It has been an extraordinary experience for me after so many years in
an emotional wasteland. A precious gift. I cannot thank you enough.
And I am glad you have had a chance to get to know me, to hopefully
view me as a man capable of being trusted with your most precious
possession.

My study door is unlocked. On my desktop computer I have left you
a video message. Simply press play and I will explain everything.

Yours, always and in good faith,
Floyd Dunn

Laurel rests the card on the table and looks through the
kitchen door. Slowly she walks toward Floyd's study. She sits in
Floyd's chair and grasps the mouse tentatively. As she touches it
the screen comes to life, and there is Floyd, dressed in the same
jumper he wore this morning, his face paused in an expression
of terrible grief. She clicks the play button and she watches his
confession.

60

Laurel, there are so many things I want you to know. But the first is this: when I walked into that café in November, when I chose the table next to yours, when I complimented you on your hair and invited you to share my cake, I was not trying to seduce you. You were far too beautiful and far too delicate and I would never have been so presumptuous.

Everything that happened after that meeting was entirely unexpected, and, I can see now, with hindsight, horribly, horribly selfish.

Earlier this year I switched on the TV to watch the news and there was a trailer for the show coming up afterward. *Crimewatch*. Not a show I'd normally watch. Not my thing at all. But they said they'd be staging a reconstruction of the disappearance of a girl called Ellie Mack and then a picture of Ellie Mack appeared on the screen and my heart stopped. The missing girl looked exactly like Poppy. Older than Poppy. But exactly like her.

So I sat and I watched the show.

"It's been ten years since Ellie Mack, a fifteen-year-old from north London, disappeared on her way to the library," the presenter said. "Ellie was a popular girl, well liked at school, in a happy relationship with her boyfriend of eight months, and the beloved heart and soul of her family. According to her teachers, she was set for a full house of As and A stars in the GCSE exams she was sitting that month. There appeared to be no obvious reason why this smiley, charmed girl should leave her home one Thursday morning and not return.

"We first launched an appeal for witnesses to Ellie's disappearance in 2005. That appeal was unsuccessful. Now, ten years on, with no sightings of Ellie and no evidence to suggest her abduction, we have staged a reconstruction. But first, here's Ellie's mum and dad, Laurel and Paul Mack, to remind us of the girl they haven't seen for ten long years."

The footage shifted from the presenter to a video of a tired-looking couple sitting side by side in a very nice kitchen. She had a sheet of vanilla-blonde hair, cut sharp at the ends and clipped back on one side. She wore a black polo neck with the sleeves pushed back, a simple watch, no rings. He was a classic city boy: pale blue shirt unbuttoned at the neck, thick graying hair parted at the side, short at the back and longer on top, a soft, spoon-fed face that was probably steam shaved in Jermyn Street twice a week.

It was you and Paul.

You started talking first, to someone off camera who had been edited out. Your voice was serious and mature, like a newsreader, and you had the same broad forehead and wide-set eyes as Ellie and Poppy. I could see the line that went straight down through the three of you; it was breathtaking. You talked about the golden light of your girl, the journey she'd been taking to the stars when she went, the laughter and the dreams, the lasagna she'd asked you to save for her lunch on her return. Your eyes turned to glass as you talked. You circled your narrow wrists with your thumb and fingers. You had beautiful hands: long, elegant, feminine.

Paul started to talk then. I don't mean to be rude but I could tell that he was a flibbertigibbet. Well meaning but ultimately pointless. And I could tell that you were no longer a couple. Your body language was all off. He talked about the bond he'd had with his daughter—with *all of his children*, he hastened to add—how she'd been an open book, always told her parents everything, didn't have any secrets. His eyes also turned to glass and flicked briefly toward you. He was hoping, desperately I could tell, for some reassurance, but he did not get it. While you spoke, pictures flashed up at intervals of Ellie: as a child at the foot of a plastic slide; on the back of a speedboat with her father's arm around her, the wind in her hair; on Christmas Day in a silly hat; and in a restaurant with her arm around an elderly lady who looked likely to be a grandmother.

The girl looked far too alive to be dead, I thought. Even in those slightly blurred photographs I could feel the essence of her, sense the sheer joy of her. But it was a coincidence, I persuaded myself, that's all it was. A young girl with a fairly commonplace name who'd disappeared a year before Poppy was born and bore a striking resemblance to her.

Then the interview faded out and the reenactment began.

And that was when I knew, that was when all the little pieces of the puzzle fell into place and I knew it was no coincidence. There was the high road, the café on the corner of Noelle's road, the Red Cross shop where she bought her nasty clothes. The camera panned across the street and I could even see the distant bloom of cherry blossom on the tree outside her house. My skin covered over with goose bumps.

Because, you see, Noelle had told me once in a fit of anger that she was not Poppy's real mother, that a girl called Ellie had had her baby for her. I hadn't been sure at the time if it was her madness that had caused her to say such a thing or if it might in fact be true. I had never seen her naked while pregnant. She had not allowed me to touch her. But still, it seemed farfetched. I hadn't given it too much credence.

And if it had in fact been true, then I'd always imagined the mythical Ellie as a desperate addict, some loser that Noelle had picked up off the street and thrown some money at to carry her fake child for her. But here on my TV screen was a beautiful young girl with her whole life ahead of her, vanished off the face of the earth and last seen virtually outside Noelle's house.

This was not a child who would have left her family behind, her boyfriend and her future, to willingly bear a baby for a stranger. And this sent my thoughts spiraling back to those days after Noelle's disappearance, when I'd gone to her house to collect Poppy's things. I thought of the weird basement room I told you about, nothing in it but the stained old sofa bed, the dead hamsters, the TV with built-in VCR, the three locks on the door.

And I knew, immediately, that Noelle was capable of stealing a child.

And I knew immediately what I needed to do.

61

You know, Laurel, all my life all I ever wanted was to feel like everyone else. I'd turn up in some different country at some new school and I'd see all the kids who'd grown up together, whose mums and dads all drank wine together at the weekends, all these laid-back kids with their in-jokes and their basement dens and their nicknames. And I'd look at them and think, How do you do that? How does that even work? I was never anywhere long enough to get a nickname. I was just "the new boy." Every couple of years. "Hey, you, new boy." And being a virtual fucking genius didn't really do me any favors either. Nobody likes a clever clogs. And I was a terrible clever clogs. My cleverness oozed out of me like goo.

Also I was not good-looking *in the least*. Plus bad at sports and completely disinterested. And of course I had these high-flying parents who clearly didn't think there was any sacrifice too big for the sakes of their careers, who genuinely, genuinely didn't seem to realize that children liked being with their parents. They threw activities at me and told themselves that as long as I was busy I must surely be happy.

There was one school, one town, in Germany. I liked that school. It was an international school, kids from all over the world; a lot of them couldn't even speak English. And a transient intake, kids coming and going all the time. So for once I had an advantage. I could speak English. And I was there for nearly four years, from eleven to fourteen. So I started off as one of the youngest and became one of the oldest. This was good stuff. Formative. Almost transformative. I'd see new kids arrive, little ones, foreign ones, tiny little Korean kids or Indian kids or Nigerian kids, struggling with the language, struggling with the culture shock. And that made me feel normal.

I had a girlfriend there. Mathilde. She was French. Quite pretty. We kissed a few times and maybe if my parents hadn't dragged me away by the scruff of my neck at that precise moment and dropped me down in the next place, maybe I'd have had a chance to develop that normality, become a guy with a core and a soul.

As it is, I don't think I ever really loved anyone, until Poppy came along.

And even now I'm not sure if that's quite the right word.

After all, I have nothing to compare it to.

∽

Why didn't I go straight to the police after seeing Ellie on *Crimewatch*, that's what you'd like to know, isn't it? And it's a very good question.

Firstly, at this juncture, I did not know whether Ellie was dead or alive. I did not know how long she'd been in Noelle's basement, assuming she had ever been there. And according to the TV show, there was a slim possibility that she'd let herself into your house four years after her disappearance and helped herself to some cash and valuables. So Ellie was potentially anywhere or nowhere and the narrative was all over the place.

But that in itself was not a good enough reason to stop me telling the police what little I knew. You see, what concerned me the most was my role in this scenario. Another thing that Noelle told me the day she told me that she wasn't Poppy's real mother was that I was not Poppy's real father. She told me that the baby had been conceived using sperm she'd bought off the Internet. I'd locked this unpalatable little nugget away with all the other stuff she told me and stuck my head in the sands of denial. Poppy was literally, Laurel, *literally* the only good thing that had ever happened to me. My pride and joy. My entire raison d'être. You know how difficult my relationship with Sara has always been. You know how she hated me as a child, spat in my face, bit me and scratched me. I thought that was what fatherhood was. I thought that was the child I deserved. And then Poppy came into my life and she was so exquisite and so clever and she adored me. For the first time in my life I had something beautiful and precious that nobody else had, nobody in the world. And if she wasn't mine, then my life no longer made any sense to me.

But after watching the *Crimewatch* special I realized that if she was mine and if I told the police what I knew about Noelle and Ellie, that there would be no police officer, no detective, no judge, and no juror that would ever, in a million years, believe that Ellie had been impregnated with my sperm without my knowledge or consent. It was preposterous. Clearly. I would be done, at the very least, for aiding and abetting. And I would be done for rape of a minor. A minor that I'd never even met.

But again I prevaricated. I did not get a DNA test done even though proof that Poppy was not genetically my child would free me to report what I knew to the police. I simply wasn't ready to let her go, Laurel. I'm so sorry.

⌘

Shortly after the *Crimewatch* special I read an interview with you in the *Guardian*. It was some kind of real-life interest story in the magazine. You said, and I quote: "The nightmare of the thing is the not knowing. The lack of closure. I just cannot move forward without knowing where my daughter is. It's like walking through sinking mud. I can see something on the horizon, but I can never, ever get to it. It's a living death."

And then a month later there were the headlines in the papers. "ELLIE'S REMAINS FOUND." You had your closure. I came to the funeral. I stood at a respectful remove. I saw your legs buckle as your husband helped you into the crematorium and saw them buckle again on the way out. Closure, it seemed, had brought you nothing but a box of bones. But I could give you something that would get you out of the sinking mud and walking toward the horizon. I could give you Poppy.

62

I became fixated on you, Laurel. I raked the Internet for articles about you, for photographs and clips of the press conference you'd given the day after Ellie disappeared. You were such a refined woman. So succinct and articulate, no words wasted, no emotional incontinence, your pretty hands always twisted together so intricately, the sharply cut hair, the tailored clothes; no lace or buttons or trim. Even in your clothing choices you wasted nothing.

And in watching you I became more and more familiar with Paul. The shirts that looked conventional at first sight until you realized that there was a contrast trim of Liberty print inside the collar. The cuff links that appeared to be tiny dog heads. The slightly unusual tortoiseshell glasses. A flash of geometric-printed silk sock inside a handmade shoe.

Further investigation of such clothing showed that he shopped primarily at Paul Smith and Ted Baker. I began experimenting with a pair of socks here and a silk handkerchief there. Then I took myself for a proper shave in a barbershop. I had never before had a proper shave. In fact I rarely shaved; I tended to let the stubble grow out until my face itched, scratch it all off with a—generally—blunt razor, leave myself with a blotchy, butchered face, and then let it all grow back again. Clothes shopping for me was a joyless affair: a whizz around M&S with a basket twice a year. I began to enjoy browsing these boutiques for gentlemen. I liked the snake-hipped sales assistants, so eager to help, to guide me in the right direction. Then I had a proper haircut, found some products that gave my rather sparse and gravity-challenged hair the appearance of volume and lift, bought a pair of clear-lensed glasses with horn frames, and the transformation was complete.

It was a gradual process, over the course of a couple of months. It wasn't as if I just suddenly popped up one day with a brand-new image like one of those awful TV makeover shows. I'm not sure anyone I saw regularly even noticed.

I just wanted to show myself to you and for you to like me. That's all it was. For you to find me familiar. To find me the kind of person with whom you could share a slice of cake. I wanted us to be friends and then I wanted you and Poppy to be friends. Because by now I had had a DNA test done. By now I knew, with only 0.02 percent of a chance of improbability, that Poppy was not my child and that the only person she truly belonged to was you.

I had not expected mutual attraction. I had not expected your hands inside the sleeves of my jumper in the restaurant, our desperate ascent up the stairs of my house that night, your head in the crook of my arm the following morning. Women like you did not like men like me. And I . . .

No. There's no defense for it. None. I took advantage. Plain and simple.

But I'm glad at least that you and Poppy have had a chance to get to know each other in relatively normal circumstances, not in the glare of a police operation, not in the strip-lit office of the social services, just as a child and her grandmother, sharing breakfast, going shopping, eating dinner with your family. I hope this means that in the days that follow Poppy will be seamlessly assimilated into the Mack family. I've given her the bare bones of the truth. I will leave it to you to decide how much more she needs to know. And remember, this house and everything in it belongs to Poppy. She'll more than pay her own way in life.

But that brings me to the final, and in some ways, most compelling reason for me not going straight to the police back in May of this year. You'll notice if you look through the window to your right that there is a flower bed in the garden, newer, higher than the others. Do you see? At the very back? I dug it out in early November, just before I met you.

Noelle Donnelly is under there.

Before that she was in a chest freezer in my cellar. She'd been in there since the night she told me about Ellie. The night she told me Poppy wasn't mine.

I didn't mean to kill her, Laurel, I promise you that. It was an accident. I went for her, I wanted to scare her, I wanted to hurt her. I mean, you can imagine, can't you, how I was feeling, with that woman, that evil woman, in my kitchen, ripping my heart out of my chest. If you had been there, you'd have wanted to hurt her, too; I know you would. But I *did not* intend to kill her. Her chair went flying and her head hit the floor and . . .

Anyway . . . I'll let you decide if you want to tell the police. If you want to tell Poppy. But I couldn't go without telling someone and I know whatever you decide to do, it will be the right thing.

Please, Laurel, forgive me. Forgive me for everything. Forgive me for meeting Noelle, for allowing her into my life; forgive me for not questioning her more when she was pregnant, for not asking more questions about the basement in her house, for not going to the police when I suspected who Poppy's mother was, for allowing myself to fall in love with you, and for taking these last few weeks with you that were not mine to be taken. Please forgive me.

The horizon is right in front of you, Laurel. March to it right now, with Poppy by your side.

63

The film stops. Silence subsumes the house once more. A quick glance through the front window tells Laurel that Floyd's car is gone, and that so, by extension, is he. She returns to Floyd's office and stares at the ceiling. A choking noise comes from somewhere deep inside her. Her baby. Her baby girl. Not tramping the back roads of England with a rucksack on her back, but locked in Noelle Donnelly's basement growing a baby for her. How long was she there for her? How was she treated? How did she die? And how could Laurel not have known? How many times had she walked those streets in the years after Ellie's disappearance? How many times had she passed that house, her eye caught by the puff of pink cherry blossom outside Noelle's basement window? How many times had she been but meters from her own daughter without somehow, through some powerful umbilical connection, feeling that she was there?

Tears of rage explode from her and she thumps Floyd's desk until her fists feel bruised. She's about to yell out again when she hears a sound behind her, the creak of the door to Floyd's study. It opens a crack and there is Poppy. She's wearing the little jersey and chiffon dress that Laurel bought her in H&M during their shopping expedition. Her hair is bunched inside her fist and she has a hairband and a hairbrush in her other hand.

"I've been trying to do a ponytail," Poppy says, moving toward her, "a high, swingy one. But I can't get it high enough. And it keeps going all bumpy on the top."

Laurel smiles and gets up from her chair. "Here," she says, turning it toward Poppy. "You sit here. I'll see what I can do. Though it's been a very long time since I did a high ponytail."

Poppy sits and passes Laurel the hairband and the hairbrush. Laurel takes the bunched hair from her other hand and starts to brush it. She finds that the act is embedded in her muscle memory. How many mornings, how many times, how many ponytails has she brushed into place? And now it seems her hair-brushing days are not behind her after all. Now it seems that she is a mother again. Something warm and delicate inside her chest opens up like an unfurling flower.

"Where's Dad?" says Poppy.

"Dad's not here," says Laurel carefully. "He's had to go somewhere."

Poppy nods. "Is it to do with what he told me last night?"

"What did he tell you last night?"

"He told me that Noelle wasn't my mum. He told me that your daughter was." She turns, suddenly, and Laurel can see that her eyes are red and swollen, that she has been crying silently in her bedroom. "Is it true? Is it true that you're my grandma?"

Laurel pauses. She swallows. "Would you like it to be true?"

Poppy nods again.

"Well. It is. Your mother was called Ellie. She was my daughter. And she was the most wonderful, golden, perfect girl in the world. And you, Poppy, are exactly like her."

Poppy says nothing for a moment and then she turns to Laurel once more, her eyes wide with fear and says, "Is she dead?"

Laurel nods.

"Is my dad dead?"

"Your dad . . . ?"

"My real dad."

"You mean . . ."

"The man who made a baby with Ellie. Not my dad who brought me up."

"Your dad told you?"

"Yes. He told me. He said he doesn't know who my real dad is. He says no one knows. Not even you."

Laurel turns her attention back to Poppy's hair. She pulls it as high as she can and then she twists the elastic band around it three times. "I don't know if your real dad is dead, Poppy. It's possible we'll never know."

Poppy is silent for a moment. Then she says, "Have you finished?"

"Yes," says Laurel. "All done."

Poppy slides from the chair and goes to the mirror on the wall outside Floyd's study. She touches her hair with her fingertips in her reflection. "Do I look like her?" she says.

"Yes. You look just like her."

She turns back to her reflection and appraises it again, her chin tipped up slightly. "Was she pretty?"

"She was extraordinarily pretty."

"Was she as pretty as Hanna?"

Laurel is about to say, *Oh, she was much prettier than Hanna.* But catches herself. "Yes," she says. "She was as pretty as Hanna."

Poppy looks satisfied with this.

"Are we still going to the party?" she says.

"Do you want to?"

"Yes. I want to see my family," she says. "I want to see my real family."

"In which case then definitely."

"Laurel?"

"Yes, sweetheart."

"Is Dad ever coming back?"

"I don't know. I really don't know."

Poppy glances down at her shoes and then back at Laurel. Her eyes fill with tears and suddenly the unnerving stoicism passes and Poppy is sobbing, her shoulders heaving up and down, her hands pressed hard into her eye sockets.

Laurel takes her in her arms, holds her tight, kisses the top of her head, feels her love for this child flow through her like a sudden, glorious summer storm.

64

I have both my passport and a handgun. I have a change of clothes in a small bag and a fully charged phone. My plan is to get as far away from London N4 as I can and then either blow out my brains or leave the country. I will see how I feel when it comes down to it. At this juncture I have no idea what is worse: to break my daughter's heart or to break my daughter's heart and then spend the rest of my life either in hiding or in jail. Plan B at least does not involve a funeral.

And so finally I have cleared up your shitty disgusting mess, Noelle. As I speak (or think, or write, or whatever the hell it is I'm doing with a dead person) Laurel will be introducing herself anew to her granddaughter and then they will go together to the twinkling Richard Curtis Christmas meal in the twinkling mews house in twinkling Belsize Park—and imagine everyone's faces, Noelle, when they walk in together, those two fine women with their strong brows and their big brains and all that golden light dazzling the bejesus out of everyone. Just imagine.

I wish I could be there to see it.

But I denied myself that privilege when I chose my own happiness and my own needs over Laurel's.

I'm out of London now, Noelle. I appear to be heading west. Yep, there goes Slough. And I'm feeling good. In fact I'm feeling amazing. I've finally shed you, like a dead skin.

I touch the gun in the innocuous Sainsbury's carrier bag on the passenger seat. I caress its solid lines, feel the cool of the metal through the plastic. I imagine the barrel of the gun, hard against the roof of my mouth, the pressure of the trigger against my fingertip. The day is still bright and clean. I imagine myself pulling off the road a few hours hence and driving into a dark-skied, sleepy Cornish village, finding a bed for the night, or sleeping in my car. Tomorrow I would awake and it would be Christmas Day. The world would fall silent as it always does at Christmas, all those big loud lives sucked up behind a million closed doors. And where would I go? Where would I be? And the day after that? And the day after that?

I feel clean and pure, purged and new. I have just done the best and greatest thing I have every done or ever will do. Do I want to be here when this breaks in the newspapers? Really? Christ, just imagine the terrifying photographs they would dig out of the two of us. Fred and Rose West would look like Brangelina in comparison.

I pass the Glastonbury Tor. The sun is beginning its descent and the sky is a pearly gray. Pale gold light shines off the stones and a few sightseers are thrown into delicate silhouette. I pull off the M5 at the next junction and make my way back to the tor. A road back I find a field. From here I can watch the sunset, can see the shadows of the Glastonbury stones shrink and grow in the changing light. I think of Laurel and Poppy in the flickering candlelight of Bonny's dining table, of their faces open and bright. And then I think again of you and me, inextricably linked for infinity, our faces side by side on the front pages of the newspapers for years to come, and I know that I do not want to be here to see that. I think of Poppy, of her brave face as I held her hands in her bedroom last night and told her the truth about herself, the solid set of her chin as she bit back on her emotions, the tiny nod of her head as she silently absorbed words that no nine-year-old girl should ever have to hear. I think of how she will learn to live without me and I know that she will. I know that she will flourish. I think of my parents in Washington, the purse of their lips, the unspoken words going through both of their minds: *We should have left him in the hospital.* And I know that this will be my last sunset, this one, here, right now, on Christmas Eve, playing out in violent flames of red and gold across the horizon. And I know that these are my last moments.

And that is fine.

That is absolutely fine.

I put my hand into the plastic bag and I take out the gun.

65

EIGHT MONTHS LATER

Theo and Hanna walk hand in hand through a bower of white roses and baby's breath. Petals of pastel-colored confetti float around their heads and a tinny recording of church bells peels across the urban streets of Finsbury Park. For a brief moment the sun breaks through the bank of clouds that's been brooding overhead since early this morning.

Laurel holds Poppy's hand in hers and watches as her newly married daughter greets her friends and well-wishers on the street outside the church. Hanna's in pure white and her hair glitters with gems. She looks glowing and golden. Her husband stands beside her handsome and assured, his hand resting gently on the small of her back, his face bursting with pride.

How, she wonders, could she have ever thought that Hanna would be Theo's consolation prize? How, she wonders, could she have allowed herself ever to feel that way?

After a short while the wedding party, only thirty strong, climbs aboard an old red Routemaster bus. Poppy sits on Laurel's knee, her hands still clutching the bouquet she'd carried into the church in her role as a flower girl. Laurel loops her arms around Poppy's waist and holds on to her as the bus lurches forward. Poppy calls her Mama. Not Granny. Not Mum. Not Laurel. Mama. She chose the appellation herself. Poppy is the bravest and most brilliant child. She has cried when she has needed to cry and she has been cross when she has needed to be cross. And she misses Floyd every moment of every day. But mostly she has been the light and the joy, the sun around which Laurel and her family all orbit. Mostly she has just been a miracle.

The atmosphere on board is high-octane and chatty. Bonny and Paul sit together at the front of the bus, Bonny's extraordinary hat almost entirely obscuring the view through the front window. Behind them sit Jake and Blue. Blue is holding a tiny puppy in a bag on her lap. It's called Mister and apparently will grow not much bigger than a small rabbit. She and Jake have been fussing over it like a newborn baby since they arrived from Devon last night.

On the seat next to Laurel is Sara-Jade. Poppy had asked if she was allowed to invite her, even though she doesn't really know Hanna and Theo. And although Poppy now knows that Sara-Jade is not her biological sister, she still wants her to be part of her family. Sara-Jade looks, as always, thin and otherworldly in a silver bomber jacket and a shapeless pink dress. She is with a bearded man called Tom, who may or may not be her partner. She has thus far introduced him only as her friend. Jackie and Bel sit opposite Laurel, with a twin on either side. The boys are only a couple of years older than Poppy and Laurel has found to her delight that her life is back in sync, once more, with those of her closest friends.

On the seats to her right are Theo's parents. Mr. Goodman looks old but Becky Goodman still looks unfeasibly young for her age. Laurel sees the drag of skin away from her jawbone and toward her ears and holds the observation inside herself reassuringly.

Elsewhere she sees friends of Hanna's from her schooldays, she sees Paul's father and she sees strangers, twenty-somethings in uncomfortable shoes and too much makeup, friends of Theo's, she assumes, or colleagues from Hanna's office.

But there are, as at every wedding, people who are not here: ghosts and shadows.

Laurel's mother finally passed away eight months ago. But not before she'd had a chance to meet Poppy.

She'd clasped her hand and she'd said, "I knew it, I knew there was a reason why I was still here, I knew you were out there. I just knew you were." A nurse took a picture that day of the three of them. It should have been four, of course, but three was better than two. Ruby died a week later.

Laurel's hopeless brother is not here either. He'd flown back from Dubai for Ruby's funeral in January and said he couldn't make two trips in one year.

And, of course, Ellie is not here.

Laurel hasn't told Poppy the full truth about Ellie. She said that Ellie ran away from home and then got run over and left in a wood and that at some point between running away and getting run over she'd had a baby and that Noelle had adopted the baby and given her to Floyd when she couldn't cope anymore.

Neither has she told Poppy about the body in Floyd's garden. She'd simply packed a small bag for Poppy and brought her to her flat in Barnet for a few days while the big plastic tent was erected over the flowerbed, helicopters buzzing overhead. As for Floyd himself, Laurel told Poppy that he'd taken his own life because he felt so guilty about pretending to be Poppy's father when he wasn't. Poppy had swallowed back tears and nodded, in that grim, brave way of hers. "I really didn't mind, you know," she said. "Because he was a very good dad. He really was. He didn't need to feel guilty. He didn't need to die."

"No," Laurel had said, wiping a single tear from Poppy's cheek with her thumb and then rocking her in her arms. "No. He didn't."

The bus pulls up outside the canal-side restaurant where Theo and Hanna will be holding their wedding reception. The party duly dismounts and smooths down its skirts and rebuttons its jackets, adjusts its hair against the sharp wind blowing in off the top of the water. Paul approaches. "Are you OK?" he asks, his hand against the sleeve of her jacket.

Laurel nods. She is OK. Her life is upended in every way. She is a mother again at fifty-five. She is making packed lunches in the mornings and writing down term dates in her diary. She is doing two school runs a day and putting someone else before her at every juncture of her life. And she is still, of course, traumatized by the revelations of the last months of Ellie's life. Some nights when she closes her eyes she is in that basement, trapped inside those pine-clad walls, staring desperately up at a window that no one will ever see her through. But the nightmares are starting to fade.

Her daughter is dead and her mother is dead and her husband lives with a woman who is nicer than her in a hundred different ways. But she is OK. Laurel is OK. She really is. Because she has Hanna and she has Jake and now she has Poppy and Theo, too. Her relationship with Sara-Jade has grown deep and strong in the months since Floyd's death. She sees her frequently, for Poppy's sake but also for her own. She sees something of herself in Sara-Jade, something important in some way, something to nurture.

Hanna lives with Theo now. She rents out the miserable flat in Woodside Park and Laurel no longer needs to be her cleaning lady. Everything about their previous dynamic has been transformed. They are friends. And Hanna and Poppy are the best thing to come out of the horror of Ellie's disappearance. Poppy hero-worships Hanna and Hanna adores Poppy. They are virtually inseparable.

Laurel catches Hanna's eye across the room as they find their way to their seats. She smiles and Hanna winks at her and blows her a kiss. Her beautiful daughter. Her golden girl.

Laurel catches the kiss and holds it next to her heart.

EPILOGUE

The woman clutches the piece of paper inside her hands and stares desperately through the glass screen at the policewoman sitting there. She'd told her someone would be along in a minute but that was nearly half an hour ago and she really needs to get going before she gets a parking ticket and the frozen chicken breasts in the boot of her car start to defrost.

"Excuse me," she says a minute later, "I'm really sorry but my parking's about to run out and I really have to go. Could I just leave this here with you?" She holds up the piece of paper.

The policewoman looks up at her and then at the piece of paper, then back at her again. "Sorry?" she says, as though she's never seen her before or been told about the paper.

"This letter," the woman says, trying her hardest not to sound impatient. "The letter I found in a book I got from the Red Cross shop."

"Right," says the policewoman. "Sure. Let me take it."

The woman hands the letter to the policewoman and watches as she reads it, watches her facial expression change from disinterest to alarm to sadness and then to shock. "Sorry," she says, "tell me again where you found this?"

"I told you," says the woman, her patience stretching very, very thin. "I bought a book last month from the Red Cross shop on Stroud Green Road. A Maeve Binchy. I only just got round to reading it last night. And this note fell out. It's her," she says, "isn't it? It's that poor girl? The one who had the baby in the basement?"

The policewoman looks up at her and the woman can see that her eyes are wet with tears. "Yes," says the policewoman. "It is."

Both of them let their eyes fall back to the letter then and they both fall silent as they reread it together, squinting to make out the minuscule words squashed tightly side by side on a tiny scrap of paper:

To anyone who finds this note [it begins], my name is Ellie Mack.

I am seventeen. Noelle Donnelly brought me to her house on 26 May 2005 and has kept me captive in her basement for about a year and a half. I have had a baby. I don't know who the father is and I'm pretty sure I'm still a virgin. Her name is Poppy. She was born in around April 2006. I don't know where she is now or who is looking after her but please, please find her if you can. Please find her and look after her and tell her that I loved her. Tell her that I looked after her for as long as I could and that she was the best little baby in the world. Also, please let my family know that you've found this note. My mum is called Laurel Mack and my dad is called Paul and I have a brother called Jake and a sister called Hanna and I want you to tell them all that I'm sorry and that I love them more than anything in the world and that none of them must feel bad about what happened to me because I am brave and I am brilliant and I am strong.

Yours sincerely,
Ellie Mack

ACKNOWLEDGMENTS

I finished writing this book in December 2016. I read it through and thought, hmm, this is either brilliantly bizarre, or just bizarre. I'd lost all objectivity and passed it to my editor with no worldly clue how she would respond.

A few days later she said, let's meet up, I have a radical suggestion. I knew then that my book was simply bizarre.

She said that she and another editor had spent ages together brainstorming my book, trying to find a way to balance out the bizarreness. And they'd had a light-bulb moment. And her suggestion was indeed radical.

I said, yes, yes, of course. That's brilliant, you're brilliant. Thank you!

And now I'd like to say thank you again to Selina Walker and Viola Hayden for being brave and clear-minded, for sitting together with my bizarre pile of paper and talking and thinking and talking and thinking and seeing exactly what needed to be done and then telling me exactly how to do it. People might think that writers are possessive of their work, think that no one but them can possibly know how it should be. But a sensible writer knows that's not true. Sometimes the writer is the least able to see the solution and sometimes the editors are the geniuses. And this was definitely the case with this book. So thank you both again. I am so grateful to you.

And thank you, of course, to everyone else at Arrow: to Susan Sandon, Gemma Bareham, Celeste Ward-Best, Aslan Byrne, and everyone in the sales team.

Thank you to my agent Jonny Geller for being so enthusiastic about this book. And thank you to the rest of the team at Curtis Brown for everything you do to support me in my career. You're all brilliant.

Thank you to my wonderful publishing team in the US, where, thanks to all your love and hard work, my career is going from strength to strength. Thank you, Judith Curr, Sarah Cantin, Ariele Fredman, Lisa Sciambra, and Haley Weaver. Finally getting to meet you all last year was beyond special. You're even better in real life!

And thank you to Deborah Schneider, my American agent (and birthday twin!). You've worked so hard on my behalf for so long and it was incredible to spend some time face-to-face with you in London last year after nearly a decade of emailing. You are amazing.

Thank you to all my foreign publishers. I am so grateful to be published so widely and so beautifully by so many incredible teams of people around the world. Thanks especially to Pia Printz in Sweden, for not only publishing me so beautifully, but for inviting me into your world, taking me for dinner, and keeping me up way past my bedtime! Thanks also to Anna, Frida, and Christoffer. You're all so lovely.

Thank you to the booksellers, the librarians, and the book buyers and to all the people who help get my books to the readers. And thanks to all the amazing book bloggers out there. Thanks for the reviews and the posts and the photos and the tweets. I love you all! Thanks in particular to Tracy Fenton of the utterly legendary The Book Club on Facebook. What a powerhouse you are, and such a boon for readers and writers alike.

Thank you to my splendid family and friends. I am blessed

with a high-quality abundance of both. And special thanks to the ones on the Board. We just get better with age!

But mostly, thank you to my readers, new ones and old ones, loyal or occasional. I am so grateful to you all for spending your hard-earned money on stuff I've written and allowing me to keep on writing more stuff. You are all amazing.

A NOTE ON THE CHARACTER NAME OF "SARA-JADE VIRTUE"

The name "Sara-Jade Virtue" was given to me by a real-life Sara-Jade Virtue, the winner of last year's Get In Character auction, which raises money for the UK charity CLIC Sargent. Incidentally, Sara-Jade is one of the greatest, most passionate, and influential people currently working in British publishing, and I was super-proud to use her name.

CLIC Sargent's mission is to change what it means to be diagnosed with cancer when you're young. They believe that children and young people with cancer have the right to the best possible treatment, care, and support, throughout their cancer journey and beyond. And they deserve the best possible chance to make the most of their lives once cancer treatment has ended.

www.clicsargent.org.uk